the Game of

Love

and

Death

Martha
Brockenbrough

SCHOLASTIC

Chapter 1

Friday, February 13, 1920

THE FIGURE IN THE FINE GRAY SUIT MATERIALIZED IN THE NURS-
ery and stood over the sleeping infant, inhaling the sweet, milky
night air. He could have taken any form, really: a sparrow, a snowy
owl, even a common housefly. Although he often traveled the world
on wings, for this work he always preferred a human guise.

Standing beneath a leaded glass window, the visitor, who was
known as Love, removed a small, pearl-headed pin from his tie and
pricked his finger. A bead of blood rose and caught the reflection of
the slice of moon that hung low in the late winter sky. He bent
over the cradle and slid his bleeding fingertip into the child's
mouth. The baby, a boy, tried to suckle, his forehead wrinkling, his
small hands curling into fists.

"Shh," the figure whispered. "Shh." This player. He could not
think of one he'd loved more.

After a time, Love slipped his finger out of the boy's mouth,
satisfied that the blood had given the boy a steady heart. He
replaced his pin and regarded the child. He removed a book from
his pocket, scribbled a few lines, and tucked it away again. When
he could stay no longer, he uttered two words, as softly as a prayer:
"Have courage."

The next night, in a small green house across town, his opponent made her choice. In this house, there was no leaded glass in the windows. No gracious nursery, no wrought-iron crib. The child was a girl. A girl who slept in an apple crate — happily so, for she did not yet know of anything else.

In the house's other bedroom, the child's grandmother slept lightly, listening from some ever-alert corner of her mind for the sounds that would indicate the child's parents had returned home: the creak of a door, the whisper of voices, the careful pad of tiptoeing feet.

The old woman would wait forever to hear those sounds again.

Wearing a pair of soft leather gloves, Love's opponent, known as Death, reached for the child, who woke and blinked sleepily at the unfamiliar face overhead. To Death's relief, the baby did not cry. Instead, she looked at her with wonder. Death held a candle near so the child might have a better view. The baby blinked twice, smiled, and reached for the flame.

Pleased, Death set the candle down, held the baby close to her chest, and walked to the uncovered window, which revealed a whitened world glowing beneath a silver flannel sky. She and the baby watched the snow fall together. At last, the child fell asleep in her arms.

Death concentrated on her essential task, relieved when she at last felt the telltale pressure behind her eyes. After much effort, a single black tear gathered in her lashes. Death removed her glove with her teeth. It made hardly any noise as it hit the floor. With her index finger, Death lifted the tear.

She held her fingertip over the baby's clean, warm forehead. Slowly, carefully, she wrote directly on the child's flesh a word that would be invisible. But this word would have power over the child, and later the woman she would become. It would teach her, shape her. Its letters, seven of them, gleamed in the candlelight.

Someday.

She whispered this into the baby's ear:

Someday, everyone you love will die. Everything you love will crumble to ruin. This is the price of life. This is the price of love. It is the only ending for every true story.

The letters sank into the infant's dusky skin and vanished as if they'd never been there at all.

Death put the baby down, removed her other glove, and left the pair of them on the floor, where they would be discovered by the baby's grandmother and mistaken for something else. The gloves would be the only things she would give the girl, though there was much she had taken already, and more she would take in the years to come.

For the next seventeen years, Love and Death watched their players. Watched and waited for the Game to begin.

Chapter 2
Friday, March 26, 1937

BENEATH A HEAVY CUSHION OF CLOUDS, HENRY BISHOP STOOD IN the soft dirt of the infield. The space beyond and between the first two bases was a fine place for thinking. It smelled like cut grass, and the Douglas firs that wrapped around the outfield sealed out the noise of the rest of the world. Henry swallowed, crouched, and socked his glove as the pitcher let loose with a fastball. The batter swung and connected — *pok!* The ball leapt off the bat and streaked through the infield. Henry jumped and reached, but the ball took its own surprising course past the tip of his mitt.

When his feet touched the ground again, Henry had an epiphany about the rhythm of baseball, and why it meant a damn to him.

It was connection. Without the answering swing of the batter, the work of the pitcher meant nothing. Likewise, the fielder's throw found its meaning in the baseman's glove or in the grass. The connection completed the rhythm. Two opposing forces crashed together with their individual desires, creating something unpredictable between them. Triumph. Disaster. Heartbreak. Joy. Baseball was a love story, really. Just a different love than the kind he'd always sought.

His feet touched the grass as the team's center fielder, Ethan Thorne, bare-handed the drive on the run, his long and loose limbs so sure of every movement. Ethan fired it at Henry in time for him to tag the runner dashing back toward second. Henry loved being part of this complicated life-form made from the hands and feet of his schoolmates.

"Nice save," called the coach, who wore a cap, sweater-vest, and necktie that almost cleared the distance from his belly to his waist. "But use your glove, Mr. Thorne. That hotdogging is going to leave you with a busted knuckle."

"Yes, sir," Ethan said. "I thought I'd return the ball faster that way."

The coach snorted and shook his head. He looked up at the sky, grimaced, and scrutinized his athletes. The practice continued a few minutes more, until something in the air shifted. Henry felt it as it happened, this sudden burst of pressure. The rain turned from a light mist to a regular shower, darkening the players' shoulders. Puddles, sizzling with falling water, filled the low spots on the diamond.

Holding a clipboard over his head in a fruitless attempt to keep the rain at bay, the coach blew his whistle. "Hit the showers! Everyone but Bishop."

Henry jogged over and looked down at his coach.

"Usual drill. Bring in the equipment and clean the mud off the bats and balls. Make sure you get them good and dry or we'll have to replace them, and that's just not in the budget." He glanced at Henry's sagging socks.

"Yes, sir," Henry said, half expecting the heat on his face to turn the rain to steam.

A sparrow lighted on the grass nearby and tugged at a worm that had been lured by the pounding drops. The bird cocked its head at Henry, appearing to study him intently. Henry pulled up his socks.

"Once you get this cleaned up, you can go," Coach said. "I'm heading in. It's a mess out here."

Henry nodded and bent to pick up the closest ball. He winged it into a bucket and did the same with the next and the next, never missing a throw, even as he moved farther and farther away from it, creating a steady *thup, thup, thup* of baseballs as they piled up. Rhythm. Connection. They went where he did, like shadows, like ghosts.

Henry whistled as he worked, the theme from a Russian ballet he'd played in the school orchestra. He lifted his cap to wipe water from his forehead and moved on to the bats, gathering them into bouquets that he swung as he walked. He rinsed them, dried them, and lowered them into a wheeled cart, which he pushed toward the storage shed with one hand as he carried the ball bucket in his other, his face angled away from the rippling curtain of falling water.

The beauty of the all-boys preparatory academy invariably filled him with awe. It was a symphony of red brick and white paint nestled in an evergreen forest. Even on a rainy day, it was a splendid thing to behold. He was glad for the scholarship that secured his spot on its edge, and hoped for another to carry him forward through the University of Washington in the fall.

When Henry arrived in the locker room, Ethan was still there, wrapped in a white towel, although everyone else had gone home.

"I should've given you a hand," he said, rubbing a smaller towel against his dripping hair. "I can be a real heel."

"My job," Henry said. "Not yours."

"Well, if that doesn't stink," Ethan said. "You're soaked clean through. And your shoes . . . I don't know why you just don't take my old pair. They're in much better shape —"

"It's fine, Ethan. Really." Henry set his cap on the bench, pulled his wet shirt off over his head, and let it fall with a slap to the concrete floor. "Don't worry."

By the time Henry finished his shower, Ethan was dressed,

looking neat and confident in his school uniform, his hair parted sharply. He turned toward the fogged-up mirror, cleared a circle with his fist, and adjusted his already smartly knotted tie.

"Malt sound good?" He looked at Henry's misty reflection. "Guthrie's is always crawling with girls this time of day."

"Nah," Henry said, ruffling his hair to peaks with his towel.

"You're certain?" But even as he asked the question, Ethan looked relieved. His expression was strange. But Ethan could be complicated, especially about how they spent their free time together. Henry had learned not to ask. He moved the fingers on his left hand, practicing the melody of a new piece he was working on. He itched to have his double bass in his arms for real. The feeling and ritual always soothed him.

"Say, you don't have other plans, do you?" Ethan asked, a vaguely hurt look in his eyes. Ethan always hated it when Henry made other plans, as if he didn't want Henry to choose any other best friend. Not that he ever would.

But Henry didn't want to admit he intended to spend the evening in the carriage house, practicing. Ethan would give him an earful. "Oh, say, I'd meant to ask about your English thesis."

"Henry, that's not due for more than two weeks and this is Friday. The weekend, for chrissakes." Ethan slung his satchel over his shoulder.

"Doesn't have to be tonight," Henry said. "I thought you might like to get started."

Ethan tugged the hair on the top of his head, ruining his perfect part. "No, no. I know what I want to say in it. There's no rush. But this isn't going to get in the way of your own schoolwork, is it? Because I can probably —"

"It's no trouble," Henry said. He balled up his towel and tossed it into the bin. "I like doing it. Stop worrying."

Ethan grinned. He drummed his fingernails against the doorframe, a quick rattle of sound, and then pushed on the door. Outside, the rain had stopped, but the world around Henry still felt as though it was about to crack open. He hurried after his friend. The world could fall into pieces if it wanted. Ethan — and everyone else — could count on Henry to hold up his part.

Chapter 3

Flora Saudade stood on the lower wing of the butter-yellow Beechcraft Staggerwing C17B, ready to refuel the plane. She ran her hands over the upper wing, loving the way it was set behind the lower one. This little detail was everything. No other biplane was crafted this way. It made the Staggerwing an oddity. Flora, an oddity herself, loved that about it.

It made the plane look fast. Even better, the plane *was* fast: blisteringly so. The previous year, a pair of aviatrixes had flown a similar model across the country and won the Bendix Trophy, along with a seven-thousand-dollar prize. The thought of speed like that set off fireworks in her chest. If only.

But this particular plane wasn't hers. It belonged to Captain Girard, who'd known her father in the Great War and who'd been something like a father to her since she was a baby herself, teaching her everything he knew about airplanes since the day she told him her dream of flight. He'd hired her on as one of his mechanics. He had an official pilot, though, a man who used the plane to ferry executives to their meetings around the country because this was faster and more impressive than travel by rail.

There wasn't a businessman around who'd trust Flora to do the actual work of flying him, although plenty had unknowingly trusted her to make sure the plane was safe, which was every bit as important. People were funny about things they couldn't see. If they couldn't see it, it wasn't there. Or at the least, it didn't affect them. But the world didn't work that way, did it? There were things all around that you couldn't see, and these things had power.

And so, even though the captain had been nothing but generous, it would take years of what she made at the airfield and at her other job, singing at the Domino, to afford a plane of her own. A Staggerwing could cost seventeen thousand dollars. She'd have to win something like the Bendix to afford the down payment. Which she couldn't do without a plane of her own.

Frustrated, as always, Flora reached up to fill the gas tank on the upper wing, inhaling the blue-smelling fumes of ninety-octane fuel. She caught a glimpse of the sky and frowned. The clouds overhead didn't look good. She hoped they'd hold off for an hour or two so she could get in a flight. But you never could trust a spring sky in Seattle.

She hopped down, her boots crunching on the gravel runway. She climbed on the other wing to fill the tank on the opposite side. Fueling the plane always took a while: one hundred ten gallons of gas was a fair amount, and the men at the airfield were about as keen to help her as they were to see her in the cockpit.

She checked the snaps on her blue canvas coveralls. Securely fastened. She had a superstition that if she wasn't buttoned up, nothing else could be. And while she was under no illusions about her own mortality — everybody and everything died someday — she aimed to keep that someday far in the distant future. Just thinking of it gave her a headache.

The plane looked good, so she turned the props over by hand to make sure no engine-damaging oil had accumulated in the pair of bottom cylinders. Satisfied, she opened the door on the port side and climbed in past the pair of seats in the back. Feeling her usual preflight giddiness, she walked forward to the front, where the polished wood on the instrument panel beckoned.

She strapped herself in and looked out the windshield. It wasn't raining yet, but it would be soon. She could feel it, the sense of change and trouble in the air. Because the plane had a tail wheel, she couldn't see the ground around her. But she'd checked and trusted it was clear. One of Captain Girard's men waved a flag and Flora accelerated. When she reached forty miles per hour, the tail wheel lifted, giving her better visibility. She pushed the engine more, and at sixty miles per hour, the plane rose. Faster still, and she was fully airborne.

Flora smiled. Every time, this separation of herself from the earth below was a miracle. She rose, and gravity tugged downward on her belly as she ascended and nosed south. If not for the clouds, she'd be able to see Mt. Rainier, a snow-capped volcano that overlooked the city like a pointy-headed god. Below her, Lake Washington extended its own limbs, a long green-gray body of water that reminded her of someone dancing. The lake's south end looked just like an arm flung skyward, where the north was a pair of bent knees. Pointed Douglas firs and brushy cedars surrounded it. And then, clustered around twisty roads, tiny houses and all the lives and chaos within.

She exhaled. The sky was hers. Hers alone. And it was forever, and when she was in it, she was part of something infinite and immortal. As long as she took care of the plane, it would take care of her. It was nothing like the jazz music she performed at night, which was never the same thing twice: sometimes wonderful, sometimes agonizing, always dependent on the moods and whims of others, influenced by the appetites of the audience.

She didn't care for this dependence. Other people were forever grating her nerves or letting her down, or just plain leaving, sometimes for good. She trusted the Staggerwing as if it were her own body. Even the drone of the engine pleased her. As dissonant as it was to her musician's ears, the steadiness of it freed her mind from heavy thoughts.

But today, she would not fly for long. A change shuddered across the sky. The engine rattled. A quick thing, as subtle as a pair of thrown dice. Then the rain. One drop, then another, and another hit the windshield until water trails streaked the glass. And while it was unlikely that this would turn into a thunderstorm, Flora knew she had to take the plane down. Thunder and ice were her enemies in the air.

She radioed her intentions and piloted back toward the airfield. As she surrendered altitude, her stomach went momentarily weightless. The runway rushed into view. She set the front two wheels down first, then the tail wheel, a more difficult kind of landing than touching all three tires down at once, but a safer and more controlled one, which she executed perfectly. She stepped out of the plane as the sky began to dump in earnest, almost as if it were overcome with the same sadness she felt returning to the earth.

Chapter 4

Not long before Flora's flight, Love had materialized in Venice, a city made more beautiful by the fact that it was doomed. He stood in Piazza San Marco, in front of an ornate church named for the man who'd run naked from the garden of Gethsemane after Jesus was sentenced to death. Mark's bones had been smuggled there in a barrel of salted pork — a strange way to keep a man and his memory alive. But what was humanity if not deeply strange?

It was from similar human bones that they'd fashioned the dice for the Game. Two of them, carved and smoothed to perfection, their dots painted in a wine-dark mix of Love's blood and Death's tears. These, Love carried with him always. They rattled in his pocket as he strolled toward the Campanile, with its bell that rang periodically to summon politicians, announce midday, and herald executions.

The bell chimed noon as he passed, his shoes tapping the stones loudly enough to rouse a flock of pigeons. Up they rose into the silvery sky, cooing and beating their wings.

Love spent a pleasant if chilly afternoon in the misty, labyrinthine alleys of the Accademia quarter, half expecting to see his opponent around every corner. At a milliner's, he purchased a handmade bowler, leaving his old hat on the head of a skinny Romany boy who would grow up to be a legendary seducer of women and men. For years afterward, Love regretted not giving the boy his pants.

At the stationer's next door, he bought a small bottle of cerulean ink because it reminded him of the shade Napoleon had used in his letters to Josephine. Love would record notes with it in the small book he always carried; perhaps it would improve his luck. Perhaps this time, unlike all the other times, he would win.

Wondering whether she had forsaken him, he stopped at a café for a snack of paper-thin prosciutto paired with a mild, milky cheese, washing both down with a glass of sparkling wine. Although his immortal body required neither food nor drink, he liked to pause for such simple pleasures. The appetite was a fundamentally human thing, and it served him to feel it, to understand it.

When he emerged from the shop, his tongue buzzing with salt and wine, the sun was low on the horizon, pulling with it all the color and warmth from the world. Fearing Death would not join him after all, Love vanished and rematerialized inside a glossy black gondola, much to the surprise of the man who'd just dropped off his last passenger of the day. The gondolier had intended to roll a cigarette and stare at the heavens a few moments before he returned his boat to the yard. And yet, here was a new fare, already making himself comfortable on a black-and-gold bench.

The man sighed and spoke. *"Solo voi due?"*

Just the two of you?

Too late, Love caught a whiff of something sweet over the fetid odor of the canal. Lilies. The hairs on the back of his neck rose.

"Sì, solo noi due," Love agreed.

She descended the crooked set of wooden steps leading down to the gondola, looking like an angel in a long coat of winter-white wool. Her gloves and boots, made of lambskin, were the same hue.

A lone spot of color hung around her neck: a red cashmere scarf. His heart sank at the sight of her in this shade.

"Hello, old friend," she said.

Love helped her into the gondola. Judging her age to be about seventeen this time, he resolved to adjust his own appearance to match. His decision to travel in the guise of someone middle-aged had been a reflection of the weariness he felt with his lot. To spend an eternity losing was enough to make anyone feel damaged by time. But the younger he felt, the more he believed Death was beatable. He would have to remember that.

"Mind if I smoke?" the gondolier asked, a skinny hand-rolled cigarette already between his lips.

Death answered, "Please do."

And there it was, her Mona Lisa smile, the one that had been the model for the artist. Then came the hiss of flame, the sour whiff of burning tobacco, the dull sizzle of the match as it sank into the canal, one more light, unlike any other, forever gone from the world.

The gondolier, now lost in smoke and thought, eased his craft from the dock and steered them from the Grand Canal through the quiet and picturesque privacy of the narrow water lanes snaking through the quarter.

"A hopeless city," she said.

Death knew he loved Venice. To deprive her of the satisfaction of wounding him, Love altered his guise so he was wearing a swooping handlebar mustache. Death sprouted a drooping Fu Manchu, but did not crack a smile. Love acknowledged the win, and both their mustaches vanished.

"You don't have to be embarrassed," she said in a language known only to the two of them. "It's appealing, your commitment to the doomed."

"Perhaps I see things you don't," he said.

"Perhaps that is true." She removed a glove and dipped a knuckle into the water.

"They're ready," he said, thinking of his player in the city far away, a city with a model of Venice's Campanile built at its train station.

"If you say so," Death said.

The sun and all its light were gone. It would rise again, creating the illusion that the world had been remade, that the cycle was starting anew. But time was not a circle. It moved in one direction only, onward into the dark unknown. Feeling his spirits teeter, Love focused on the sound the water made as the boat sliced through it. A series of small kisses.

He looked into the heart of the gondolier and discovered the woman the man loved most. He cast that image overhead so that it might settle over the boat like a soft blanket. Surely Death would not object to that small comfort. The gondolier extinguished his cigarette in the canal and opened his mouth to sing. " 'O Sole Mio." My sun.

Love's light spread overhead, and the darkening sky revealed a moon whittled to near nothingness. Reflections of human-made lights stretched across the water, beautiful fingers that stroked the slender boat as it passed, its captain singing of the glow of his heart's sun on his lover's face.

Love's pulse steadied. He took Death's hand so she could better see into his mind, and together, they looked at the city on the young edge of the world. Seattle. There was a wildness to it. Oceans of corruption, yes. But imagination and hope and wonder that attracted people who yearned to remake bigger and better lives. There were vast fortunes to be cut from forests and chipped from gold mines.

There was also opportunity for the poor to rise. The landscape itself reflected this. Still, deep lakes and frothing rivers. Snow-covered mountains whose beauty belied their explosive origins. If ever there were a place where the old might give way to the new, where Love could beat Death, it was here.

He wished he could see into Death's mind the way she peered into his. He did not know the secret of it. The ride ended, and Love paid the gondolier extravagantly. Arm in arm, the two immortals glided off the boat, up the steps, and onto the arc of the Ponte dell'Accademia, their steps barely audible over the insistent slap of water.

"Paper?" She held out her hand.

Love tore a sheet from the book he always carried.

"You first," she said.

Love pricked his finger and offered it to her. She lifted a tear from the corner of her eye and rubbed her fingertip against his. Love handed her the paper and the pen he'd purchased earlier. She dipped the metal tip into their strange ink and wrote two names. The ritual was quick, almost anticlimactic, but they'd performed it many times, and what's more, knew each other well.

She blew on the ink. "This binds the players to the game. They live as long as this is intact. When the clock runs out, I'll destroy the paper and claim my prize."

"Only if you win," Love said.

"When I win. And what constitutes victory?"

Love paused. In the past, he'd said a kiss. Or consummation. But neither seemed enough. "They must choose courage," he said. "They must choose each other at the cost of everything else. When they do that, I win."

"I do not even know what that means," she said.

Love chose to show her with a picture painted in thought. He put his hands on Death's cheeks and concentrated on the players. On the surface, they were an impossible pair. From two separate worlds. But Love knew something Death did not, at least when it came to hearts. Theirs were twins. He sent her an image of what it would look like when they locked on to each other. The light within them would burst out and rise, two columns of flame winding like the strands of matter that are the stuff of life itself. The image echoed both the creation of the universe in miniature and the elements of life on earth writ large. It was the source of everything, including Love and Death themselves.

If Love won, it would remake the world, at least for the players.

Death pulled her face away. "Don't ever do that again." She put a hand on her cheek. "We of course cannot tell the players about the Game."

He nodded. To tell them would change everything. "And the stakes this time?"

Her answer was swift. "When I win, I claim the life of my player."

"When I win," Love said, "both players live on."

She shrugged. Her powers were far greater than his, and the Game was only something she agreed to for the fun of it.

"Is there anything that isn't allowed?" she asked.

He hated this question. He'd made the wrong choice many times. "The usual restrictions. Before time runs out, you cannot kill either player with a touch, just as I cannot instill love."

"Unless." Death held up a finger.

"Unless what?" She was a slippery opponent.

"Unless your player chooses me. Then I can kill him with a kiss."

Love laughed. Henry would never choose death. Not over life. And certainly not over love. He'd been born for this. "As you wish. Have you chosen your guise?"

"You're looking at it. At one of them, anyway."

In the near darkness, Love studied Death's face. Star-white skin. A smart, wavy black bob. Dark eyes. The wide, insolent mouth. He'd seen her face before, but where? She'd also undoubtedly appear as the black cat. How her guises would affect the players was ever a mystery.

"And now to determine the length of the Game," Death said. "You have the dice, I trust."

Love removed the dice from his pocket. The bones clacked against each other. "You first."

"I'll roll the month, then." She rattled the dice in her hands and tossed them on the boards of the bridge. "Three and four. The Game lasts until July. Which day is up to you."

He could add the sum of the dots or multiply them, so long as their product did not exceed the length of the month. He hated having the choice. He would rather blame fate.

He squeezed the dice, kissed his hand, and let them fly. Their clatter echoed over the water.

Death read them. "How droll. A tie."

Even the numbers were the same, a four and a three. Love nearly chose the twelfth of July as the day the Game would end. That would give him more time, the thing he always wished for. Sometimes, even minutes would have made the difference.

But there was something about the symmetry of the seventh that called to him. So he trusted it. The Game would end at midnight on the seventh of July.

"When will I see you again?" He liked to know what she was doing so he could adjust his interventions to match.

"Two days," she said.

Love nodded. A pair of days felt right.

Death disappeared, as she did when she'd tired of his presence, and Love wandered, dazed, in the other direction until he found himself standing in front of a nearly empty café. He ate alone in the ancient square, a simple plate of gnocchi with a tart red wine, watching the stars find their way out of the darkening night sky.

The Game had begun. He ached for the players.

Chapter 5
Saturday, March 27, 1937

ETHAN'S FATHER SAT AT THE DESK IN THE STUDY OF HIS SEATTLE mansion, sucking an unlit pipe. A New York City newspaper lay open before him. He scowled at it, folded it, and shoved it aside. Outside, a sparrow landed on the windowsill and peered in.

"Ethan!"

No reply.

"Ethan!"

Mrs. Thorne stepped into the room and issued an eloquent sigh. "Ethan's teaching Annabel how to play croquet," she said. "Henry's in the carriage house."

"Don't tell me," he said. "That boy and that infernal thing. It's at best a waste of time. At worst, it will ruin —"

"Oh, Bernard," she said, putting her hands flat on his desk and planting a kiss on his shining forehead. "There's no harm in it. Not considering the world's real menaces."

"It's a piece of —"

"Bernard."

Mrs. Thorne walked to the bookcase beside the desk. She made a small adjustment to an arrangement of framed photographs, angling one of a smirking, black-haired, black-eyed girl so that it faced the room directly.

"Get Ethan for me," Bernard said, lighting his pipe. "Henry —"

"Henry's just as interested in the newspaper," she said.

"Henry's interested in *music*." He said the word as if it were a curse. "And he's not —"

"He's just as much your son as Ethan is. Honestly, after all these years. His father was your closest friend. He was the best man at our wedding."

"Fetch Ethan," he said.

"Please?" She tilted her head, looking amused at her husband's foul mood.

"Get Ethan now, dammit, *please*," he said. "Tell him I have an assignment for him."

Sunlight burst through the carriage house windows, illuminating the edges of Henry's sheet music. It made him squint, but he kept playing. He pulled his bow along the lowest of his bass strings, digging blood-stirring notes from their depths. He was working on Edward Elgar's Enigma Variations for the school orchestra, and as he moved his way through the song, he filled in the rest of the parts from memory: the singing violins and violas, the keening cellos, the trumpets, and the thumping percussion.

He'd been obsessed with the piece since Mr. Sokoloff had handed out the music a few weeks earlier. It wasn't the best thing he'd ever played. Mahler, Tchaikovsky, Shostakovich, Rachmaninoff, Beethoven, Mozart . . . there was a long list of more thrilling composers. But it was the first thing he'd played that was *more* than music — it was a code of sorts. A riddle. A mystery to solve.

He felt sure a secret lay beneath the melodies that linked one movement to the next. There was the obvious place to start: Each movement was dedicated to people identified on the sheet music only by their initials. But that hardly deserved the title of

"Enigma." Anyone who knew the composer could solve it in an instant. There had to be something more. And so, over the last several days, Henry had worked the mystery over in his mind.

Curious, he'd gone to the newspaper archives to find an interview with Elgar, and what he read puzzled him. The man had compared the song to a drama where "the chief character is never on stage." Henry couldn't think of any example of such a play. Even in *Hamlet*, the ghost appears. Henry paused. Outside, a wind kicked up, rustling the spring-bright leaves. He caught a whiff of new grass.

He picked up his bow again, pouring himself into the music. He let it speak for him, ignoring the perspiration that rose from his forehead, gathering and traveling in a bead that carved a slow path down his cheek. He even ignored the fly circling his head like an airplane looking for a place to land. There was so much he wanted to say with the notes.

Henry played until there was a knock on the door. The rhythm of it, from a song called "On the 5:15," was Ethan's code. Henry was supposed to return two taps if it was okay for Ethan to enter, but Ethan never waited for that and Henry didn't want to stop anyway. The door creaked open and the fly spiraled outside.

"Sounds fine." Ethan stood in the rectangle of afternoon light that polished the carriage house floor. His shadow reached for Henry's feet.

Henry finished the movement. He would have liked to be alone a little while longer, but if anyone were going to interrupt him, Ethan would be his first choice. He certainly preferred him to little Annabel or either of Ethan's parents, who'd made it clear that they found his love of music decidedly unwise in uncertain financial times, a waste of time, a distraction from what was important, namely his education and his future. That's why he'd been consigned to the carriage house in the first place: They'd told him they didn't want to give him the idea that they approved, although they'd certainly tolerate it at a distance provided he met his obligations with school.

The last note came, low and long. Henry let it hang in the air a moment. After the sound faded, he lifted his head and caught Ethan staring at him in a puzzling way.

"What's that look for?" Henry said. "I happen to like this piece."

Ethan shrugged. He leaned against a worktable that ran the width of the room and was covered with sawdust, lanterns that needed oil, and the odd bent nail. A window behind his head framed it perfectly, casting a halo of light around his blond curls. It was no wonder girls were always batting their eyelashes and whispering to each other whenever Ethan walked into a room. He looked like he belonged in a Hollywood picture.

"The tune — it was great," he said. "You're getting all right on that thing."

Henry laughed. "Thanks for that ringing endorsement of my *tune*."

"I don't want your head to swell or anything is all. You know you're good." Ethan pushed himself up so he was sitting on the table. "So, we have an assignment."

"We do?" Henry said. It was common knowledge that Ethan was heir to the *Inquirer*, and that Henry was . . . well, he was a charity case.

"Yes, my father said it's fine if you go along."

Henry tried not to bristle. It wasn't Ethan's fault how his father always set them on different levels.

Ethan grinned. "It's a good assignment too. About airplanes."

Ethan guided the Cadillac toward the airfield with the fingertips of his left hand while he draped his right over the front seat, near where Henry sat. They'd driven from the Thorne mansion on

Capitol Hill and were crossing a green drawbridge that arched over the Montlake Cut, offering views of mountains on either side of the lake.

"So this is the situation," he said, looking at Henry out of the corner of his eye. "The *Inquirer* was scooped and Father's spitting nails about it. There's some airplane at Sand Point that's supposed to be one of the fastest on the planet. A New York paper covered some modifications a mechanic made to the engine, and now our job is to show those East Coast boys they aren't the only ones with ink in their veins."

"Sounds straightforward," Henry said.

"It's straightforward all right. The beat reporter had his backside handed to him in his hat, and Father is using us cubs to heighten the humiliation. I feel lousy about it, actually. It's not as though the poor sap missed a story about an airplane that could fly to the moon."

"As if that would ever happen." Nothing sounded more horrible; Henry far preferred to have his feet on the ground.

"You bring your notebook?" Ethan said.

"Of course."

This was how they worked together. Ethan asked the questions, Henry wrote the answers. Then Ethan composed the story in his head and dictated it to Henry, who typed it so that it would be free of spelling and mechanical errors. It was their system, their secret.

Mr. Thorne thought his son had long ago won his battle with the written word, but Ethan continued to struggle. It wasn't due to a lack of intelligence or effort. He was one of the brightest people Henry knew, quick to see patterns and connections between things, quick to form a rational argument. But through some accident of wiring, the letters on the page confounded him. Henry had been secretly reading and writing Ethan's work long before he'd come to live with the family — since the day he'd found him crying behind the school, the backs of his hands bloody where he'd taken a lashing from a teacher who'd accused him of laziness.

Neither Henry nor Ethan was certain what would happen when Ethan took over the family business. A publisher who couldn't read or write — it was unthinkable, unless they found a way to stick together. For now, they pretended that day was in the impossibly distant future, and that an answer would materialize when it was most needed.

"There she is." Ethan pointed out a yellow biplane with a glass cockpit and thick rubber tires. He stopped the car a distance away and hopped out, running a hand through his hair. Henry followed, but he wasn't looking at the plane. He was looking at the girl crouching on its upper wing. Something quickened inside him as he studied her, and he wasn't sure whether the feeling was good or bad.

"Do you know her?" Henry said.

"What? Who?"

"The girl you were pointing at," Henry said. Though he couldn't imagine where he'd seen her before, he felt as if he knew her the way he knew the sound of a low D.

"What girl? Where? I was pointing to the plane, numskull."

Of *course* Ethan was focused on the plane and the assignment. He never let himself get distracted by girls. Never. Henry tried not to, but without much luck. He was forever looking at them, forever looking for the one who'd make him feel as if he'd met his other half. He'd yearned for it his entire life, not that he could talk to anyone about it. And this girl . . . there was this . . . *quality* about her, something so alive. She walked from the tip of the upper wing to the middle, and then lowered herself to the bottom one as if it were nothing.

"Don't be ridiculous," Ethan said.

"Come again?"

"Henry, you can be such a dope." Ethan gestured toward his own face.

Henry had no idea what Ethan was trying to communicate.

"She's not a possibility, Henry. Stop dreaming of your wedding. You'd give my mother a conniption if she saw you gaping like a salmon."

"I wasn't. It's just . . ." He'd noticed the color of her skin, of course. To his surprise, he did not care, even though he knew everyone else would.

"Well, at least close your mouth."

Henry clamped his jaw shut, but Ethan was already walking toward a man in a navy-blue suit, his smile in place, his right hand extended. He dropped it immediately when he noticed what Henry had just observed: that the man in the suit had no right arm.

"I am Captain Girard," the man said in French-accented English. His tone was light, as if he were used to such gaffes. "I regret I cannot shake your hand, but mine was lost to me in the war. I see you've noticed the real story, though. The one those boys from New York missed."

"How's that?" Ethan asked.

"That girl right there. She's a fantastic pilot. The best of her kind in the state. Perhaps even better than Amelia Earhart. It is not just the plane that is fast; it is the skill and daring of the pilot, and here, she is unparalleled. It is because she understands the workings of the engine as if they were an extension of her mind."

Henry pulled out his reporter's notebook so he could take down what the captain said. Ethan, who did not have much of a poker face, was irritated. They were there for a story about a plane, not a girl. There wasn't a teacup's chance in a tornado that Mr. Thorne would let them write about a female pilot, especially one with skin the color of hers. But Henry didn't care about that either. He wanted to hear everything the captain had to say about her.

"Her papa fought with me in the war, when our troops joined forces with American ones. He was a brave man. Very good with his hands. Without him, I would have lost more than my arm. And the thing is, I cannot get any of the journalists interested in her. The reason for this is obvious, you see. Flora has the brown skin, and here in America, you pay so very much heed to that. And so they spend all their ink on Miss Earhart, who is also a courageous woman and almost as fine a pilot. But they are missing out on something here, something almost magical."

Henry wanted to volunteer to write the story himself, just so he could observe Flora at closer range, but the offer would get him into all sorts of hot water with Ethan, who worried endlessly that people would figure out Henry was helping him if the paper ever carried his solo byline, and who always changed the subject when Henry wanted to talk about girls.

"That is fascinating, of course," Ethan said, sounding not at all fascinated. "What can you —"

"And so, she needs a sponsor," Captain Girard said. "Someone to provide enough for a plane and a trip around the globe. I pay her what I can but the times, they are bad. Nobody works harder. She takes the night shift to support her *grand-mère*. . . . I honestly don't know when she sleeps."

The captain tucked a cigarette between his lips, took a matchbook out of his pocket, and offered it to Henry. "Do you mind?" he said, shrugging apologetically at his empty right sleeve. "I forgot my Zippo in the office."

Henry struck a match.

"Here," the captain said, showing the matchbook. "This is its name."

"Come again?" Henry asked.

"This is the club where she works. The Domino. It used to be her parents', but alas, they were killed in an accident with an automobile when she was just a baby. She has the place now with her uncle. I am ashamed to say I have never been, but I am past the age of music and dancing. She does keep me in matches, though."

Captain Girard took back the matchbook and Ethan shot Henry a look. Henry shrugged and phrased a careful question to regain control of the interview: "What can you tell us about her airplane?"

As the captain described a change Flora had made to the engine mounting so that the plane was better balanced, Henry took notes, but his mind was elsewhere. The captain seemed to notice.

"The girl," he said, smiling widely. "You really should take an interest. There is something there. Her name, it suggests she is rooted to the earth, but in truth, the girl has the heart of a bird." A breeze kicked up, ruffling Henry's hair, sending a gentle thrill down his spine. Henry swallowed. He looked at her, just as she looked at him. Neither looked away. For a fraction of a moment, it felt as though the earth had ceased its spinning, but his body moved on, dizzy with some unseen force.

"We're here for the plane," Ethan said. "But maybe we'll do another story later. You were telling us about the Staggerwing. . . ."

Henry transcribed the captain's answers to the questions Ethan asked. But his curiosity had traveled ahead to the Domino. No matter what Ethan wanted, Henry planned to attend a show there, and soon. In a strange way, it felt as though his life depended on it.

Chapter 6
Sunday, March 28, 1937

THE DRESS HAD BEEN HER MOTHER'S, AND SO IT WAS THE SLIGHT-est bit old-fashioned: a black-and-white harlequin-patterned halter that plunged in the back and made Flora feel self-conscious. The entirety of the silky fabric had been covered in sequins, so it was heavy on her skin in the way a fur coat might be, like something that had once been alive. She inspected her reflection, turning to make sure the seams were intact and that she wasn't going to give more of a show than she intended. One of the waves in her chin-length hair was misbehaving, so she pinched it back into place, sighing in exasperation. She would have preferred to wear her flight coveralls everywhere, along with the braids she wore as a child. Such things were comfortable, practical, and practically invisible. Being togged to the bricks made her feel like a Christmas display.

She'd asked Uncle Sherman probably a thousand times if she could just wear something simple and stay in the kitchen with Charlie, reminding him to go easy on the salt in the brisket rub, telling him to cut smaller pieces of corn bread because too much of that makes a customer too sleepy to drink.

But Sherman wasn't having it. "The Domino's half your club, baby," he'd told her. "You got to be out in front and on that stage. Nobody comin' to hear Charlie's corn bread sing. And there ain't nobody in town who sings like you, and you don't even half try."

She wasn't bad-looking, she knew, but far from the stunner her mother had been. She compared her reflection to the woman in the picture frame on her bureau, glad to be not as lovely. Her plainness had shielded her from the interest of boys, except for Grady. Her own absence of beauty made her miss her mother more.

She had no true memories of her parents. But she'd imagined being hugged and sung to so many times the memories felt like something made of truth.

"Flora!" Sherman's voice, calling from the parlor.

"Almost ready." She opened her top drawer, removed the pair of kid gloves that had been her mother's, and slipped them on. Though it was no longer raining, the night was still cool. And she liked the look and feel of them, the way they still carried the shape of her mother's hands.

Sherman, dressed in his master of ceremonies tuxedo, whistled at her when she emerged from her room. "I always liked that dress."

"Thank you." Flora felt embarrassed by the praise, although she knew it was his way of remembering his sister.

On their way, she passed Nana, who was working on a quilt with patches of red and white.

"Hello, love," Nana said. "There's a cake for you in the icebox."

"Chocolate?"

"Does coleslaw give Sherman heartburn?"

"Hey!" Sherman said. "It's not my fault your slaw is so good I can't stop eating it."

Flora gave him a friendly shove and stopped to kiss her grandmother's head. "Thank you, Nana. I'll eat it after the show. But you should have your piece now."

"I can wait," Nana said. "I'm not so close to the end that I need to take my dessert first, you know." She looked up at Flora over the tops of her glasses. "Don't you look just like your mama."

"Not half as pretty," Flora said, waving it off.

"Half again prettier, child. But she would have liked for you to stay in school. Graduate. Not have to work two jobs the way you do. You're only seventeen. Not old enough to be carrying the weight of the grown-up world on your shoulders."

"Oh, Nana. We've talked about that." There was no point in school, not when the club was her future and most white folk were hell-bent on keeping colored folk in their place, even if they were polite about it. And not when Nana needed her the way she did. Taking care of the house by herself would be far too much of a burden, and Nana moved so slowly these days, as if every inch of her ached.

"Girl's right," Sherman said. "The club needs her. We'll be able to turn things around and be more like we used to be. And just wait till she sets that record in the airplane. Flora's got all of Bessie Coleman's fire, and all of Amelia Earhart's ice. Miss Earhart won't know what hit her, and people will line up around the block to hear her sing. There's no kind of bad fame, you know."

"Tell that to Bonnie and Clyde." Nana returned to her quilt.

Flora waited until Nana had finished a slow, careful stitch. Then she bent and placed one more kiss on top of her grandmother's head. "Don't stay up too late."

"Sing your heart out tonight, child. Your mama's buttons would burst if she could see you now, all grown up."

Flora found a light coat and stepped into the night. A black cat, the strange but elegant one that had stopped by every so often for years to beg a little supper, skittered from the shadows and wove through Flora's ankles.

"You again," she said.

The animal had odd black eyes and seemed to prefer affection on her own terms, never coming when she was called, often hovering near the edges of things, as if she merely wanted to observe. The strangeness of the creature softened Flora's mood. She'd feed her when she got home. Maybe even some cake.

"Come on, Flora." Sherman jiggled his keys. "We got to go."

The cat blinked slowly before turning abruptly and disappearing into the night, as if she were done with Flora. But she'd be back. Flora was sure of it.

On the short ride to the club, they went over the set list, adjusting things here and there based on how the audience had responded the previous night. They arrived a good thirty minutes before the rest of the band. Because Saturday was their biggest day of the week, Charlie had been at work since dawn, slow-cooking pork shoulder, brisket, and ribs. The scent was warm and wonderful, as much of home to Flora as her nana's house.

"Hit the lights, baby," Sherman called out from the kitchen as the double doors swung shut behind him.

Flora turned and walked into the heart of the club, a room painted black to hide the many scars in the walls and woodwork — and to make everything in the room disappear save the stage. She flicked on the chandeliers that hung over the dozens of round tables filling the floor. The room went from dark to dazzling. She found a box of matches and struck one, and carefully set about lighting the sea of candles that lay before her, their wicks hungry for the light and heat that would by night's end consume them. Then she went to her dressing room to warm up her voice.

Chapter 7

ETHAN ROLLED HIS EYES AS HE STEERED THE CAR TO THE CURB. Down the hill, past the International District, rose the Smith Tower, its lights glowing against the black sky. Beyond that, Puget Sound. It had taken the better part of two days, but Henry had convinced Ethan to go to Flora's nightclub. His fingers twitched, playing the notes of the Enigma Variations.

They exited the car and put on their hats, swirling mist into the light of the streetlamps. All along the sidewalk, sharply dressed couples strolled arm in arm toward a low brick building with a black awning that read THE DOMINO.

"I don't know why we're doing this," Ethan said. "We've got school tomorrow, and besides, Father won't even let the arts reporters write about this music. He says it reduces people to an animalistic state. We're not writing the story about the girl pilot anyway, so all of this is a waste of time."

"It's just jazz," Henry said. "We've listened to it a thousand times."

"Au contraire," Ethan said. "We've listened to the uptown stuff. This is something else entirely. You of all people ought to hate it."

Henry wasn't so sure. The notes that found their way outside intrigued him. There was a call-and-response aspect to them, the same thing an orchestra did when the melody circulated from the strings to the winds and brass. But this was simpler. More elemental. More like one person chatting with another, one hand reaching out to touch another. He didn't know whether it was the music or something else, but the air felt electric, almost alive.

They headed toward the line of patrons entering the club. Most were older, in their twenties. Some even as old as thirty. Only about half were white. The rest came in all shades. There was even a couple from somewhere in the Orient. Each pair stopped before entering, chatting briefly with a bouncer who weighed at least three hundred pounds.

Closer to the door, the music grew louder, complicated with rhythms he'd never encountered. His fingers moved along with these new sounds, trying to pick out the notes he'd need to hit if he were playing along. Not that he ever would. It was one thing to dream of playing in an orchestra, which had ties to history and respectability and a connection to the world he was used to. There was no way he could set his hopes on playing in a place like this. The Thornes would toss him right out, and he'd be alone in the world.

They reached the bouncer. "You eighteen?" he asked.

"Yes." Ethan offered the man some folded bills.

The man laughed, taking the money into a hand that looked like it could remove a head as easily as it could uncork a bottle. "Happy birthday, then." He unclipped the velvet rope drawn across the double-wide door.

The music swelled and the boys stepped inside, passing a huge oil painting of a couple dressed to the nines, their brown skin burnished with tones of red and gold. Henry and Ethan headed down a staircase. The song ended and a ripple of applause reached them.

"Ugh, it feels like anything goes here," Ethan said. "Which is to say, a perfect recipe for everything going wrong."

Henry didn't respond. He couldn't. They'd reached the bottom of the staircase and now stood at the edge of an enormous room filled with round, candle-lit tables, a long bar lined with bottles and glassware, bustling cocktail waitresses, and waiters carrying trays of food and drink on their shoulders.

On the far side rose a stage flanked by red velvet curtains and pearly lights. Everything had seen better days, to be sure. But it was the biggest, brightest thing Henry could remember since before the Crash, and for a moment, he almost felt as if he were back in that old world, the one he'd lived in with his family before the influenza took his mother and sister, before his father . . . Henry stopped the thought in its tracks. Now wasn't the time.

A group of musicians stood on one side of the stage, and the drummer kicked off a new song. Center stage, stepping down a wide white staircase with curving handrails, was Flora, looking paradoxically the same and yet so different from the way she looked on the airstrip. She smiled as she walked, but it was clear she couldn't care less about the audience clapping and hooting on the floor below. A spotlight pinned her in front of a nickel-plated microphone.

"Something wrong?" Ethan said. "Don't tell me you've come to your senses."

"It's not that. I just —" Henry shook his head. "The singer."

"Not that it matters, but she's not bad-looking out of that canvas getup," Ethan said. "I'll grant you that. Even if her dress looks like something that was in style twenty years ago."

Henry didn't care about the dress. It looked fine to him. More than fine.

Flora opened her mouth to sing and Henry swallowed hard. He'd never heard anything like her voice, which made him wish he had his bass in his hands, just so he could return the sounds, a mix of chocolate and cream, something he wanted to drink through his skin.

Once upon a time I dreamed
Of how my life would go . . .

He recognized the song: "Walk Beside Me." But her voice nailed him to the floor. It made him feel as though something had slipped under his skin and was easing everything nonessential straight from his bones.

I'd span the globe, a lonely soul
Beneath the moon's white glow . . .

"Cigarette?" A blond wearing a short red dress and a tray of Viceroys slung from a strap around her neck leaned in toward them, blocking Henry's view.

On that day I saw you
It wasn't love at first sight
But slowly, like a sunrise
You revealed your light

Henry craned around her as Ethan waved the cigarette girl away. "Your kind always says no to mine," she muttered as she left. The maître d' approached holding menus.

"Follow me, gentlemen," he said. "It's your lucky night. We have a table right up front by the dance floor."

Henry had heard "Walk Beside Me" many times on the wireless. But he had never heard it like this, slow and tender. And the accompanying music was nothing like the orderly, upright way the Ozzie Nelson Band played it. This was something unsettling here, something unpredictable, as if some set of rules, both written and unwritten, was being shattered like glass. The awareness of it dampened his forehead and made his blood sing, raising all the tiny hairs on his arms and the back of his neck.

Flora moved on to the chorus.

> *I may have dreamed before you*
> *Of how my life should be*
> *The only thing I want now*
> *Is for you to walk beside me*

Beneath her voice, a skinny young bass player plucked a steady rhythm, holding her on a sturdy web of notes. For some reason, Henry immediately hated the man, his mustache, his pompadour, his trim tuxedo, the way he looked at Flora as though she were a thing he owned. The music picked up a notch, taking Henry's pulse with it as the song traveled back to the main melody, now with the full band. It was a conversation with a piano, a guitar, a saxophone, two trombones, and a pair of twins playing trumpets that turned the reflection of the chandeliers overhead into movable stars.

Henry felt as though he'd dived deep into the water of Lake Washington on a hot day, braced by the coolness of it, knowing he'd have to surface to breathe. He was vaguely aware that next to him, Ethan was saying something and gesturing with the menu.

"Beg pardon?" Henry said, unable to take his eyes off of Flora.

"I was saying," Ethan said, his voice edged with something sharp, "I ordered you a gin fizz and a rack of ribs with collard greens on the side. This place is supposed to be the best, if you like that sort of food."

It took Henry forever and a day to process Ethan's words. It was as though his mind was forcing him to untangle the letters, as though they were unspooling from a knotted ball of twine.

"Yes," he said. "I do."

"What's with you?" Ethan asked, his expression dark. "The eating had better be good because this music does nothing for me. And this club is a shambles. It's worse than her dress." He flicked his hand toward the stage, and his gesture extinguished the candle burning on their table.

Henry looked again at the gown, wondering what Ethan could see that he couldn't. Under the spotlight, the sequins followed Flora's curves in places he wanted to touch. And the club, well, it had seen better days, but what place hadn't? Ethan and his family might not have felt the full weight of the hardship that had afflicted most these long eight years, but it was never far from Henry's mind that he was one friendship away from nothing.

A waiter set down their order and leaned in to reignite the candle, and Henry focused on Flora, hoping she'd see him too. The moment the flame caught, there was a flash of recognition in her eyes, a quick stiffening in her shoulders, the slightest break in her voice. She looked away, and Henry leaned back in his seat and forced himself to breathe.

Ethan's voice cut in. "I suppose that's the thing with real life. It has a way of not living up to the one you imagine."

Henry downed his drink so he wouldn't have to reply. As far as dreams went, his imagination had never conjured anything as powerful as the hold Flora's voice had on him, and the only thing he could do was sit still and swallow it whole, trying not to feel Ethan's disapproval too sharply.

Chapter 8

After the show, Henry stood in the alley outside the club and rapped on an unmarked door while Ethan, making no effort to hide his mortification, turned to face the street. No one answered. Henry waited a minute before knocking again.

"Come on, Henry." Ethan glanced back over his shoulder, his car key in hand. "You can't afford to get yourself into trouble. Let's get out of here before that happens. At best, you're going to make a fool out of yourself. At worst . . . at worst, this might be the stupidest idea you've ever had. We're not writing an article about her. Not now, not ever. Nothing justifies your curiosity here. Let's go."

Henry had just raised his hand to knock one final time when the door opened and the emcee, a tall man with front teeth gapped wide enough to hold a nickel, burst out.

"Club's closed, gentlemen," he said. Stripped of his tuxedo jacket, he crossed his muscular arms over his chest, his shirtsleeves rolled up to his elbows.

Ethan took a half step back, leaving Henry by himself. Henry stammered, and the man laughed and shook his head, as if he'd seen the same scene unfold a thousand times before. "Her name is Flora, but it's Miss Saudade to you. She's my niece. She doesn't date the customers, especially not turkey-necked white boys who only have one thing on their minds."

"I know. That's not what —" The words clogged his throat. "I — we were at the airstrip yesterday. For an article. I wanted to say hello. I wondered if I might —"

The man exhaled, uncrossed his arms, and grabbed the doorknob. "Much as I am a fan of publicity, I don't believe a word you're saying. There hasn't been a white newspaper that's written about the likes of us unless some sort of arrest was involved. You wouldn't have any proof you are who you say you are, would you?"

Henry looked at Ethan, who had such proof in his pocket. Ethan, stubborn as ever, shook his head.

"Just as I thought," the emcee said. "How about you make yourself scarce before I pound you into a pudding."

"But —"

The man slammed the door in Henry's face.

"Cripes! There you go," Ethan said. "I knew I should have talked you out of this ridiculous business. My parents would be apoplectic at the thought of you coming here. Nothing good can come of this, Henry. You'll thank me later."

He turned on his heel. "Are you coming?" he called over his shoulder.

"Yes." Henry felt a crack in the ground open between him and his best friend. He wouldn't say another word about Flora to Ethan.

I'll come every night, he thought. *Every night, just to listen.* He had to. He'd focused on being useful and dutiful and respectable for so long. He couldn't do it. Not when it came to this girl, this music, even if it wasn't something Ethan could understand.

Chapter 9

Finished for the night, Flora sat in her small dressing room, holding a tall glass of lemonade against her forehead. The stage lights were always so hot she felt like something out of an oven after a performance, and nothing was better than something cold, tart, and sweet to drink. As she lowered the glass to sip, she tried not to think about that one moment in her performance . . . the moment she lost control.

Focus on what went well, she told herself. *Your club was full. No fights broke out. The tax inspectors didn't drop by with their notebooks to count the bottles of liquor.*

Probably no one even noticed the ruined note — well, no one but Grady, who'd no doubt bring it up with her later, thinking he was doing her a favor. He was that way with her. Because he was older, he considered himself her teacher, her protector, and her superior. He could be a real jackass.

She blamed the boy, though. The one from the airstrip. The one doing the article on the plane. Henry or Ethan. She wasn't sure which was which. Either way, he wasn't the sort she usually saw in the Domino, which was perhaps why he stood out in his tuxedo, his eyes glittering in his white face. It needled her that she couldn't ignore him during the show. Usually, she looked over people's heads. The audience couldn't tell the difference.

This time, though, it was as if some force had lashed her gaze to his. The moment of connection felt the way it did the instant the wheels of her airplane touched ground. There was a solidity, an inevitability to it, as though her body had been built for it, even if she wanted only to be back in the sky. It had never happened before. Never. But it was over and done. He wasn't the Domino type, and surely he'd gotten what he needed for whatever article he'd planned.

Flora shivered and set down the lemonade. She had no business looking twice at a white boy, or he at her, especially if he was the sort who felt entitled to take what he wanted. She'd seen it happen before, sometimes with the waitresses, sometimes with the cigarette girls. Deep in her center, a sense of danger planted itself. She trusted — she hoped — the feeling would disappear.

To let in a bit of air while she waited for Grady to come fetch her (as if she were a child), she stood on a low bookshelf and cracked open the high window, the only one in the whole club that hadn't been bricked shut. Sherman was scolding someone in the alley. Not the authorities. With them, he was nothing but honey, smiles, and free cocktails. Whoever it was, he was handling it. Flora smiled and jumped off the shelf. She took one last sip of her lemonade, letting the ice rattle in the glass. Then she felt ready to call it a night, and maybe feed the cat, poor thing, and then eat some of that chocolate cake Nana had made.

Right on cue, Grady knocked and stuck his head inside the door.

"Time to go," he said, as if she might not have realized. Jackass.

"Fine." She put on her gloves and felt better, more grown-up than girl.

"Let's feed you some supper at Gloria's," he said, referring to the all-night diner that served their people. "A little sustenance for my girl."

"It's late," she said, although she was famished just thinking of the cake. "And I might be coming down with a cold. It made my voice break during 'Walk Beside Me.'" That was to keep him from saying anything about the flaw in her performance, or worse, trying to kiss her.

Grady's face fell. "You should just let me take care of you." He pulled her close. "You need taking care of."

"It's kind of you to offer, and I do appreciate it," she said, trying not to breathe in his heavy cologne. "But not tonight. Please."

"Let's get you home," he said. She took the arm he offered, wishing he didn't hold her so tight. It made it hard to walk.

"On second thought, considering how I feel, I'll ride with Sherman." She dropped his arm.

"Flora," Grady said. He looked more irritated than hurt. She gathered her things in silence. Then she went to find her uncle.

Chapter 10

Tuesday, September 13, 1927

ONE MORNING, WHEN SHE WAS A NEWLY MINTED SECOND GRADER, Flora stood over her nana's bed. She wasn't supposed to wake her grandmother, but a small, scared part of her wondered whether Nana had gone to heaven in the night. Flora watched carefully until she saw her grandmother's chest rise and fall under the quilt. The relief at the sight felt as sweet as water on an August afternoon.

Perhaps she would stir if someone made the tiniest noise. Flora whistled, clapped, and stomped her foot. Just the one time. Then she stood as still as a statue, hardly even daring to breathe. Even so, Nana lay on her back, her chest rising and falling, a little quicker now, but still her eyes stayed closed. Flora moved closer to the bed. And then, like lightning, Nana's hand shot out from under the covers. Her papery fingers gripped Flora's wrist, and one of the old woman's eyes popped open.

"Caught you." She grinned and pulled Flora under the covers. It was the softest thing, and Nana was warm and cozy, the way she'd always been when Flora had bad dreams. But bed was the last place she wanted to be. Charles Lindbergh was going to land his *Spirit of St. Louis* in the city and visit Volunteer Park later that morning. Flora's school was going. It was her first field trip, and she was to take lunch in a pail and to wear her second-best dress, and there was a chance that Mr. Lindbergh would stop and shake some of the children's hands. She aimed to be one of those children, knowing that if her hand touched his, it would be a blessing on her that meant she'd learn to fly a plane and be up there in the blue sky herself.

"Why so squirmy?" Nana said. "And heavens to Betsy if your feet haven't been carved from a block of ice. I'm shivering from my toes to my teeth!"

"Nana," Flora said. "It is time to get up."

"Oh, but I thought I'd keep you home from school today," Nana said. "There's laundry to wash. All of Uncle Sherman's under-clothes. And so many socks to mend. You'd think they were aiming to join the hallelujah choir, they're so holey."

"But Nana!" Flora sat up.

"Oh, and the last of the pickling," Nana said. "I know how you hate the way it shrivels up your hands and makes your eyes water, but it has to be done." She sat up next to Flora and turned the girl's face toward hers. "Where should we start? Socks, britches, or cucumbers?" Flora was too stunned to speak. "My goodness it's a lucky thing your jaw has that hinge on it, or we'd be scraping your chin off the floor."

She pulled Flora in closer and started laughing, and that's when Flora knew Nana was teasing.

"Let's start with the britches," Flora said. "There are only thirty pairs, after all." It was Sherman's bachelor notion that he'd do less laundry if he had underthings for every day of the month. It worked, in a way: Nana did all of his wash.

"On second thought," Nana said, sliding Flora out of bed, "I think we had better pack you a pilot-size lunch."

While Flora ate a bowl of porridge, Nana's practiced hands heated the iron, straightened Flora's hair, and smoothed it into a pair of braids. Then she buttoned Flora into her dress, put the pail in her hands, and shoved her out the door.

"You say hello to Mr. Lindbergh for me," she said. "I packed an extra square of gingerbread in case he looks hungry."

"I will, Nana! I will!" There might have been sidewalk beneath Flora's feet as she ran, holding her pail as steady as she could. But she did not feel it.

At Volunteer Park, there was so much noise — the shuffle and murmur of the thirty thousand children in the crowd, the bright urgency of the marching band. Even so, the sound Flora heard most was her own heartbeat thumping in her fingertips and ears. She looked up. The sky was a perfect blue, with just a pair of clouds sliding across, as if swept along by God's broom.

She watched them, hoping, as always, that she'd see her parents looking down at her. She'd memorized their faces from the small photograph framed on her dresser. Every so often she was certain she'd seen them up there, the fringe of their fingertips fluttering over the edges of the white, waving down at her as she lay on the grass, holding things she wanted them to see: the doll Nana had made for her out of rags and a tea towel, the first book she read, the first tooth she lost.

"Is that so," her nana would say when Flora would report her sighting.

Those were the words Nana always used when she thought Flora was stretching the truth to better fit her imagination. But if it was possible that her parents were up there, perhaps Mr. Lindbergh had seen them from his airplane. And maybe when she learned to fly herself, she could visit them. Just that one moment it took for her plane to pass the cloud . . . that would be enough.

The sky's brightness flared, making Flora's vision swim. Sound rippled through the crowd, and Flora turned to look, wiping her eyes. Mr. Lindbergh had arrived in a long black motorcar. All around, the shout arose from her schoolmates. "I can't see! I can't see!" And it was true. The children enrolled at Flora's school had been positioned on the far side of the huge crowd, where there wasn't any sort of view. She couldn't help but notice that all of the white people had been given the best spots to stand, and she wondered if Mr. Lindbergh had asked for it to be that way.

The din of the thousands of children rose as the pilot approached the front, surrounded by a group of men from the city and the mayor herself. From Flora's spot, she could see a row of hats skimming the surface of the gathered children. But then, across that sea of bodies, an uncovered head attached to a man wearing a baggy leather jacket emerged. He raised his tanned hand to wave it at the throng. Flora glimpsed his face, the same face her parents had seen when he flew by.

She knew she would not get to touch even his sleeve, let alone give him her extra piece of gingerbread. But she'd gotten something. "And somethin' ain't nothin'," as her uncle often put it.

Then Mr. Lindbergh was guided back into his motorcar. Its engine faded and the crowd's roar broke into a quilt of individual voices again. The scattered laughter of children shoving each other in jest, the muffled sound of feet trampling the lawn, the occasional shout from a boy or girl who needed to find a restroom. The roar diminished, creating pockets of silence where Flora could once again hear her own thoughts.

She was not yet ready to leave, and when the opportunity for her to slip behind a sweeping redwood presented itself, she took it. She could make her own way home. The teacher probably wouldn't even miss her. She set her lunch pail down. Uncle Sherman could eat the gingerbread. The comforting scent of rich earth, a blend of growth and decay, rose up and surrounded her. Beneath her hands, the tree bark felt rough. Through its swaying branches, she could barely make out the blue overhead. But even that view was enough, and every inch of her strained upward as if she'd been created to be part of it, with threads of her left nice and loose so she might be pulled more easily into the blue.

At that same moment, Henry was on his bicycle, heading home from the same park, holding his cap on his head with one hand and the handlebars with the other. He whistled a happy tune, as much from the thrill of shaking Mr. Lindbergh's hand as from being permitted to skip school that day. Having recently lost his father and moved in with the Thornes, he was allowed a variety of small freedoms such as this. He never took them if Ethan objected, but Ethan was home that day with a fever, so he couldn't possibly mind.

Henry was tired of people looking at him with sad eyes. He planned to spend his free afternoon riding his bicycle around town, breathing in all the non-school air, the best kind there was. As he passed through the shadow of a giant redwood, a black cat chased a swooping sparrow across the street. Henry swerved to avoid the cat and bumped up onto the sidewalk, where a girl in a blue dress and pigtails had appeared.

He squeezed the brakes, sending up an awful squeal. The bicycle skidded, its wheel sliding forward until the whole thing tipped, taking him with it. He scraped his palms and tore the knee of his pants. The girl, meanwhile, tumbled backward with a shout. He hadn't hit her, but nearly so. Henry lifted the bicycle off of himself and sat on the sidewalk, dazed.

"Are you all right?" he asked the girl, who was looking at her own skinned hands.

She nodded. "But my dress is dirty. And it's my second-best one."

"I'm awful sorry," Henry said. "Let me help you home."

"I don't need any help," she said. "It's just down the hill."

Henry thought about letting her go. He didn't know her, and her expression was anything but friendly. But it didn't seem the right thing to do. "I ought to walk you home." He stood and held out his hand. There was a long pause. The sparrow, which had escaped, flitted overhead and trilled.

"I'm fine," she said. She brushed the dirt from her dress. The cat lowered itself onto the sidewalk next to them and started cleaning its back leg shamelessly in the way that cats do.

"How about if I just walk next to you?" It felt like a competition now, to see which one of them would give in first. He looked into her eyes, and she returned his gaze just as fiercely. There was no instrument to measure the slight change in the atmosphere between them. They were scarcely aware of it themselves. Neither would remember the meeting until years later, except in the vaguest of ways. But both would recall the feeling of being brought into something, even as neither had the word for it or the experience to understand what it meant.

After a pause, she shrugged and stood. "I have some gingerbread. It was meant for Mr. Lindbergh, but if you want it, you could have it. It's probably smashed, anyway."

"Oh, I couldn't," Henry said, falling into step beside her.

"Are you saying that to be polite?"

Henry was so relieved he laughed. "Yes. I love gingerbread and I'm hungry enough to eat a goat, beard and all."

They shared the cake and talked about airplanes until they arrived at Flora's small green house, which was about a mile from the park. He told her how it felt to shake Mr. Lindbergh's hand, which, in all honesty, was pretty much like any other grown-up's hand. But she seemed interested, so he told her everything about it, including the fact there was a small cut on one knuckle.

It wasn't until he delivered her to the porch steps that he remembered to ask her name.

She bounded to the top of the steps and put her hand on the doorknob. "Flora."

Flora. The only Flora he'd met before had been an elderly aunt who smelled like powder and Sloan's Liniment. But he liked the name for this girl. And she smelled nice.

"Look what followed us." He pointed to the black cat.

"She's around a lot. I'm not supposed to feed her." Flora stood in the open doorway and, for the first time, smiled. "But I do. Don't tell." She put her index finger to her lip.

"Your secret's safe with me." That smile, that gesture. He liked them. But he couldn't think of a reason to stay. She didn't ask his name, which he took to mean she didn't care to know. It was surprisingly disappointing.

"Good-bye, I guess," he said, wishing he could think of something else to say.

She waved and shut the door behind her. Then he got back on his bicycle and headed home, whistling a melody of his own invention, one to which he would someday return.

Chapter 11
Monday, April 26, 1937

WEEKS PASSED. LATE-NIGHT JAZZ MUSIC, LOOKS GIVEN THROUGH candle- and stage light, schemes whispered into the ears of tax inspectors. Why had Death consented to this Game again?

Ravenous, she stood in a small Spanish market town wearing a simple black dress. She could have been any young woman sent by her family to pick up food for the evening meal: a loaf of bread, a bit of meat, something leafy and green, a bottle of red wine. She was as far as she could be from the modern city by the Sound, and deliberately so. When the hunger was this great, the players were in danger. Her control over the Game was in danger.

As she walked through the market, stopping to inhale the perfume of flowers, Death felt a fingertip on her forearm. A light touch, as swift as the closing of an eye.

"For you, beautiful one." A young man stood before her, offering her a red tulip.

"I did not ask for this," she said.

"But you are so lovely, I cannot help myself." The man, who was no more than eighteen, looked down, his face turning red.

Death understood what he meant. She accepted the flower and noted the dirt pressed into the ridges of his fingertips. These were the hands of a person who spent his days working the earth, coaxing life from the soil. He'd seen a million flowers. Even so, each new bloom could make him smile, and unlike all the other humans who'd passed her, he noticed her. He saw her.

He is the one who is lovely.

The tulip was fragrant and beautiful. But, she noted, it was also dead. She would not be able to help herself. She moved on, and after a moment's thought, turned and looked at him over her shoulder.

"When you hear the engines in the sky," she said, "run."

She brought the tulip with her when she took to the air in a Stuka bomber. This time, she wore the guise of a young Nazi Luftwaffe pilot who'd left his plane momentarily because he was literally sick with nerves. He would return, pale-faced and sweaty, to discover that the dozen Stukas and half-dozen Heinkel 51 fighters had already risen like a cloud of insects, casting their awful shadows in the late-afternoon sun. Much as he did not want to be part of a German experiment to determine how much firepower was required to bomb a city into oblivion, he also did not want to be executed for dereliction of duty. And yet, why was his plane not still on the ground? The man wondered this the rest of his days.

Now his plane was above Spain, lighting the sky with reflections of the firestorm below. Death marveled at the noise, at the sudden lightness of the aircraft as it dropped a bomb from its belly. Every so often the roaring of the swooping Stuka was overtaken by the tatter of machine guns strafing the fleeing townspeople below. The noise, the heat, the color, the smell, the buzz of her hands on the yoke. It was almost like music, and she bombed herself senseless, unaware of anything save the plummeting thunder and fire.

Eventually, all of the town, except a church, a tree, and a small unused munitions factory, had been pounded to bits. The smoke of charred bodies rose, setting the stage for a bloodred sunset. By the time she landed the plane, the sky was smoke clogged and dark, lit only by the reflection of fires that would burn for three days. For each of those days, she returned to the village in the guise of the Spanish girl, walking quietly through the smoking ruins. The soil had been stunned to silence. All around lay the harvest, so many lives. Too many to reap at once.

She twisted time like a kaleidoscope, suspending the crucial shards until she could visit them one by one, lifting souls from their scorched and shattered cases. The sensation of so many lives rushing into her was deliriously good, so much so that she was insensible to anything beyond it. The enormity of what she'd done hadn't yet hit her, although she knew it would, ribboning her essence as though it had been run through the blades of an airplane propeller. White-eyed and insatiable, she consumed these souls as one might pick up scattered cards in another sort of game, scraping them into order, fanning them out in front of her, feeling their perfectly balanced weight in her hands before flinging them into the beyond.

At last, she found the one she had been looking for. He lay beneath a stone from a building that had once held hand-blown drinking glasses. Shards of their remains, some as small as stardust, surrounded him.

There was life left in him, but not much.

She knelt beside him, her hand on a stone too heavy for him to remove, for any human to lift alone. His face was sweaty, caked with dust and the dried blood from a cut on his forehead. He shivered.

"I told you to run," Death said as she put her hand on his brow. His skin was hot, his eyes delirious.

"I —"

If she removed the stone, it was likely he would die. If she didn't remove the stone, his death was a certainty.

"I —"

His eyes focused on her face and she remembered the flower tucked into a pocket of her now filthy dress. Its crumpled petals were still as soft as an infant's skin. Soft, scarred, ruined.

"I was looking," he said. "Looking . . . for you."

"Here I am." She pinched the stem in her cold fingers.

His lashes fluttered. Death saw something in his eyes: recognition. And something else: desire.

"What do you have to live for?" She weighed his soul in her hands, wondering why humans wanted to live so when in the end, everything would be lost.

She could feel him trying to wrap his mind around her words, trying to shape an answer with his dry lips. Water. She wished she had some. Footsteps echoed off of broken buildings, and rescuers called out for survivors to hear. There wasn't much time.

She moved the stone and touched his cheek, and as she did, the images in the man's mind splashed over her. A field of blooming flowers. The shape of a woman, a woman whose face he could not yet see, but one whom the man wished to marry when he found her at last. Then the man himself silhouetted against the setting sun on a pleasant spring evening to come, the man and his someday child walking hand in hand through the field.

"This," he said at last. "This."

Death laid the broken flower where her hand had been. The man gasped.

"Hay uno por allí," a rescuer called out. *There's one over there.*

There was a scuffle of running feet, the gust of an anxious breeze heaving the smoke aside. Death disappeared behind the broken stone skeleton of a church before they found the man and put their quick hands all over him, probing him for injuries, brushing away gravel and bits of glass, putting a tin cup of water to his lips, lifting him into the long shadows of early evening.

She walked the cobbled streets one last time and reimagined herself a dress, a new style, cut close to her frame, unadorned, and also free of blood and dust and smoke, as if none of it had ever happened. The light of the setting sun turned its black edges red. She stood until the pain quieted itself within her and the color of her clothes was at last the same black as a starless sky. Then she brought herself to New York, where she had someone to observe.

Chapter 12

Monday, May 3, 1937

MR. THORNE SAT BEHIND HIS DESK, SUCKING HIS PIPE AND READING a stack of newspapers from cities across the continent. He looked up when Ethan and Henry walked into the room in their shirt-sleeves and trousers, their hair still wet from washing, their chins glowing pink from the razor. Henry suppressed a yawn as he watched Ethan's gaze travel over Mr. Thorne's collection of untouchable tin windup toys from his childhood: cars, clapping monkeys, a painted minstrel, and even a small automaton.

"Fine job on the Staggerwing story, Ethan," Mr. Thorne said. "You look like hell, Henry. You get any sleep?"

"Plenty, sir." He hoped his lie wasn't obvious. His was an exhaustion built of late nights listening to jazz music and dreaming of Flora. He'd been every night for weeks. He still hadn't worked up the nerve to speak to her again. Even so, sitting at his usual table near the stage, he'd watched her, memorizing every inch of her. And he'd felt her stealing glances at him, always looking away whenever he'd try to catch her gaze. It had almost begun to feel like a game.

"Eat some meat, why don't you. You look low on iron." Mr. Thorne set his pipe in a stand and snapped open a newspaper from

Washington, DC. He cleared his throat and pointed to a grainy photograph on page A2. "See this?"

Henry and Ethan leaned in, but it was obvious neither knew what Mr. Thorne's point was.

"Hooverville. Below the 59th Street Bridge in New York City," he said. "It's nothing compared to ours. We have eight encampments. Our largest is ten times the size, easily. But because it's out west, these newspapers think it doesn't exist." He slapped the paper closed.

Mr. Thorne clamped his pipe between his molars. "You're going to write a story about Seattle's Hooverville, Ethan. The big one by the water. It's a human-interest story, at least. Especially on this new fellow" — he consulted a typewritten sheet of paper on his desk — "a Mr. James Booth, age twenty, who arrived out of nowhere a few weeks back and claims to be their de facto mayor. But here's the thing. I hear tell they're brewing liquor in those shacks of theirs. No doubt this Booth character is behind it, trying to build himself a quick fortune. I wouldn't be surprised if he has connections to the mob. If that's the case, and if the buyers aren't paying liquor taxes, then it's more than a human-interest story. It's a scandal. And it's something to show those East Coast clowns that news doesn't drown when it hits the Mississippi."

"Thank you for the assignment, Father," Ethan said. "It's all right if Henry accompanies me, isn't it?"

Henry braced himself.

"I suppose, if he can tear himself away from that music. Start by sussing out this Booth character. Where there's power, there's most likely corruption."

Behind them came the tap of high-heeled shoes on parquet floors, followed by the slapping soles of Annabel's patent leather Mary

Janes. Lydia Thorne entered the room holding a small, yellow rectangle of paper. Annabel followed her, carrying a porcelain doll.

"I have news," Mrs. Thorne said, lifting a pair of reading glasses on a bejeweled chain and putting them on her nose. "Two pieces, in fact."

"We have news!" Annabel said. "Two newses."

"Quiet, dear." Mrs. Thorne patted her blond daughter on the head. Even with the reading glasses, Mrs. Thorne was still a beauty. It was from her that Ethan and Annabel had inherited their fair hair and clear eyes.

"We're to have a visitor," she said, relishing her moment as the important person in the room. Mr. Thorne wound his right hand in a circle, as if to tell her to get on with it.

"A visitor!" Annabel said.

"Quiet, Annabel," she said. She pressed her lips against each other, as if to hide a smile. "It's Helen."

"But her debutante ball. I thought —" Mr. Thorne set down his pipe and leaned forward on his elbows.

"Apparently she made the wrong sort of debut." Mrs. Thorne's nostrils flared.

Mr. Thorne grunted and settled back in his captain's chair, with one hand behind his head. He picked up his pipe with the other, most likely so that he could better exude thoughtfulness.

"Helen. Helen is a hellion," Annabel said.

"Annabel! Where did you hear that word?" Her mother shot her a scolding look.

"May we be excused?" Ethan rolled his eyes for Henry's benefit. "If we're to —"

"I learned it from Ethan," Annabel said.

"That couldn't possibly be true." Ethan pretended to look shocked. "I'd never!" He walked to the bookshelf, picked up the clapping monkey, and twisted the key in its back. The clicking revved Henry's already taut nerves. Ethan pinched the key, no doubt waiting for the perfect moment to release it.

"When does she arrive?" Ethan asked.

"We're to pick her up at the King Street Station" — Mrs. Thorne adjusted her glasses and studied the telegram once more — "next Tuesday at two forty-five."

Mr. Thorne whistled low. "They didn't waste much time, although I'm surprised your sister didn't have her on the first train west."

Mrs. Thorne nodded and removed her reading glasses. "They've probably had all sorts of fires to extinguish . . . and there's the issue of managing the gossip. And apparently they are departing for Europe to —"

"Ride out the storm?" He sucked his pipe and exhaled a plume of purple smoke. "Europe's lousy these days. Spain especially."

"Well, now," Mrs. Thorne said, "let's not overdramatize things. And Spain is lovely, despite what happened to that one little town."

"Spain is lovely if you like fascists."

Ethan caught Henry's gaze and shook his head, smiling slightly. Ethan sometimes called his father a fascist for his domineering ways. Henry drew his finger across his neck so Ethan would cut it out.

"She's traveling unescorted?" Mr. Thorne said. "Or will we play the hosts to a companion, as well?"

"She's traveling alone." Mrs. Thorne fanned her face with the telegram. *"It's come to that."*

Ethan set the monkey down and it clapped wildly. Annabel handed Ethan her doll, took one of her father's newspapers, and fanned herself as well. Henry, mortified by the monkey, gestured for Annabel to come over and scooped her up. Mrs. Thorne lifted a photograph of a black-haired girl in a navy sailor's dress from a gathering on a shelf.

"She's a handsome girl, Henry, wouldn't you say?"

Henry, his arms full of five-year-old, cleared his throat and looked away from Ethan, who stuck a finger in his open mouth and pretended to vomit.

"Yes." He blinked, starting to grasp Mrs. Thorne's point.

"Henry likes her," Annabel said. "He's turning red."

"She's older now," Mrs. Thorne said. "This was taken while my sister's family vacationed in Switzerland three years ago. She and Ethan — and you, of course — are of an age. We haven't seen her since they were children, but she and Ethan had a marvelous time playing together on the island."

"She kicked my shins," Ethan said.

"Ethan, put the doll down," Mr. Thorne said. "You look ridiculous. Like some sort of nancy boy."

Ethan set the doll on the shelf and Annabel wiggled down so she could retrieve her baby. Then he started juggling a group of fossilized trilobites. "Helen wears really hard shoes."

"Ethan," Mrs. Thorne said. "Those aren't toys."

"Well, we're not even supposed to handle the ones that are," he said. "Besides, I never drop things."

"You have to be able to withstand a bit more than hard shoes in the pursuit of procreation," Mr. Thorne said. "Your mother said to put down the fossils."

"I was five when she kicked me," Ethan said, catching the fossils one at a time with a flourish. He set them back on the shelf. "And Helen" — he shot Henry a warning look — "Helen is not particularly lovable."

"Kicking isn't nice," Annabel said. "I do not kick."

"Run along to the kitchen, Annabel," Mrs. Thorne said.

Holding her doll by one leg, Annabel galloped out of the room.

After a moment, Mrs. Thorne tucked her hair behind her ear. "Helen isn't a match for Ethan, of course, but we'll see what Henry says about the matter. She might . . . he might enjoy her company."

She set down the photograph and wiped imaginary dust from the edge of the frame.

"He's in the room, Mother," Ethan said. "And he's not like one of Annabel's dolls for you to play with. He's a person."

Henry wanted to say something on his own behalf. But what? This was what he was supposed to want. A way to become an official part of the Thorne clan. He'd complete his schooling and become engaged to a girl damaged enough to say yes to a penniless orphan but still a good enough match to give him connections that would lead to a respectable job. It was a life that promised him everything that was supposed to matter.

"The second bit of news involves Henry," Mrs. Thorne said. She held up an envelope, addressed to him, which had been opened. "The scholarship to the university came through. Isn't that wonderful?"

It was good news. Truly. Pieces of his life were falling into place all around him.

"Excellent, excellent," Mr. Thorne said. He turned his attention back to the newspaper in front of him.

"Now, boys, both of you may be excused," Mrs. Thorne said. "We're going to have to get the house ready. There's so much to do." She clasped her hands together. "So much to do."

"She probably won't kick you in the shins," Ethan said as they hustled out of the library. "But if I were you, I'd be careful."

"What?" Henry said. He was thinking of one thing only: getting to the carriage house so he could play music and think. So many things were happening, and so fast.

"I was joking," he said. "But I do imagine she's outgrown kicking boys. She might even be nice now. And for certain, she's not bad-looking. I wouldn't blame you if . . ." He let the thought trail off.

Henry looked at Ethan in disbelief.

"I'm on your side, of course," Ethan said quickly. "You don't need a marriage to be part of this family. You're important." His face turned a bit pink. "You're like my brother. It doesn't matter what anyone else says."

Henry was glad to hear it even if he and Ethan weren't the sort for soppy stuff. He felt the same way, despite the fact he was feeling the limits of their brotherhood for the first time. He wouldn't talk about Flora with Ethan, not after that first night, although he'd been to the Domino many times since. He'd waited until after Ethan had gone to bed, then he'd sneaked out, borrowing Ethan's car on the sly.

Now that he knew this Helen person was on her way, it felt as though someone had planted a bomb in his life and lit a fuse. As soon as Helen arrived and Mrs. Thorne put her plot into motion, this life he'd begun to hope for — one with late nights in jazz clubs and the dizzying presence of Flora — would be annihilated. Ethan's words confirmed it.

"But think of it, Henry," he said. "If you married her someday, not now or anything — and I'm not saying you have to, I mean, you ought to get to know her and see if she's your kettle of fish. And maybe neither of us will ever marry. But if you did, and you chose her, you'd really be part of the family. My father might even write you into the will or give you a share of the paper. I'd always have you with me. It would solve so many problems —"

"Look, I know," Henry said, louder than he'd intended. "There's something I have to do, so if you'll excuse me."

He ignored the hurt look on Ethan's face. This one time, he couldn't bear being responsible for disappointing him.

"Hooverville tomorrow, though, right?" Ethan called behind him. "We'll crack that story wide open."

"Yes." Henry didn't bother to turn around. When had he ever let Ethan down?

Henry spent the rest of the afternoon in the carriage house. He started off playing the Enigma Variations but lost interest before he made it through the second movement. Without thinking, he began to play his versions of Flora's music, eventually setting down his bow so he could focus on jazz-style plucking, varying the lengths of his notes to create a rhythm that felt entirely new. He imagined her voice replying to the voice of his bass, and he wished she were there so they could talk to each other without the peril of words.

This wasn't like classical music, where every note was written, every movement with the bow prescribed, every dynamic meant to be the same every time. It was more like real life: unpredictable, unrepeatable, sometimes lousy, but something you loved all the same.

Working with a melody he'd heard in his head since he was a child, Henry played until the quarter moon rose and his fingertips ached. He burnished the tune until it felt right, and then pondered lyrics that matched, words about the yearning the sea has for the moon. The song that took shape felt like something that had existed for a long time. He played it over and over, setting his bass down only when Mrs. Thorne came out to make sure he'd finished his homework.

"Nearly," he said. It wasn't true, but he did not care.

"Wonderful," she said. "You've always been such a fine boy. So diligent and reliable."

Henry swallowed. Then he followed her through the cool night air into the warm, well-lit mansion.

Chapter 13

Tuesday, May 4, 1937

THE NEXT DAY, AFTER BASEBALL PRACTICE ENDED, HENRY AND Ethan traveled to Hooverville in pursuit of their story.

"Father was right. This is a big encampment." Ethan shut off the engine and stepped out of the car. He shaded his eyes and scanned the nine acres of dried mud and misery. The air reeked of sweat and waste and burning wood. A nearby train rumbled by, spewing black smoke.

"Can you imagine trying to sleep through that noise?" Henry said.

"I'm sure they're used to it." Ethan reached into his satchel and handed Henry a fresh notebook and pencil. The two walked past flimsy plywood houses, small fires in metal barrels, and staring men. "Which one do you suppose is James Booth?"

"Haven't a clue." Somewhere, someone strummed an out-of-tune guitar. A small group tossed dice in the dust, occasionally lifting their hats from their heads, wiping away perspiration. People stopped whatever they were doing to stare as Henry and Ethan passed in their clean, well-constructed clothing. Every so often, a whistle rose above the crunch of gravel underfoot. It took Henry a moment to realize these whistles were a signal to let someone know they were there.

"Welcome, newcomers!" a clear, sharp voice called out. Henry and Ethan turned toward its owner.

A golden-haired man who couldn't be more than twenty walked toward them, his arms extended as if he were Christ on the cross. Despite his youth, there was something powerful about him, something you couldn't help but stare at. His voice was almost hypnotic, even if his suit had seen better years. Embarrassed, Henry looked down at the man's shoes, and noticed they were oddly clean.

"I'm James Booth," the man said. "Mayor of Hooverville. I welcome you to our community, although I can tell from your attire you're not looking to move in."

James Booth clasped his hands over Ethan's and gave them an enthusiastic shake. Ethan's expression changed, and Henry felt something effervesce from his scalp to his fingertips.

"Do you have a name?" Mr. Booth said.

Ethan looked flustered. "Ethan. Ethan Thorne."

"And who's your friend?"

Feeling Mr. Booth appraise him, Henry stood straighter as Ethan introduced him. Mr. Booth did not offer his hand, and the whole experience left Henry feeling pinned like a butterfly under a lepidopterist's magnifying glass.

"We're from the *Inquirer*," Ethan said. "Here to do a feature story. If that's all right by you, sir."

"It's more than all right," Mr. Booth said. "But you must call me James. I insist."

Henry glanced around, wondering whether he was the only one who felt unsettled about this welcome. The other residents of Hooverville had resumed their business tending their fires, flinging dice, mending the soles of their shoes with cardboard, leaving Ethan and Henry to talk with the mayor.

"You and I — we'll go someplace private." James put a lightly freckled hand on Ethan's shoulder. "Your friend can walk where he likes, taking notes, making observations. That's how it's done, isn't it?" He addressed someone behind Henry. "Will, show this young man around."

Henry expected Ethan to object. He couldn't very well write down what was said in an interview that he didn't hear. But Ethan nodded and allowed Mr. Booth to steer him toward one of the larger shacks Henry had seen in the encampment. It was made of straight, sturdy boards and capped with a roof of corrugated tin. There was even a small porch on the front.

Henry tried to tamp down his anxiety as Ethan disappeared inside. He'd come with Ethan on newspaper reporting jobs before, although nothing this important or — he realized — this danger-ous. What if Mr. Thorne was right and James Booth was a mobster? Up until now, the greatest danger they'd faced was covering the Shriners' parade, when an irritated llama spit on Ethan.

Feeling ill and overwhelmed, Henry turned to face a man who looked about forty-five. He wore a moth-bitten three-piece suit, along with an old hat pulled low over his forehead. His entire ward-robe appeared held together by nothing more than dirt. Behind him stood a few more men who looked equally destitute.

"Got any jobs at that paper of yours?" The man pushed his hat up.

"I don't know," Henry said. "I'm just —"

"Figures," the man said. "Careful with what you write. All the stuff before's been lies. We want work, not charity." He paused and looked away from Henry. "We're not criminals. Not most of us, anyway. Will Barth."

The man extended his hand and Henry shook it, feeling stares from all directions. The place was a regular melting pot. People who'd come from around the world and across the country look-ing for something better only to end up here because they had no place else to go, no family to turn to, no Ethan Thorne as a best friend.

"Boy's from the newspaper," Will said. "He's going to tell our story. Maybe then people that got jobs and such will think about hiring the likes of us."

"Fat chance," said one with an Irish accent.

"Don't mind Rowan," Will said.

"How do you know he isn't a copper?" Rowan shoved himself away from the shack he'd been leaning against and advanced toward Henry. "Gatherin' up information that'll be used to bust this place up."

"He's not," Will said, "he's a kid." He gave Henry a hard look. "Right?"

Henry felt uneasy, knowing what Mr. Thorne wanted. "I'm not with the police," he said. "Here." He reached into his pocket and pulled out his wallet. Inside were the two dollars he hadn't spent the previous night at the Domino. Rowan snatched the bills, inspecting them before tucking them into the pocket of his coveralls.

Will shook his head. "Come on, Henry. Watch where you walk. The ground isn't level and not all of the men use the privy at the end of the dock."

As they wove through the maze of shacks, across depleted, gray soil scarred with ruts, Henry learned Will's story. He'd grown up in the Skagit Valley, where his family had a tulip farm. He'd fought with the Second Infantry Division in the Great War, and lost the farm a couple of years after the Depression. He'd come to Seattle to find work, and had ended up in Hooverville.

They stopped walking. "Each of these," he said, "is a house for one man or two, depending. Duck your head in here. No one'll mind."

Henry peered inside a small, mud-spattered shack with a tar-paper roof. It had no windows, and at night would be as dark as a cave.

"Bed's there," Will said, pointing to a piece of plywood covered with a well-worn scrap of burlap and a few sheets of newsprint. "There's the table and chairs." By those, he meant two overturned boxes that had once contained apples.

"A man can have a house for twelve dollars or so — four if the seller's drunk." Will chuckled grimly. "No women and children. Not anymore, anyway, although from time to time you do see one. Found a little tyke all curled up in a crate once, but took him back to the orphans' home. Wouldn't have lasted two weeks here, not with some of the characters who mix with us."

They made their way to the center of the once vacant lot, where the largest building in Hooverville stood.

"This here's the church," Will said. More care and better building materials had gone into its construction. On the front stood a porch with wide, horizontal rails. The front rose to a shallow peak, where a cross had been nailed above a decorative lattice capped with a curving beam. "Most days, though, doesn't feel like God bothers to show up, even though our new mayor acts like he's God's gift, if I do say so."

Nearby, men argued. When it became clear the dispute was getting worse, Will held up his hand. "Wait here a moment."

He strode toward the source of the scuffle, which now included grunts and the thuds of fists meeting flesh. Henry followed, intending to sneak back to the church once he learned what was going on. Peering around the rough edge of a shack, he saw Will holding two red-faced men apart. In the air, the sharp scent of alcohol. In the background was a contraption with rusting pipes and barrels. A still.

Henry slipped back to the church and wrote a quick description of what he'd seen and where. If he could prove the men weren't paying taxes — and they almost certainly weren't — Ethan would have his story. But Henry wished he wouldn't want it.

Will returned and registered Henry's stricken look. "A dozen gallons a day pays for a lot of bread and meat. Those soup kitchens? Dinner only and not much of it. Without this, these men would starve." He paused. "It'd be better if they drank less and sold more. But I'd challenge any man to live here and not want to take the edge off a bit. What we want is a chance, not charity. So you'll keep that part out of your story, right?"

Henry considered this, and thought about all the alcohol that was consumed at the Domino, and even the glasses of wine and tumblers of Scotch at Ethan's house. What made this so very different, aside from the matter of taxes?

Before he'd worked out his opinion, Ethan and James returned.

"I'm glad to see you've shown our guest the church," James said. "We do like a spiritual moment now and again in Hooverville." He turned to Ethan, extending his hand. "I'll see you again next week?"

Henry expected Ethan to decline. They had all the information they needed, and Ethan was never the sort to come to a place like this when he didn't have to. But Ethan tucked his notebook into his shirt pocket and said, "Next week. See you then." His voice was nonchalant, and Henry knew him well enough to know that meant he was anything but.

Inside the car, Ethan shut Henry down before he had a chance to say what he'd seen. "We're not writing about the booze. James told me all about that. I'm interested in something different. It's hard to explain. And do me a favor," he said, casting Henry a sidelong glance. "Don't tell my father."

Henry glanced at Ethan, curious about the look in his eyes. It wasn't one he'd seen before. But he didn't question it, he felt so relieved.

"I won't say a word."

Chapter 14
Wednesday, May 5, 1937

HENRY AND ETHAN CAME HOME AFTER A DISAPPOINTING BASE-
ball game to the spectacle of Annabel in a sobbing, facedown heap
by one of the columns holding up the porte cochere. With anyone
else, Henry would have worried there had been a death in the family. In all likelihood, Annabel had stubbed her toe.

"What's wrong this time, Bell?" Ethan said.

"Mother. She's what's wrong." She rolled onto her back to sob
sunny-side up, flinging an arm across her forehead.

"Don't say that so loudly," Ethan said, laughing.

"Don't laugh at me."

"Ethan's right." Henry stifled his chuckle. "She might make
you eat Brussels sprouts. Or worse."

"She won't teach me how to ride a bicycle," Annabel said. "She
said ladies don't do that."

"She doesn't know how to ride a bicycle is why," Ethan said.
"But I'll teach you this weekend."

"I need to know *now*," Annabel said. She sat and brushed gravel
from her dress.

"Sorry, kiddo," Ethan said. "It's a school night. And we're worn
out from our game."

"I'll teach you, Bell," Henry said.

"Really?" Annabel asked. She stood, wiped her nose, and launched herself into Henry's arms. He caught her and pretended to stagger backward, but really, she was as light as anything.

Ethan shrugged. "You're spoiling her. Not that I give a darn about that."

"Dry your face," Henry said, offering her his handkerchief. "Let's get Ethan's old bicycle and go to the park." He felt like having a little adventure before drilling calculus into his skull.

Once they'd arrived and he'd helped her carry the bicycle down the steps leading to the path, Henry explained to Annabel how her feet were meant to push the pedals, and how forward momentum would make it easier for her to keep her balance as she rode from one of the circular ponds to the other, landmarks that reminded him of the day he'd seen Charles Lindbergh. He'd been about Annabel's age at the time. Strange. He hadn't thought of that moment in years.

"I'm not a dummy," she said. "I know how a bicycle works. I've watched you and Ethan do it a thousand times. I just need you for the push."

"All right, then," Henry said. He helped Annabel onto the seat. "Ready?"

"Ready."

"On the count of three."

"Don't let go."

"I thought you knew how to ride a bicycle."

"I do," she said. "I just don't want you to get lost from me."

"One," Henry said.

"And don't go too fast."

"Two."

"And don't let go," she said.

"Three!" Henry started jogging beside the bicycle, holding tightly to the seat. "You have to pedal, Annabel." He had visions of her tipping and falling into the pond and getting tangled in the lily pads.

"I am."

"You're just moving your feet," he said. "I can tell. Use your muscles."

"Is this better?"

"Perfect," he said, running faster to keep up.

"I think I am a natural," she said.

"You certainly are. Keep going." His plan was to have her pedal from one pond to the other, down the straight sidewalks connecting the two.

As Annabel pedaled, a sparrow trilled. Henry looked up and caught a glimpse of a young woman in a green coat, white gloves, and black hat. It was Flora, coming down the steps just ahead. Of course it was. It felt as though he'd willed this moment into being. She was all he could see when he closed his eyes, and he knew at some point or another, he'd open them and find her in the real world, away from the club and away from Ethan, where they could just be two people together, standing under the same sky.

"Annabel, let's practice stopping," he said, trying to mask his nerves.

"I don't want to."

"Annabel," he warned, "you're going to have to." He tugged gently on her seat, but she pedaled harder, breaking away. He took off after her, but wasn't fast enough to stop her before she crashed spectacularly in front of Flora.

Annabel turned on the waterworks. "Henry. You let go of me. You let go."

Henry crouched next to her and put his hand on her shoulder. He glanced up at Flora and remembered a long-forgotten moment from that day in the park. He'd nearly run over a girl on his bicycle. In his mind's eye, that girl's face and Flora's were one and the same. They had the same name too. The coincidence of it seemed equally impossible and necessary. Did she remember? Had it been her? He couldn't bear to ask. And there was also the matter of Annabel's dramatic meltdown. She had a definite future as a radio star. The situation was feeling more like a disaster every moment.

"I'm sorry," he said, wiping Annabel's tears.

"Girl's got a good voice." Flora looked even better than she did onstage. Definitely less serious as she crouched down to talk to Annabel. "Do you know any songs?"

"Lots," Annabel said, hiccuping.

"Like what? Can you sing me one?"

"No," Annabel said. "Ladies don't sing in public. Mother says."

Flora laughed. "Some do. I'm pretty sure of it."

"Henry sings sometimes," Annabel said, "because he is not a lady."

Flora laughed again. "You look as if you could use something to clean up that flood on your face." She opened her pocketbook and took out a handkerchief with her name embroidered on it.

"Flora," Annabel read. "Henry talks in his sleep about someone named Flora, even though he is supposed to marry cousin Helen the Hellion."

"Annabel!" Henry said. "That's not true!" He wondered what the odds were that the earth might open up and swallow him then.

"Yes, you do," she said. "I heard you last night when I was getting a drink of water. And Mother says you and Helen are a perfect match even if I am not to say *hellion*."

"I'm sure he doesn't do any such thing." Flora looked as if she'd like to be anyplace else.

Henry stood and brushed off his slacks. This was not going well, and he wanted to make a quick escape. Maybe a unicorn would materialize and he could gallop away in style. "It's been swell to run into you again. I mean, not the almost crashing part. But just seeing you. I hope you liked the article."

"Are you a maid?" Annabel said.

"Annabel!" He wished for invisibility or time travel or just a really big box to climb inside.

"I'm not a maid," Flora said. "I fix planes and I fly them. And yes, I did like it. Ethan got most of the facts right."

"Well, you *look* like our maid."

"Flora's a singer too," Henry sputtered, wondering which facts he'd botched, feeling a shameful level of relief that Ethan was taking the blame for the errors. "A great one. And your mother is wrong about ladies singing onstage, just as she was wrong about girls riding bicycles." This was not how he'd imagined telling Flora that he admired her voice. Oh, God.

"You and our maid are both colored," Annabel said. "And Mama says the colored people make the best maids. Sometimes our maid sings. She only knows church songs, though."

"Well!" Flora said. "Isn't that an interesting story." She looked as finished with the meeting as Henry. He hoped Annabel had exhausted the opportunities to mortify them.

Almost, but not quite.

"Can I keep this?" Annabel held the handkerchief out.

Flora's face softened. "Yes, you may keep it."

"I'll share with Henry. I promise."

Flora laughed again. "I'm sure he'd love that." She adjusted her hat, tugged at her gloves, and gave a relieved smile that almost countered the strange look in her eyes. "And now I have to be off. It's been nice to see you again."

She turned toward the nearby cemetery, and as she walked away, Henry called after her.

"Flora! It was —" What did he want to say? That it was nice seeing her too? He'd already said that, and it would ring false anyway. He pushed his hair off of his forehead. "I'll — I'll see you around. I hope."

She looked back over her shoulder and gave him a small wave. He wanted to say something else, something more definitive. Or even suave, to salvage the scraps of his dignity. But he couldn't find the words. Though they stood only a few yards apart, what felt like miles of embarrassment stretched between them.

She turned toward the path and was on her way.

Chapter 15

From the floor of the Domino, the white steps leading to the stage looked substantial. Like the kind of marble used to carve an angel for a church or graveyard, the kind of thing that could withstand eons of rain and lightning. From the top, they were anything but. They were wood, coated in glossy paint to reflect the most light from the chandeliers, and flimsy enough to vibrate with the music of the band. Flora had to be careful not to step in the wrong place, or they'd sag. So many things in life were not what they appeared. It was a wonder she trusted anything.

But she trusted herself as she made her way down the steps, aware of the audience, aware of the steadiness of Grady's bass line supporting her. That reliability. It was supposed to be enough. She put one hand on the microphone, then another, as if she were cradling a face. Only it wasn't Grady's she was thinking of.

She opened her mouth and let the first note rise, acutely aware that Henry wasn't there for the first time in weeks, probably because of their run-in at the park. What a disaster, even if it had broken the weird spell between them. She was more disappointed at his absence than she could have believed, and the feeling leaked into her song. But she didn't mind. There was little difference between disappointment and yearning.

She closed her eyes and sang, focusing on technique. Shutting out the audience helped, and by the end of the number, she felt more herself again. She opened her eyes, and there he was, at his usual table. The surprise made her miss her cue for the next song by a half beat, and she had to rush to catch up. The band covered for her, but Grady shook his head and looked at her with pity.

As her irritation hardened into anger, she could feel it color the song. She worried she might lose control of the performance. This only frustrated her more, so she was surprised to notice the effect it had on the audience. People leaned forward. They set down their cocktail glasses. Some held their forks midway to their mouths. Encouraged, Flora focused on the notes, making each as heartfelt as she could. The full disaster of her feelings spread from the deepest part of her and flooded the room. The band responded, Grady especially, turning heat into sound.

She avoided looking at Henry until a thought struck: That was just another way of giving him — and whatever was between them — power. She remembered when she'd first started flying and feared contact with the earth and the danger it represented. The way to conquer that, Captain Girard had taught her, was to remember she was the one in control. The plane would do what she told it to. She would not be harmed. It was that simple.

She turned her face to his and sang to it, wishing she hadn't noticed him in the first place, but a mistake like that, she could recover from. Her blood was just a bit of fuel she had to burn off. Burn it, she would.

By the time she finished the tune, sweat coated her back. The last note out of her mouth soared overhead and then dropped, ringing against the hard surfaces of the room, burrowing into the soft ones. The crowd erupted. Her heart felt lighter. She'd done it. She was safe. She looked away from Henry and let herself smile as she disappeared backstage, ignoring Grady's hurt and perplexed look.

She'd faced Henry and stayed in control. This thing that was happening — whatever it was — she would survive.

Chapter 16
Thursday, May 6, 1937

THE GAME HAUNTED LOVE AS HE WALKED THE STREETS OF Seattle in the guise of James Booth, past hollow-eyed men holding cardboard signs begging for work. Days had passed. A week, and April turned into May, bringing longer days and soft earth, warm with growth, along with a visit from Death. She materialized without warning at the shanty in Hooverville, where he lay looking at the sky through the cracks in the ceiling.

"I don't see how you expect to create any sort of love from this vantage." She sat on an overturned peach crate, her face lit by a candle on the floor. The shadows underscored a haunted expression, even as her voice radiated arrogance. "Honestly. You're making it too easy."

"You might be surprised." Love found a bottle of wine and two glasses. It was a good wine, one he'd picked up on a quick trip to France.

"Red?" she said.

"I'm not going to be superstitious about things anymore. I won't give you that power."

She sipped from her glass. Love put his to his lips, but he could not drink. "What you did in Spain." His voice cracked.

"Stop." She held up a hand. "You don't know what I go through."

"Sometimes . . ." He paused, weighing his words before he tossed them across the table at her. "Sometimes I feel as though you haven't any heart."

"You know nothing of my heart."

"Why are you here?"

Death sipped her wine. She was hiding her thoughts, as ever. Love tried to read her face, but couldn't.

"To tell you that it's not too late," she said.

"Too late for what? It's certainly too late for all of those people in Spain."

"Let me have her now," Death said, "and I won't take any others from either player."

"Call off the Game? Is that what you're saying?" She'd never done this before. Then again, she'd never looked so awful. He was almost concerned enough to ask after her, to ask if there was anything he might do. But then he chided himself for the foolishness. She was worried, worried that he might win.

He laughed and finished his wine. Death reduced herself to the form of a cat and slipped out into the night. The candle flickered out. Love refilled his glass and let the darkness surround him as he drank. He'd made a mistake, laughing at her. He'd have to be more careful.

Chapter 17

No one likes to be laughed at, Death least of all. This time she did not venture as far as Spain, but rather to the East Coast, where she had two errands. If he didn't want to call off the Game, she'd make it worse. Far worse.

Her first stop was Lakehurst, New Jersey, where she waited at the edge of a naval airstrip, watching the sky. She looked clean and modern in her smart black suit and red cloche, even if she felt as though she'd been stuffed with the ashes of an apocalypse.

The afternoon was stormy. A charge hung on the air, reeking of dirt and ozone. Clouds gathered; humans did the same. At seven in the evening, a silver airship glided into view, its shadow a swath of black below. The craft looked like a blind whale and was the biggest thing that had ever flown. Humans had already conquered land and sea. With the *Hindenburg*, they'd rule the sky.

Death adjusted her hat and allowed a smile to stretch her lips. The ground crew waved the ship off, so the captain turned it sharply toward the sinking sun. The man's emotions spilled down on her just as surely as the shadow of his ship. He was on edge. Her smile now had teeth.

Four minutes later, he renewed his approach. Death dropped her gloves into her handbag. She gestured, bare fingered, and the wind shifted. None of the humans standing near her noticed the way her hands trembled, or the slight sheen that developed below the brim of her hat.

The captain, fighting the wind, turned the dirigible away from the swiftly fading daylight. Death held out her hands, palms facing upward. The crew dropped massive quantities of water, first six hundred pounds, then another six hundred, and finally more than a thousand, to right the listing beast. Liquid crashed down, sounding like a falling sky. No one on the ground spoke as the mist settled against shoulders and faces and hands, mixing with sweat and dust.

For a moment, the strategy appeared to have worked. The airship held steady, limned by the last filtered light of the sun. Two mooring lines dropped, tumbling nearly three hundred feet to the ground. Workers would attach these to a winch that would bring the *Hindenburg* down.

The first line was secured. The ship bounced on it, and the ground crew raced for the second line. The air shivered, and overhead, the cloud-bruised sky continued to darken. Then, on the upper edge of the great ship, the chemical-soaked cotton cloth that had been stretched over the zeppelin's aluminum frame fluttered. The movement was small enough that it might have been some trick of the failing light.

It was anything but. And in the helter-skelter thirty seconds that followed, the ship was gone, swallowed by a mouth of fire that ate its skin and turned its metal skeleton into a pile of twisted, glimmering red bones. Lashed to the ground, the wounded ship writhed. The screaming from all quarters was intense. Death watched the ravenous flame, another for Love to get sentimental over, no doubt.

Death plucked the rising souls like flowers, decorating her mind with the residue of human experience while the fire lit and warmed her face. Hungry, she searched for the captain through the smoke and flame. His life's essence would be infinitely satisfying at a time when she needed all the strength and comfort she could get.

She walked the length of the scene looking for him, worrying he'd been consumed too quickly to be noticed. As she turned to leave, disappointed, she sensed something behind her. She stopped walking and peered over her shoulder, which was dusted with still-warm ash. And there he was, the burnt skin on his face smoking in the glow of the fire. He was trying to go back on board so that he might save a few more hopeless souls.

It would taste splendid to kiss that face directly, to feel the heat and ash on her lips, to inhale the heartbroken entirety of him. She was about to set upon him when his first officer lurched forward and pulled the captain away from the wreckage. He struggled and then collapsed on the ground. Alive! He would be scarred inside and out. But he could live, so she let him.

She would catch up to the captain later; she preferred to, in fact, when he would be seasoned in the bittersweet brine of survival.

Meanwhile, she had a train to catch.

Chapter 18
Saturday, May 8, 1937

FLORA WAS COOKING BREAKFAST WHEN HER GRANDMOTHER HELD up the morning paper.

"My merciful heavens," Nana said. "Did you see this?"

Flora glanced at the headline. HINDENBURG BURNS: 35 PERISH.

"May I?" Reading over Nana's shoulder as sausage sizzled in the pan, Flora read about the accident that had occurred two days earlier. No one was certain what caused it, although several commenters were happy to suggest it was God objecting to human incursions into the heavens. She doubted that. Sometimes, bad things happened for no reason. The deaths of her parents, for example.

A photo of the zeppelin the moment after it caught fire sickened her, though. It was no stretch for Flora to imagine the terror people must have felt with flames racing toward them as they hung some fifty feet in the air, suspended by an explosive gas.

"I worry about you in the sky like that." Nana accepted the plate Flora offered. It was Saturday morning and she was still in her housecoat, as was her tradition. So was their breakfast of cinnamon French toast and fried sausage.

"I'm not flying a zeppelin," Flora said. She bit into a sausage. "I stick to the airplanes."

"Don't talk with your mouth full," Nana said. "Airplanes, blimps. All the same thing, taking over God's blue sky."

Flora swallowed. "If God felt that way about the sky, we wouldn't have all those birds."

"God put birds in the sky," Nana said. "He did not put man there. Or girls. What if this article is right? What if God doesn't want you to do what you're doing?"

"If God didn't want me to fly," Flora said, reaching for her coffee, "why on earth would God have made me want to fly so much?" She took a sip of coffee and it felt fantastic on her throat, soothing and invigorating at the same time. She was so glad Nana had finally given her permission to drink it. "I'm not going to die in a plane, Nana. I promise."

Nana pushed herself away from the table, tipping her nose up the way she did when she was feeling ignored. "Those are not the kinds of promises a girl can rightly make, Flora. You keep your humility about you or it will kill me from worry."

"I'm sorry, Nana," Flora said. She held out her hand and Nana took it, giving her three squeezes. *I love you.* Flora returned four squeezes. *I love you more.* "I'll wash the dishes, Nana. You sit down. Put your feet up."

She couldn't help but worry; her grandmother was getting shorter of breath every day, it seemed. And she was forever rubbing her swollen ankles. She never complained, but Flora could tell they gave her pain.

"We'll wash up together," Nana said. "Many hands make light work."

"Sit, Nana. Please," Flora said. "I can't eat if you're not resting."

"Just a minute." Nana opened a cabinet and pulled out a canister marked SUGAR. She reached inside and pulled out a wad of bills, mostly small denominations that had obviously been saved over a long span of time.

"Do you really want to fly?" she said.

"More than anything."

"Then here. Let me help you. I know it's not all you need, but I do believe a girl needs to follow her heart."

Flora interrupted. "No, no. That's your money, Nana. You might need it."

Nana sat and Flora could hear the wheeze in her lungs. "It's for your dreams. Those are what I live for." She set the money on the table. "That is all I have to say about it."

The look she gave made it clear she'd brook no argument. Flora surrendered. She'd accept the money to make Nana feel better, but she'd never use it. She'd slip it back into the canister later, when Nana wasn't looking. As much as she wanted to fly, she wouldn't take a cent from her grandmother. She couldn't. This wouldn't be enough, anyway. She could hardly bear the thought of the many things that stood between her and her dream of flying around the world. First, she'd need enough money to enter the Bendix. Then, she'd need to persuade Captain Girard to lend her a plane. After that, she'd need to win, and even when she did, the purse still wouldn't be enough money for a plane of her own, let alone fuel and a navigator's salary for the grand trip. It was enough to make Flora want to yank out her own hair. She ate a few bites of breakfast, though she no longer had much stomach for it. Then she led Nana to a comfortable seat in the parlor, as far from the dishes as she could get.

"Bring me my quilt, lamb. I am so close to finishing," Nana said.

While her grandmother hummed and sewed, Flora cleaned the kitchen. As she did, she remembered something she hadn't thought of in years: that day Charles Lindbergh came to town. That boy who almost hit her with his bicycle. As she scrubbed the pan, she wondered what became of him. There was something so likable about the boy who'd walked her home when he didn't need to, who was so happy to eat Nana's gingerbread. And he was so eager to tell her what it was like to shake Mr. Lindbergh's hand; it had given her the feeling that she'd done it too.

Though this boy was still a child in her memory, he'd be almost grown now. She tried to imagine what he'd look like, and the face that came to mind was Henry's. No doubt because he'd watched her perform so often at the club, he was fresh in her mind. A bit irritated by his intrusion into the quiet of her mind, she turned her thoughts to other things: a thousand errands to run, a million things to do before work that evening.

She bathed and dressed, and on her way out, she took one last look at the ball of flame that had once been the biggest thing to ride the clouds — and then she put it out of her thoughts. It was a tragedy, but it was all the way across the country. Such a disaster wasn't in the cards for her. She saw no reason to waste energy on worry.

Chapter 19
Thursday, May 6, 1937

AN APPLE. AN APPLE THAT HAS BEEN PLUNDERED BY A WORM. THAT'S what Ethan's cousin Helen Strong thought of herself. There was something wrong with her, something on the inside. How had everyone else grown up clean and pure? she wondered. *How dare they?* This bewildering resentment made her prone to lash out at everyone around her. She did not want to be like this, but she could not figure out any other way to be.

And it had been a bad couple of weeks. Helen didn't regret the incident at the debutante ball. Jarvis Bick deserved to be kneed in a certain trouser seam, particularly when he told her no one would marry her after he walked in on her kissing Myra Tompkins in the coat closet — just when the getting had started getting good. (Myra had the sweetest mouth. Like fresh cherries.)

Helen had never wanted to be married in the first place, but how dare he say such a thing. It was his fault she was being shipped west to be dangled like a piece of chocolate in front of icky old Ethan. Let's just say there was a reason she'd intended to be blind drunk and irredeemably late for her train. She'd wait in the Kissing Room beneath the Biltmore Hotel in Grand Central Terminal until the last possible moment and see what happened.

"I'd rather be dead than doing this," she muttered. She glanced up. Someone who looked exactly like her, right down to the polka-dot travel suit, looking altogether too pleased to see her. Helen took a drink from a pewter flask she kept in her pocketbook. She squinted and tried to fix whatever was wrong with her eyes.

Her second self didn't scram like a good little hallucination. Instead, she sat next to Helen, removed her gloves, and held Helen's hand. Something flowed out of her. Something heavy and awful she was glad to be rid of.

"Follow me," the Other Helen said.

Helen was delighted to. It felt good, what had just happened. What had been troubling her before? She could not remember. They walked beneath Grand Central's soaring turquoise ceiling with its strange backward constellations. A lone helium balloon pressed against the stars. The women approached the track, and the rumble of the approaching train shook the ground beneath their feet. It pushed a gust of cool wind toward them, stirring their hair, lifting their hems. Helen put a hand on her forehead and stumbled. Other Helen wrapped an arm around Helen's waist.

"This," Helen said. "I don't . . . what?" It was all so confusing.

They stood at the edge of the track. The wheels of the oncoming train squealed in the distance. The woman turned to face her. It was strange, seeing herself in someone else like this. But it was also wonderful, almost as if she might finally be understood. She extended her hand to touch her reflection. They stood, palm to palm. Helen's knees buckled and the woman, her eyes white, held her gaze. Helen felt her life drain away; she saw scenes from her own past travel through the eyes of this strange other.

And then she stood on the platform in numb confusion as a woman who looked like someone she ought to know boarded the train.

The girl — what was her name? — could not remember what she was doing there. Where she had meant to be going. She remembered nothing of her future plans, but also none of her past sorrows. Not even the look of her own face.

People came for her, people who put her in a white room in a quiet hospital with barred windows. They whispered that someone so finely dressed would have family searching for her. But for the longest time, no one came for this girl. Not until it was far too late.

Chapter 20
Tuesday, May 11, 1937

WHEN THE TRAIN PULLED INTO THE KING STREET STATION FIVE days later, screaming and billowing steam, Death could barely contain herself. She could have traveled back to Seattle instantaneously, but she did not wish to face Love so full of souls from the *Hindenburg*, or so charged with what she'd consumed of Helen's life. She rode west on the train as a human would, drinking tea and eating stale sandwiches, looking at a crowd of souls through their flesh cases, pretending they held no appeal, making conversation whenever she was called to.

Her self-control was not aided by the fact that the station in Seattle had been modeled after the Campanile in Venice, reminding her that the Game would end where it began. What's more, it was just blocks from the Domino, and not much farther from the Thorne mansion, where she would be living, or the small green house she'd first visited so long ago. Every element was gathering in the neck of an hourglass, and it would not be long before the ground opened up for the final plunge.

She stepped out of the train, one delicate shoe at a time. Henry and Ethan were there, waiting, and ready to welcome her into their home.

"Kiss kiss," Death said.

Ethan put his hands on her shoulders and faked a peck on her cheeks.

"Don't look too happy to see me or anything, cousin," she said.

Behind them, the huge train breathed steam on their hands and faces.

"I'm always happy to see you, Helen," Ethan said. "Shin-kicking, name-calling, things done with spiders in the middle of the night. You're a treat. I can't believe so many years have passed since your last visit."

"We were *children*," Death replied. The name *Helen* had long held significance for her, and Love had never forgiven her for the whole business with the thousand ships. How was she to know the war would last ten years and kill a demigod? "We're all grown up now."

"That's an awful lot of luggage you brought," Ethan said. "Just how long are you planning to stay?"

"As long as it takes," Death replied. Then she looked toward Henry and gave him her most seductive smile. "Who's your friend?"

Death was happy to devour Henry with her eyes. He wasn't movie-star pretty, like Ethan. But there was something about him she liked even better, from the slight gap between his front teeth to the way his dark hair refused to obey a comb. She liked the curve of his cheekbones and the square of his jaw, all the better to envision the skull beneath the skin.

Taking her time, she removed an enameled compact from her bag. She snapped it open and appraised the face in the mirror from a variety of angles. It was a face she'd grown to like. She powdered her nose, applied a swipe of red lipstick. Then she reached for Henry's arm and readied herself. She was nearly home.

The Thornes no longer had a houseboy due to the changing nature of the times, just a maid and a cook, so Ethan and Henry carried

Helen's luggage upstairs to her suite of rooms. When they finished, Helen and Mrs. Thorne were standing at the bottom of the stairs. Mrs. Thorne held a basket of cut tulips.

"Yes, those are divine," Helen said. "Very fresh. Almost as if they're unaware they've been cut." She smiled coyly at Henry. "I'm just going to dash upstairs and change."

"Ethan, dear," Mrs. Thorne said. She shoved the basket of flowers at him. "I'll need you to hold these while I make arrangements. Helen is changing into her tennis garb. She said she'd so love to play. I thought Henry —"

As Helen glided up the steps, Ethan held his hands behind his back, as a soldier might stand at ease. His mood was anything but. "You know what Father would say if he saw me arranging flowers with you."

"Oh," Mrs. Thorne replied, too irritated even to get out a sentence.

"I'll help," Henry said. He reached for the basket. Mrs. Thorne held tight.

"I'd rather play tennis," Ethan said. "Even with Helen."

"Ethan," she said. "How rude."

"I'd love to help." Henry held out his hands once more, and Mrs. Thorne reluctantly set the basket in them. Helen reappeared at the top of the steps, dressed in a white skirt and sleeveless blouse.

"Who's up for a match?" she said. "I'd kill for some fresh air." She looked pointedly at Henry.

He shrugged and held up the tulips. "I'm afraid I have my hands full."

"On second thought, I can surely manage this myself," Mrs. Thorne said. She picked up a leaded glass vase and nodded toward the flowers. "Just set them on the console, Henry."

"I'll play," Ethan said. "Give me a moment."

"You too, Henry," Mrs. Thorne said. "I insist."

"After we're finished here," Henry said. The truth was, Helen made him uncomfortable. He wasn't sure if that was a good thing or a bad thing. But he wasn't inclined to spend any more time with her than he had to.

"Do you ever wonder," Helen said, walking down the stairs toward him, "if flowers feel pain when someone cuts them?" She lifted one from the basket. "Does it look like it suffered?"

"Oh, Helen," Mrs. Thorne said, "what a curious thing to say. I'm sure Henry has thought no such thing."

It was true. But, he realized, he would not be able to look at a flower again without wondering whether it had suffered, and whether anyone had cared.

A minute later, Ethan bounded down the stairs holding two racquets and a fresh box of Slazenger tennis balls.

"Don't you have any Dunlops?" Helen said. Ethan shot her a look of disgust. "Oh, but I'm just teasing. I'll play with any old thing."

"You're stuck with me," Ethan said. "Henry's busy."

Helen took one of the racquets from Ethan's hand, tipped it over her shoulder, and looked back at Henry with a wink.

"Isn't she lively?" Mrs. Thorne said, after Helen and Ethan had disappeared outside. "Lively and intelligent." She slid one tulip after another into the vase. "This whole thing with the — it's just — she comes from good stock," Mrs. Thorne said. "That should be what matters. But back east, they're a little —" She sniffed, and somehow managed to elongate the space between her nose and lips just enough to look like an insulted horse.

Even with all the half-finished sentences, Mrs. Thorne's meaning was clear. The prospect made him feel — he looked at the tulips before him — as if he were about to be severed from something vital.

"Did I tell you about the school she attended?" Mrs. Thorne

chattered as she led Henry to Mr. Thorne's office. She wiped her already dry hands on her white linen apron.

"You did," he said. *Twice.* "It sounded like a rigorous environment."

"And she would've had top marks there." Mrs. Thorne tilted her head to examine her work. She nudged one flower to the left and moved the vase to the corner of Mr. Thorne's desk.

Henry nodded and watched the flower drift back to its original spot. *Top marks but for all the time she spent in the office of the headmistress accused of things for which they had no proof.* He'd heard Ethan's parents whisper about it.

Seeming satisfied with her arrangement, Mrs. Thorne lifted the old photograph of Helen off the shelf. She held it up and regarded Helen's and Henry's faces side by side. "Well," Mrs. Thorne said, after she'd set the photograph down. "I think we're finished here. Can you please send Ethan inside to do his schoolwork?" She smoothed her apron and left the room with the empty basket, a satisfied smile on her lips.

"Of course."

He walked to the west-facing window. Late-afternoon sun spilled across the grass and through the trees, bathing everything in a green-gold light. Helen returned a serve, a cigarette dangling from her lips. Ethan lobbed it over the net and Helen threw her racquet at it. Both the racquet and the ball made it over the net. Ethan picked them up, looking exasperated, as Helen flopped down on the grass, laughing, her cigarette in her left hand. Ethan tossed the ball at her. She caught it with her right, and winged it into the cypress hedge.

"Hey!" Ethan yelled. "That's practically new." He jogged after the ball. Helen caught Henry staring through the window. He ducked into the shadows, and then realized this made him look more foolish. When he looked out again, she blew him a kiss, holding her nearly spent cigarette between her fingertips. By the time he thought to wave, she'd already turned back to Ethan, who'd emerged from the hedge, looking ready for revenge.

When Henry went outside to fetch him, Helen came inside as well. He wondered if he'd ever grow used to her arm in his — stiff and cold, even through his sleeve. It wasn't what he thought it would feel like, and, if he were being truly honest with himself, he didn't care much for her perfume or how it smelled mixed with tobacco. But maybe this was what a person was supposed to get used to. Maybe accepting it was what it meant to grow up.

At dinner, Henry sat across from Helen, who took the seat of honor at Mrs. Thorne's right.

"You must be starving, my dear, after your long journey," Mrs. Thorne told Helen, who'd changed out of her tennis whites and into a black-and-white-striped dress with an enameled red rose pinned over her heart.

"I confess I am rather hungry," Helen said. She sipped red wine from a goblet. "Though I did eat quite well on the way." She lifted her fork, letting it hover over her plate.

"It's curried lamb," Mrs. Thorne said. "And Waldorf salad. There's chocolate cake for dessert."

Annabel pointed at the lamb dish. "I don't want . . . the yellow. May I just eat bread and butter?"

"That's prison food, Annabel," Mr. Thorne said. "You'll eat what your mother planned and you'll like it. Even if it is . . . never mind. I don't know why you didn't just have Gladys bake a ham. Everybody likes ham."

"I think it's terribly modern," Helen said. "Well, except for the salad. That's been in New York for ages and ages. But curried lamb! My!"

Henry marveled. Everything that came out of Helen's mouth in front of the elder Thornes was perfectly polite. And yet something about the way she spoke, the way she carried herself — maybe it was her slow, wide smile — felt off. Dangerous, even, as silly as that notion felt.

"It looks like cat food," Ethan said.

"Ethan!" Mr. Thorne choked back a laugh, even as he rebuked his son.

"Well, then I must be part cat," Helen said. "I think it's delicious." She put a huge forkful in her mouth and chewed, closing her eyes with pleasure.

Mrs. Thorne looked pleased to have found an ally. "Henry," she said, "don't you have anything to say to Helen? Ask her about her journey?"

"I'd rather talk about ham," Ethan said. "Helen, is ham also terribly modern?"

"Or bread." Annabel slid down in her chair until only her eyes were visible above the tablecloth. "I like rye bread best. It is terribly delicious."

Henry tried to think of a question for Helen, preferably one that didn't involve food. He felt Helen's gaze, looked up, and had to turn away in embarrassment. She laughed and emptied her wine glass. Her lips and teeth were stained.

"How was the weather on your journey?" It was the best question he could conjure.

"Inside the train?" Helen dabbed her red lips with a napkin. "No storms, I suppose. Though there was some bad weather on the East Coast just as we were leaving. Thunder and lightning. I was frightened half to death."

"Electrical storm," Mr. Thorne said. "Took down the *Hindenburg*. If they'd launched it here, where those sorts of storms are a rarity, that tragedy might have been averted. But no, it was Germany, and Rio, and New Jersey. New Jersey!" He said it as if New Jersey were the waiting room of Hell itself.

Everyone was silent for a moment, except for the scraping of forks against china. Henry glanced out the window into the twilit sky, and he felt something tug at his core, as though someone had called his name from a great distance.

"Mother," Ethan said. He had his hand on his chest and his face was pale. "I'm not feeling well all of a sudden."

"Why, Ethan," Mrs. Thorne said, "whatever is the matter?"

Ethan reached for his water goblet and drank until he coughed. "I might go outside and get some air. Maybe even go for a drive." He did look unwell.

"May I come?" Helen asked.

Mrs. Thorne looked alarmed. "Ethan, if you're feeling ill, then you should go straight to bed."

"All right, Mother," Ethan said. He laid his napkin on the table, pushed in his chair, and left.

"What about you, Henry?" Helen asked. "Would you take me for a drive?"

"That's a wonderful idea," Mrs. Thorne said.

Henry panicked. That would scotch his plans to go to the Domino.

"You can use my car," Mr. Thorne said. "Special treat."

"After the cake," Mrs. Thorne said. "It was made especially for Helen."

"Lovely," Helen said.

"It's your grandmother's recipe, dear," Mrs. Thorne said. "God rest her soul."

"Yes," Helen said. "God rest her soul."

Henry steered Mr. Thorne's car along Fairview Avenue and toward downtown.

"Are you nervous?" Helen asked. "You seem twitchy."

"Nervous? No. Just thinking about schoolwork, I suppose."

Henry wasn't thinking anything of the sort, but what Helen didn't know wouldn't hurt her. He'd resolved to keep her away from his usual haunts, and instead, was driving her to Queen Anne, where they could ride a cable car to the top of the hill and see the city lights and the waterfront from above.

She laughed lightly, but Henry could feel her watching him. They parked at the bottom of the hill, and he guided her onto one of the cable cars, his hand lightly — politely — on her elbow.

"I don't understand how they run," Helen said. She covered his hand with her gloved one.

"Think opposing forces." Henry took the opportunity to liberate his hand as he demonstrated how these particular cable cars worked. "There's a counterbalance underneath. It's sort of a weighted car that runs through an underground tunnel about three feet high. At the top of the hill, they release the weighted car. As it travels down, it pulls the passenger cars up. Then, when the streetcar goes down, it pulls the counterbalance up."

"Interesting," Helen said. "I do love opposing forces. They keep things exciting, don't you think?"

"I suppose." It seemed like a lot of bother when so many people had automobiles. They boarded the cable car and took their seats. Helen leaned her head out the window. The wind pushed her hair behind her, and Henry couldn't help but notice how lovely she looked in the evening light.

She came back inside. "It seems terribly dangerous."

"The cable breaks sometimes," Henry said. "That's why they have all those sandbags down there. They stop the crash. As long as you plan ahead, you can manage the danger pretty well."

"Sandbags," Helen laughed. "Sacks of sand against an elemental force and a cable car that weighs thousands of pounds."

"Well, it's not going to break now, if that's what you're worried about." Henry felt as though he should reassure her, even though he had no idea whether it would break. If that could be predicted, then there would be no need for the sandbags and other precautions.

Helen seemed to consider the likelihood of such a disaster. "No," she said, her hands in her lap. "I don't believe it will."

They made their way down from the crown of the hill to Kerry Park, which had been given to the city by friends of the Thornes a decade earlier.

"What are we looking at?" Helen said.

Henry pointed out Elliott Bay and downtown. "In the daylight, you can sometimes see Mt. Rainier." His gaze swept the mud flats and he considered mentioning Hooverville and James Booth and the story they were researching, but something made him hold back.

"Don't you just love the feeling of being on top of the world?" Helen said. "I adore heights."

Henry didn't feel any particular need to impress Helen, but neither did he care to say the truth.

She persisted. "Such a romantic view. Thank you for bringing me."

Henry swallowed. "It'll be dark soon. I should be getting us home."

"Only if you can't think of anything else to do." She looked up at him with her dark eyes. He looked away.

He hoped his discomfort wasn't obvious. "Oh, I wouldn't want to keep you out too late."

At some point, maybe he'd become used to her, or less embarrassed by the see-through scheme of Mrs. Thorne. Yet he felt no connection to Helen. Nothing in common, besides maybe their age. And there was this sharpness to her, not just in the line of her smile, but somehow beneath her. It reminded him of the smell of food that had just turned bad. There was an underlying menace to it.

And, though she was clearly on best behavior with Henry, she'd been prickly with Ethan. She didn't seem like someone he could trust.

"It was a lovely tour," she said, when they returned home again. The dark, chilly sky was moonless and thick with high clouds. A row of streetlamps lit the driveway. The air smelled of fresh earth and spring blossoms. Even a hint of lily, though none grew in that part of Mrs. Thorne's garden.

Helen stopped to pick a tulip. She ran her fingers down its pale green stem. Then she put her nose inside the cup of the flower and inhaled.

"I'm not sure you should be doing that," Henry said. "Mrs. Thorne is pretty particular about her garden."

She bent and picked several more. Each, she placed in Henry's arms, until he held a bouquet. "She won't notice. And you look darling standing there with your arms full of dead flora."

Henry shuddered.

"Cold?" Helen said.

"No. Just tired, I suppose. Either that, or a bird flew over my grave."

"What an expression," she said. She feigned a yawn and held out her arm. "I'll no doubt sleep like the dead tonight. I haven't adjusted to this new time zone. My body thinks it's midnight already."

"Let me take you inside, then." Henry felt the lightness of sudden possibility, adjusted the bouquet, and took Helen's arm. They walked to the house. "I'm going to put these in water."

"I'll see you in the morning," Helen said, as she turned to head upstairs. Henry hurried into the kitchen, in search of a vase. But as soon as he was alone, he changed his mind about what he'd do with the flowers. He still had Mr. Thorne's car keys. He found some paper, wrapped the tulips, and slipped out the side door. He headed for the Domino, wondering what little thing nagged at him as he drove.

He'd just arrived at the club when he figured out what it was.

Ethan's Cadillac was missing. Wherever could he have gone?

Chapter 21

LOVE HAD FELT HIS OPPONENT RETURN TO THE CITY HOURS EAR-
lier. And disguised as the cousin. No wonder the face had been
recognizable. It was clever, devilishly so. When her train pulled in,
he and a small group of men at Hooverville were standing around
a burning barrel full of wood scraps and trash, discussing the best
meals they'd ever eaten. He could hardly mention oysters in Paris
or chocolate in San Francisco, so he'd made something up about
his mother's biscuits. He felt a darker sort of hunger, and he knew
it was hers.

His first impulse was to join her. He was desperate to harangue
her for what she'd done to the zeppelin. This would not change
what had happened, though. He stilled himself by watching the
flames gorge themselves on the sad heap of scraps. Then Love
directed his heart toward Ethan's, calling him across the miles.

He was fond of the young man, surprisingly so. But he was
equally conscious of the fact that Ethan stood in the way of the
players. It wasn't just Ethan's unspoken attraction to Henry, but
also his growing interest in an alliance between Henry and Helen.
Love wouldn't break the rule against interfering with the players'
hearts directly. But with one close to them? Especially one so full of
charm? It would be his pleasure.

Ethan knocked on James's door at sunset, still pushing the ruse that he was researching the newspaper piece.

"You're not writing anything down," Love said, after they'd spent two hours inside his shack discussing philosophy and politics.

"I have a good memory."

"Just what the forgotten men of Hooverville need. Your memory."

Even in the weak light that found its way through the doorway, Love could see Ethan did not know what to make of the remark. He touched the young man's forearm to reassure him it was not meant as a jab. He meant it truly: to be seen, to be remembered, to matter. It was what these men, and all others, needed.

The gesture undid Ethan. Love meant no harm by it, and he'd so sunk into the skin of James Booth that he'd forgotten the power of his touch, particularly on skin as electrified as Ethan's. Love removed a small lantern from its spot on the framing of the shack. The Zippo clicked, the flame caught, and there was a smell of burning oil and smoke. Ethan held his breath.

"There," Love said, his voice low and soft. "A bit of light."

Ethan exhaled. His hands shook. Love regarded him in a way that said, *I see you*. Ethan looked downward, then back at Love. Their hearts began to keep time with each other. Henry would have appreciated the rhythm, the connection. Love did. More than he had anticipated. It meant there were more depths to Ethan.

"I should go," Ethan said. "I —"

"Or you could stay," Love said.

Ethan did not object as Love ran a knuckle down his cheek, slightly sandpapered with stubble where his beard was beginning to come in. Like a rope, the air pulled tight between them. The tension was excruciating; Love could almost feel the fibers snap.

He closed the makeshift plywood door, sealing the space so Ethan would not have to hear any sounds from the outside world:

not the voices of men, not the scream of steam engines as they arrived at the nearby station. The only sounds would be of their bodies breathing, of their clothing rustling, of skin moving against soft skin.

The shack was small and humble, but it was cozy and private, and lit with a light that did not seem to come entirely from the lantern.

Afterward, Ethan wept, and Love whispered things meant to make him feel safe. Were it possible, he would have traded his immortality to remain with this beautiful soul, to concentrate all that love on a human who needed it so.

Chapter 22

THE BOUQUET OF TULIPS SAT NEXT TO HENRY ON THE FRONT seat. He was having second thoughts. What was he going to do, give them to the bouncer and ask him to deliver them? Better to throw them away.

The air outside blushed with humidity. Summer was coming, with its long, hot days. He slipped into the alley behind the club and found a trash can by the door where he'd first encountered Flora's uncle. As Henry lifted the lid, a black cat dashed from behind the can and looped around his ankles. He nearly had a heart attack; he wasn't much of a fan of cats.

"Sorry," he said, not unkindly. "I don't have any food for you."

The animal meowed plaintively. Henry turned to discard the flowers. The door opened, and Flora emerged holding a saucer of milk. She wore a robe, though her hair and makeup were done. Seeing Henry, she started, spilling liquid on the cobbles. They stared at each other a moment until Flora broke the silence.

"I brought you this saucer of milk." She held it out to him, her face deadly serious.

"And I brought you this lid." Henry offered it to her. "A very rare item. A similar one sold for millions at auction."

Flora laughed and the cat meowed again. She set down the saucer. "Sometimes she follows me here."

Henry put the lid back on the trash and held out the flowers. "I know it looks like I might have pulled them out of the rubbish, but I didn't. I was too much of a coward to deliver them. But now that you've caught me in the act, I might as well get credit for the gesture."

She laughed again, pulled her robe tighter around her rib cage. "They're lovely. Thank you. I give you full credit."

"Am I getting more embarrassed or less as this conversation progresses?" He shoved his hands in his pockets.

"If we're talking relative levels of embarrassment," she said, "one of us is standing here in a bathrobe." Her expression changed. "Wait! I do have clothes on underneath. I would like the record to reflect that."

"As I thought," he said. "More embarrassed every second."

Flora smelled the tulips. "Can we pretend this never happened?"

The cat meowed again. Henry shooed it aside gently. "Let's pretend I walked up to you in a better place than an alley, and I wasn't tripping over stray cats or holding garbage can lids, and I gave you flowers because I like the way you sing, and no one was mortified in the process. That way, I still get some runs up on the board."

"Runs on the board? I didn't realize we were playing a game," Flora said.

"It's a baseball thing. Sorry. I'm going to stop talking now. In fact, I'm about ready to agree that this never happened."

Flora smiled. "Sherman's going to have my head if I'm not ready to go. We're onstage again in a few minutes."

"And I am going to pay the cover charge and find a table, and not say another word. You didn't see me. I'm a ghost."

Flora reached the door. Then, looking over her shoulder, she said, "I'm glad you came back. I've gotten used to seeing you out there in the crowd."

The door clicked behind her, as solidly attached as Henry's heart.

Chapter 23

Afterward, Flora mopped her brow in her dressing room. She leaned into the tulips, breathing their clean perfume. What had happened onstage? She'd become aware of Henry in the audience again, of his eyes on her, of his hands on the table, of the way the candlelight gilded his face and hair.

This time, though, her immunity was gone. She had an overwhelming urge to look at him, to sing to him, and it terrified her. She fought it. But when the time came to sing "Walk Beside Me," it was as though someone had found the source of music inside her and was pulling the notes out of her harder and faster than she intended. She was only able to resist for a moment more before giving in absolutely.

She sang to Henry, and to him alone. And once she gave her voice like that she couldn't remember any more of the performance. What she'd sung. What it sounded like. Whether she'd been good. There had been applause at the end. That she knew, although the spotlight had disoriented her enough that she'd rushed offstage. It would be the last time she'd allow her feelings to get the better of her.

Needing fresh air, she left the dressing room and hurried through the narrow, carpeted corridor. The light was dim; only a few sconces with single bulbs lined the walls. She put her hand on the doorknob beneath an exit sign.

The night air was like a splash of cool water. She thought about going back for a coat, but decided against it. She slipped out and closed the door behind her, making sure it was unlocked. The fire escape was within reach. Glad she was wearing a shorter dress, she stepped onto the trash can and climbed to a small second-floor window. Someone had been tuck-pointing the bricks and left a ladder against the wall. She pulled herself over the lip of the building and onto a flat, tar-covered roof.

And then she heard his voice.

Sitting on the roof's edge, she leaned forward. Henry stood in the alley, looking every direction but up. Her breath caught in her chest. What was he doing?

"Flora!"

She couldn't bear the sight of him down below. He needed to be answered. "Look up."

Henry's eyes found her. "What are you doing?"

"Getting air."

"There not enough on the ground?"

"It's better up here," she said.

"If you say so." He scratched his head and glanced back at the door.

"Are you coming up?"

"Up? I don't know —"

"Don't tell me you're afraid of heights."

"It's not that."

"What is it, then?" Did he not want to see her, after all? She tried to figure out whether that hurt or relieved her, or both.

"It's that . . . it's that I am *deathly* afraid of heights."

She grinned and swung her legs back around the edge. After

that confession, it would be rude to send him away. "This is an easy climb. Meet you on the balcony."

"No, it's fine. It's not that bad." There was a grunt as he jumped for the fire escape.

"Don't look down," she said, trying to sound lighthearted.

Henry, hanging tight to the ladder, looked down and then up at her. His face looked pale.

He scaled the fire escape and then the ladder, pulling himself over the ledge in a single, fluid motion. He hurried away from the edge. "How's the view from the center? Whew. Safe. Now, about your singing." He turned to face her.

"Shh," she said. "Nobody likes a critic." Her heart pounded. "We have to stop meeting like this. The stray cats will talk." She found a seat on the rooftop a few feet away from him and caught his scent on the night air. Lemons and spice.

"Maybe I'm writing another article and I need an interview," he said.

"Are you?" she said. A hope flickered that he would, and she'd find a sponsor. But she knew that was nonsense.

"No, but I'd like to." He sat next to her. "Tell me about it. Why you like to fly. Where you'd like to go."

She leaned back on her elbows, turning her gaze up. He was close, though not so close that their bodies touched. She couldn't bring herself to face him. Nor, it seemed, could he look at her. But she felt him all the same.

"Ever hear of Bessie Coleman?" she asked.

"No, was she a singer?"

The disappointment that he was unaware of someone so remarkable, so important to her, pricked her like a needle. Flora tried to keep her voice light as she explained.

"She was the first colored woman to fly a plane. And the first of my people to have an international pilot's license. No American schools would teach her to fly, so she went all the way to Paris to learn with money she earned doing people's nails."

She glanced at Henry as she spoke, gratified to see he looked embarrassed.

"Why haven't I heard of her?" he asked.

She shrugged. She had a theory, but didn't want to talk about it just then.

"Well, what happened to her?" Henry asked a moment later. "She sounds like a good news story."

"She died," Flora said. "In an accident."

"That's terrible," Henry said.

Flora didn't know what to say to that. It was terrible. But death happened all the time. It didn't do to dwell, or you'd never get anything done for the sadness. This was why it was better to care less, at least when it came to others.

They were silent for a long while, looking at the cloud-muffled sky, hearing noises from below — people talking and leaving the building — as well as their own gentle breathing. She briefly wondered about Grady, and hoped he'd assumed she'd made her own way home.

And then they talked about their families — Nana and Sherman. And the fact that Henry lived with Ethan and the Thornes, because he'd lost his family. Flora didn't ask Henry about his newspaper job, whether that was his dream, as flying was hers. She didn't need to know any more about what was in his heart.

Time passed. It was hard to tell how much. There were no stars or moon visible to measure the spent minutes. Light from the streetlamps reached the roof, polishing the planes of Henry's face. She studied it and concluded that she liked it. Very much. What would she be thinking if Henry weren't white? Would he be a possibility?

She scolded herself silently, first for thinking in terms of possibility, and second for thinking she would change anything about Henry. She'd never want anyone to try to change anything about her. What's more, there was something so right about him. The way he'd been with Annabel. The way he paid attention to her music and asked her about flying and her family. And something else she couldn't identify. Some people, like some songs, simply added up to more than the sum of their parts.

She pretended to inspect her fingernails, embarrassed that her teeth had started to chatter. She stood.

"You're cold." He stood next to her.

She nodded. Her body shook, but more from trying to keep herself from pressing against him. He put his coat around her shoulders.

"Thank you." It was a miracle that she'd been able to control her voice, especially when a shy grin spread across his face and he pushed that one stray curl on his forehead back up where it belonged. The gesture pierced her. He just wanted to keep things in order. She could relate. She concentrated on the warmth and scent of his coat until her body stopped shaking.

"We should probably head home, shouldn't we — back into our regular lives and such. Believe it or not, I have a test tomorrow. Then a baseball game."

She nodded, surprised that, for once in her life, she wasn't the one pulling away.

"Unless," he said.

She looked at him, puzzled.

He whistled the opening line of "The Blue Danube."

"A waltz? You can't be serious."

"As serious as scurvy for pirates," he said. "I know we should go, but I want just one more minute of this, and I'm cold too. One more minute, a tiny bit of warmth. It's all I ask." He put on a grave look. "Please?"

She laughed. "You're such the tragic figure." Still, she hesitated. What would it be like if she were still in school, studying for tests and going to dances and such? Would it be like this? Or would she still be chasing other, bigger dreams?

She reached for his upraised hand and looked into his eyes, whose color reminded her of that sharply curving part of the sky at the horizon's edge, the part she always aimed her plane toward. But it wasn't just that. It was the openhearted kindness in them, so much that she forgot the loneliness that overwhelmed her most of the time.

He closed his left hand over hers. He moved his right to the hollow of her back and it was almost more than she could take, the warmth of his touch, this connection in two spots. He moved his feet. She moved hers in response. And then they were dancing together on the rooftop, wrapped with an invisible thread that she needed to snap before it killed her.

"A request, Henry."

"Anything." He looked into her eyes and it was a moment before she could work her mouth.

"No more whistling."

"But we need music."

"How about you leave that to me? Music's more my thing than yours, after all." If she could find her voice, she could find her equilibrium.

He smiled and looked as if he was about to speak, but he didn't. Then she hummed the rest of the song as he moved her in circles. She put her own spin on the melody, so it was more swing than waltz, and he picked up on her cue, releasing her only to draw her back in, closer than he had before. Behind her, the black cat that had found its way to the edge of the rooftop meowed.

The sound brought her back to herself. What she was doing? It was a mistake for so many reasons, not the least of which was the fact of Grady. And then there were their different backgrounds, the wrongness of thinking of a white boy as anything other than someone to be wary around. But this wasn't just any boy, or any white boy. There was something about him. Something worth knowing. That much was certain.

The cat hissed and slipped over the edge of the roof, and the feeling that had overcome Flora during her performance rushed back. She pushed away.

"What did I do?" he said.

"Nothing. We can't. I'm sorry. I don't know what I was thinking."

"Maybe," Henry said, "some things just aren't meant to be thought about."

"Still," she said, "we can't do this. We can't. For so many reasons."

"What about someday?" he asked.

She couldn't help but wince, as if the word itself had been formed to hurt her. Henry did not reply, but the look in his eyes shattered her.

As they made their way down the ladder, Henry looked straight ahead. He was glad Flora still wore his jacket. He'd have perspired clean through if he'd been in it. His fear of heights embarrassed him. He'd long wondered how something that existed only in his mind could so affect his body. But then again, fear wasn't the only emotion that worked that way. Love was nothing you could see or touch. It lived entirely inside of you, invisibly. Even so, it could change everything.

One step at a time, one step at a time. And then he was down and walking behind Flora, reveling in the scent of her hair, feeling happier than he had in ages. She reached for the doorknob, jiggled it, and looked at Henry.

"Was it locked when you went outside?" she asked.

"Honestly? I haven't a clue. My only thought was catching up with you."

"It wasn't. I made sure. And now it is. We're locked out."

"Is that a problem?"

"My pocketbook is in there," she said. "My money and keys. I won't be able to get into my house, or pay anyone to take me."

He took her hand. "Let's go around the front and knock like crazy," he said. "Maybe someone will hear us. And I can always give you a lift."

She wrested her fingers out of his, ignoring his suggestion that he drive her himself. "They'll be gone. They'll be gone and we'll have no place to go until sunrise. And now this." She held out her hand. "Rain."

Henry looked up. A warm raindrop smacked his face. "Maybe it won't turn out to be as bad as all that."

As he spoke, the door swung open. In its dark mouth stood the bass player.

"Grady!" Flora said. "I thought you'd gone home."

"I would have," he said, staring at Henry with eyes full of hurt and malice. "But you left your things and I was worried. Who's this, Flora?"

"This?" Flora said. "This is Henry. He helped write that newspaper article, the one on the Staggerwing —"

Grady interrupted. "I looked for you. Everywhere. What's going on?"

"Nothing," she said. Henry looked away. "Just talking."

"Do you know how late it is?" Grady said. "I've been waiting."

"Grady," Flora said. "I'm sorry. I don't know what came over me. I needed some air, and I ran into Henry in the alley." She

115

slipped out of Henry's coat and handed it back to him. Henry could hardly bear the look in Grady's eyes.

"Let's go," Grady said. "Let's get you home where you belong. Your grandmother will be worried sick, just like I was."

Grady pulled Flora into the Domino. Henry held his coat overhead as the sky started raining in earnest. He stood in the deluge until he was drenched. But he couldn't be miserable. The soft hands of the rain on his skin made him feel as though he stumbled on the edge of someplace magical. He wasn't sure which direction he should move next. And he wondered how serious Flora was when she said such things couldn't happen, not even someday.

Chapter 24

HENRY ARRIVED AT THE THORNE MANSION, EVERY NERVE IN HIS body alight. He felt Flora in his arms, still breathed her essence in his jacket. He assumed everyone was asleep when he slipped inside, grateful the front door always swung on well-oiled hinges. He removed his shoes and crept toward the curving staircase.

Then Helen called his name.

Her voice had come from the kitchen. He found her sitting at the counter, which was laden with enough food to feed a hungry family. Cold cuts, soft rolls, sliced apples, cheese, a wedge of four-layer chocolate cake, and directly in front of her, a jar of strawberry preserves with a spoon sticking out of it.

"You're out late." Her tone was sharper than it had been earlier. She took a huge spoonful of jam and slid it into her mouth. "You could've invited me, Henry."

It hadn't occurred to him. But he was glad he hadn't, even as he regretted Helen's wounded feelings. "I thought you'd be far too tired. I apologize."

"Oh, Henry." Helen wiped her mouth with the back of her hand, pushed the jam away, and scanned the table for her next victim. "I'll always rally for you."

Henry's collar felt tight.

"So where were you, anyway?" Helen shoved nearly half of her sandwich into her mouth. Henry's eyes widened. "What? I get hungry. So hungry. You wouldn't believe it."

He had to look away a moment.

"There's plenty to go around."

Helen shoved the plates of rolls and meat in his direction. Henry, not one to decline food, put together a sandwich of his own.

"So you simply must tell me. Where were you? There's something different about you right now." She finished her sandwich and dragged the cake toward her. "Should I be jealous?"

Henry bit into his sandwich to buy time. A conversation with Helen must be what a tomato felt like when encountering a blade. He chewed and swallowed. "Listening to music."

"Judging from the looks of you, it must have been" — she licked something red off her finger — "quite a show. Next time, you simply must take me."

He took another, smaller bite, intending to shield himself with his sandwich for as long as he could. Helen tucked an enormous amount of cake into her mouth. The way she was looking at him made him check his fly, just to be sure.

"Of course," he said, wishing he actually wanted to, wishing it didn't feel like the single worst idea in the world. What if — he studied Helen, her hands, her wrists, and her heart-shaped face — what if he did choose her? He tried to imagine that life he was supposed to want, the security it would represent, the way it would please the Thornes and spare Helen's feelings. And Flora had said they could never be together, not even someday. He shook his head and fought to focus.

Helen smiled and lifted another forkful of cake. "Wonderful. When shall we go?" She filled her mouth. As she chewed, she didn't blink, even once. She reached across the table and tapped the back of his hand with a light fingertip. The room darkened and Henry lost feeling in his feet and legs. He gripped the table's edge.

"What's wrong?" she said.

"Nothing, I don't think. I'm probably just tired." The feeling passed. He yawned. Then there were footsteps, and Ethan appeared on the far side of the kitchen, looking rumpled but surprisingly awake. His eyes widened.

"Well, now," Helen said. "There's our other night owl."

She sniffed the air, and it gave Henry an overwhelming sense of something predatory about her.

"I was working, Helen," Ethan said. "Give it a rest." He took an apple from the bowl and bit it savagely.

"I don't doubt it," she said. "Henry and I were just making plans to listen to some of that cunning jazz music he likes so much. Won't you join us?"

"Not interested," Ethan said. He took another bite and rubbed juice from his chin with his thumb.

"You could bring a friend," she said. "The person you've been working with so late. Goodness, I hope you're not exhausted at school tomorrow. You know what your parents will say if your grades drop."

Ethan squared his shoulders. "Fine. But only to make sure you don't devour Henry like you're going after that cake."

Helen bent over her plate, shoveling cake into her mouth the way a laborer endeavors to fill a hole.

"You haven't changed since you were a little girl eating sweets with your bare hands," Ethan said, surveying the wreckage of her snack. "Do you ever stop with your disgusting devouring?"

"No," Helen said, her mouth dark with frosting. "I do not."

Not long afterward, as Henry lay in bed and felt his body succumb to sleep, he practiced a jazz riff in his head, one he hadn't yet been able to get right. As his mind unclenched, he understood what his fingers needed to do and how his hands needed to work with each other, and he felt certain that in the morning, he'd be able to play it for real, if only he didn't have to get up and go to school.

He breathed deeply. In his last moments of consciousness, it occurred to him that he'd never talked with Helen about what sort of music he'd been listening to.

Ethan must have said something about jazz. Surprising, given how much he hated his cousin. But Helen could rip anything out of you that she wanted.

Chapter 25

Wednesday, May 12, 1937

FLORA WOULDN'T ADMIT IT FOR ANYTHING, BUT SHE LIKED CLEAN linens. Loved them, even. Unwrapping them from the crinkling brown paper Mrs. Miyashito used. The smooth feel of their ironed surfaces. The act of putting them in the closet next to the bar, their edges aligned like bones. The sheer impersonal order of them was a thing of beauty. And while it was true that the cycle of laundry was as futile as the cycle of life, it was equally true that no one ever dropped tears over a dirty napkin. Maybe Mrs. Miyashito, but she was the exception.

Because there was no one to hear her, Flora sang as she worked, a sweet little lie of a love song. "Easy Living."

It was Grady's new favorite. Grady. She felt guilty even thinking of him, after the time she'd spent with Henry. His friend Billie had recorded it for a motion picture that was set to open in the summer. It was the latest in a line of songs he'd taught her after he'd started courting her. She wasn't quite sixteen when it started. She'd just left school so she could take care of Nana during the day, and she hadn't even imagined such a role for herself until Sherman informed her he'd given Grady permission to come courting. *Permission.* As if that had been his to give.

She'd protested her lack of interest, which had only increased Grady's. At first, she'd let him teach her the songs so they'd have something besides flowery nonsense to talk about. Then, she'd consented to see him outside of the club so he would stop bothering her about his feelings when they were at work, calling attention to the whole situation in front of the entire band. After that, it just seemed easier to keep things simmering along, never reaching any sort of emotional boil, because it would protect her from the interest of any other boy.

Oh, Grady. He was a decent musician. Nice-looking. Attentive. Polite to Nana. But their relationship was nothing like the easy living in the song. It felt forced, and she felt watched. Watched and managed. Like when they'd attend church together on Sundays . . . it bothered her to know that everyone looked at them as a couple who would one day be married. Or they'd take a walk in the park and he'd hold her elbow and lead her along at a pace that didn't quite match hers, and he'd smile and shake his head when she wanted to pause and steal a glance at the sky.

All those times he'd tried to kiss her, she'd pushed him away. He once even asked her to marry him, probably thinking that's the sort of thing that would make her finally consent. She'd panicked and said not yet, by which she meant not ever. He was waiting until she turned eighteen to make things official. She intended to hold him off until she made her flight, and then, if everything went according to plan, she was free. She could leave the club in Sherman's hands and spend the rest of her days as Bessie Coleman had done. She'd have left already if it weren't for Nana and the matter of money.

Whatever she thought of Grady, "Easy Living" was a good song. Quite possibly too good, because she'd closed her eyes so she could really feel the second verse. As she did this, she saw Henry in her mind's eye. She couldn't think about what it meant, not when she was singing.

The slam of a door in the distance saved her from dark thoughts. Then came footsteps on the stairs. She stopped mid-note.

"Don't quit on our accounts." The voice belonged to the first of three men in suits who stood in formation at the bottom of the staircase. "That was a hot little number you were singing."

He opened his coat to reveal a badge clipped to the inside pocket of his jacket. It glinted in the half-light of the club. Tax inspectors.

"My uncle isn't here right now." Flora regretted her choice to work in solitude.

"Well, isn't that a shame," the tax inspector said. He stuck out his hand. "Edgar Potts. Alcohol Tax Unit."

His palm was moist, and she wished she could wipe her hand on her dress without seeming rude.

"Can I help you, Mr. Potts?"

"Probably so." His slow voice dripped with something worse than sweat. He gave a look to the two men flanking him. It was clear that whatever joke Mr. Potts was making was at her expense. They wouldn't get a rise out of her that easily. Flora waited. If Mr. Potts wanted something, he'd have to spit it out. The silence thickened as the seconds passed, a technique she'd learned while stalling Grady.

Mr. Potts finally broke. He pulled a dingy handkerchief from his pocket and mopped his forehead. Flora wished he'd get to the spot on his upper lip. Even in the low light, it was damp enough to gleam.

"We're here about your taxes," he said.

Flora didn't reply straight off. Taxes weren't her turf, and Sherman usually shooed her away the moment these sorts of men appeared. Now she understood why. There was something snaky about Mr. Potts's eyes. He was looking for an opportunity to strike, and Flora didn't want to say anything that accidentally brought trouble to the club. The two men with Mr. Potts took a half step forward so that the three of them formed a wall between her and the exit. Her pulse throbbed in her temples.

"I'm sure my uncle Sherman would be happy to go over those with you tomorrow afternoon when he's here." She kept her voice smooth and calm. "Can I offer you a bit of something to eat?" The leftover corn bread would still taste good, even if it was meant to be taken to the poor. Mr. Potts hesitated, and Flora hoped she didn't look as jittery as she felt.

"We'll take you up on that," Mr. Potts said, finally. "And we'll have a bit of something to drink. And then" — he paused and coughed into his wet hand — "we'll take a look at your books. Today. Right now, even. We know it's your club as much as it's his. Your name's on the tax rolls, after all."

Flora stared hard at him, certain he'd purposely chosen to come on a day when Sherman wasn't there, thinking she'd be an easy mark. He was in for a surprise. Their books were as clean as the laundry, and she had more life experience under her sash than most people her age. Other clubs might try to cut corners on the liquor taxes, but not the Domino.

"Fine, then. Won't you please follow me . . . gentlemen?" They weren't the only ones who could make a joke.

She headed through the swinging kitchen door and felt the warm weight of someone's hand on her backside. Gritting her teeth hard enough to crack stone, she stepped out of Mr. Potts's grip and walked to the long wooden counter in the middle of the room without saying a word.

She chose the largest knife Charlie had to cut the corn bread. It didn't make the job easier, especially as her hands were shaking. But it sent a message, she hoped, as she used its tip to set three squares of yellow onto three white plates. She poured three glasses of milk, knowing it wasn't the type of beverage Mr. Potts had in mind. He couldn't exactly complain, though. He wasn't supposed to drink on the job. Her breathing deepened as she felt herself take control of the room, much as she did when she was onstage, creating a barrier of notes between her and her audience.

"Won't you please sit?" She pointed the knife toward a round table in the corner where she and Sherman and the rest of the staff ate during their breaks. Mr. Potts and his flunkies let her serve them corn bread and milk, which he eyed as if it was from a one-eyed goat. Flora let herself smile fully. Maybe she'd get lucky and he'd choke. "I'll be back with the books in a moment."

She felt their eyes follow her into the safe in the storeroom, where Sherman kept the records. Someone wolf whistled — not Mr. Potts, who was in the middle of a spongy cough. Oh, to cut the three of them into squares and serve them up on clean white plates. That would be something. She found the ledger and stood a couple of paces from the table, holding the book, bound in marbled cardboard, to her chest.

Mr. Potts snapped. "Let's see it here."

She set it in front of him and moved his milk and corn bread away.

He flipped it open and found the most recent entries. "How do I know you don't keep a second set of books?"

"A second set? I don't know what you might mean. But I believe my uncle would tell you it's work enough to keep the one."

Mr. Potts made a show of studying the numbers. He nodded and grunted as he reached across the table and stuffed his mouth with corn bread, dropping greasy crumbs on the pages that Sherman had labored over.

"Got anything else for us?" he asked. "Any other source of income to report? Your *uncle*" — the way he said the word indicated he didn't believe the relationship was true — "hasn't gone into an older line of business, has he?"

It took Flora a moment to understand his suggestion that Sherman was a pimp and she was his prostitute. And by "anything else," Mr. Potts meant a bribe.

"Unless you gentlemen would like some more corn bread, that's all I have. Most folks say it's the best thing on the menu. My grandmother's recipe."

Mr. Potts flipped the book closed. He dabbed his lips with his dirty handkerchief, once again missing the perspiration beneath his nose.

"See, that's just the thing," he said. "Taxes are complicated, and I wouldn't expect a young . . . lady . . . such as yourself to understand them fully. Your uncle being unavailable during working hours makes me certain he's hiding something or up to some other unlawful business. So we're going to have to shut this place down. Unless —"

"Unless what?" Flora looked at her pocketbook. She'd forgotten to put Nana's money back in the canister. Mr. Potts registered the glance and a smile slithered across his lips.

"Well now," he said. "I can see that you might be more savvy about business matters than you've let on."

Flora looked away. The thought of giving this man what he wanted made her blood smoke. But if it would get rid of him, it was maybe worth it. She hesitated, wishing Sherman were here to handle things. This was her grandmother's money. Money Nana meant for her to spend on her flight, not that she intended to. But if she didn't pay, they'd shut the club down.

Flora panicked. In that moment, the thing she most wanted was for those men to be gone, and she wanted the Domino to keep its doors open. She could pay Nana back, eventually. She opened her pocketbook and pulled out half the bills. Mr. Potts made a show of eyeing what remained. Flora, her hands shaking, gave him all of it.

"Satisfied?" She couldn't resist spiking the word with venom.

"I don't have a clue what you might be talking about, miss." Mr. Potts opened his jacket. His badge flashed as he tucked the bills inside and smoothed the bulge from his chest. She looked toward the door.

"If that's all," Flora said, "I have work to do. I hope you'll be coming back for the performance." She also hoped her tone made it clear she wanted them gone for good.

"No offense intended," Mr. Potts said, "but your kind of music . . . it just isn't our thing."

As he headed for the stairs, Mr. Potts slowly brushed against Flora's chest. He grunted as he did, and she swallowed her protests. You had to pick and choose your battles with men like these. It wasn't so much about winning as surviving.

When they'd gone, she leaned against the storeroom door. Her whole body shook, but she did not cry. Even if they weren't there to see it, she wouldn't give them the satisfaction. She hoped Sherman wouldn't be disappointed with how she'd handled the situation. The day she was free of all of this could not come soon enough.

Chapter 26

Not long afterward, Love followed Grady Bates into a rough section of town a few blocks south of the Domino. At first, he'd appeared as James Booth, in his shabby suit, his golden hair glowing in the light. Worried about witnesses, Love broadened his frame, ruined his posture, and added a bit more history to his clothes and face. He stayed two blocks behind Grady, following him through the benign rays of an early-afternoon sun.

The neighborhood was bleak compared to other parts of the city, especially compared to where Henry lived. A row of skinny maple trees planted along the sidewalk offered little in the way of shade or ornament. Crumpled bits of yellow newsprint tumbled through vacant lots, and shards of glass from broken bottles glittered in the dirt.

A single thought circled through Love's mind as he walked, a mad idea, one he should have spit out like a piece of bad meat.

Kill Grady Bates.

It unsettled him, to say the least. He doubted this was how Death felt stalking her prey, exposed and quaking. But it was the right choice. Grady was a danger and an obstacle, and the way to remove him permanently was to steal a play from Death's book.

She would be furious, of course. Love wondered briefly why that bothered him more than the prospect of a man's imminent murder.

Grady stepped inside a shop that carried newspapers, magazines, and tobacco. Unsure how long the man's business would take, Love leaned against a lamppost and waited. He was halfway tempted to go inside and buy a newspaper, but something held him back. Instead, he considered murder methods. What would he do if he were human? Use his fists? Wield a broken bottle like a knife?

How intimate fists and blades were. Almost as intimate as love itself. Death often used a touch, but Love couldn't imagine it was anything like love, what she did. Her powers also far exceeded his own. She could manipulate matter, bring down an airship, and stop time. By comparison, his gift felt pathetic. All he could do was fill a heart with love.

He removed his hat and rubbed his forehead, squinting against the sun. The door opened and Grady emerged with a newspaper folded beneath his arm. Love peered inside Grady's heart. The man's next desire? A gingersnap — and a moment with the pretty girl who worked behind the bakery counter.

This small infidelity ordinarily would have bothered Love. Now, he relished it. He followed Grady into the bakery. The young woman behind the counter — she was perhaps two or three years older than Flora — regarded him with a flicker of suspicion before she turned her attention back to Grady and smiled. It stung to be treated differently for his skin color. To think of how often the white majority of the city looked this way at the small population of brown-skinned residents was worrisome. As ever, Death had been shrewd in her choice of player.

He perceived a third human in the bakery. The baker, a quiet, middle-aged man, shuffled out from the back, his face dusted with flour. He looked hot, no doubt from standing by ovens all day long. With regret, Love plumbed the depths of the baker's heart, adding layers to it as a brick mason might construct a wall. He needed to insert an overdose of the wrong type of love, the sandpapery, possessive sort that rubs a heart raw. He folded this twisted love into the soft spaces, and he held it in place so the man's mind could not shake it free.

The baker believed he was eternally in love with the girl behind the counter, the girl who was laughing and flirting with Grady as though such things came with every cookie sold. Love whispered the baker's name, knowing it was the single word most likely to send him over the edge. The man opened a drawer beneath the cash register. He pulled out a revolver. Grady backed up against a rack of freshly baked loaves of bread, holding his hands high.

"Now," Love whispered.

The baker swung the gun toward Grady. Love held his breath as the safety clicked off.

Just then, a figure materialized in front of him. His mind registered who it was as her hand flew against his cheek. The blow broke his hold on the baker, who dropped the gun. It discharged, blasting through the sweets display case. Both the baker and Grady covered their heads to protect themselves from raining glass.

The girl dropped to her knees.

"Please," she whimpered. "Please, no."

Embarrassed, Love felt his blazing cheek. Death stood inches away, her eyes narrowed to slits, her mouth a slash of red lipstick. She looked like Helen and she looked like herself at the same time. "What do you think you are doing?"

"You, of all people, ought to know." Love worked his jaw, half expecting it to break to pieces. There was a flash as the baker bent to retrieve the gun, which he examined like it was something alive.

Death froze time.

"Of course I know *what* you were doing. What I'd like to know is *why*. How *dare* you."

"How dare I what?" Love said. "How dare I do what you do every day?"

Death clenched her hands, and Love braced himself for another blow. Grady stood frozen, holding the folded newspaper across his chest as if in defense, his mouth parted because he'd been about to speak.

"He's in the way," Love said, unable to say Grady's name.

"He's a human being," Death said. "A living soul. And this isn't how you play the Game."

Love couldn't quite read the expression on her face. As ever, her mind was closed to him. "What do you mean? It's how *you* play the Game."

"Exactly," Death said. "You are not me. You don't —"

"I don't what?" He lifted his hat and smoothed his hair. "I don't want to win? Is that what you think?"

Death made a noise of frustration. She stepped outside. Love followed. "Leave them alone. You don't need to do this," she said.

Love looked back at the humans, still frozen in the shop. "Fine. I won't."

Death released her hold on time. A look came over the baker's face. He gazed at the gun, and Love remembered, too late, that poison remained in the man's heart, more than enough to be dangerous.

The girl flinched. "Please, no!"

Love looked to Death. Her irises flashed white as the baker took aim. She materialized inside the shop as the gun flashed. Too late to save him, Death caught Grady from behind. The bullet had torn through the newspaper. An unholy crimson flower bloomed through the paper and ink. Grady coughed blood, and Death set him gently down.

The baker cried out, his heart drumming a frantic beat. He rushed toward the girl, who'd backed up against the sacks of sugar and flour.

There was second shot, then a third.

Love closed his eyes. "No," he whispered.

A few moments later, Death stood beside him. Through the shop window, three bodies had been laid neatly side by side by Death, as if sense could arise from this small gesture of order. Blood spattered the bakery walls and floor. Her knees buckled. Love held her up, marveling at how small she really was. She lifted her head and looked at him, her eyes still the silvery white they turned when she was feeding. After a moment, the color flowed back. She pushed away and wiped her eyes.

She'd abandoned her Helen guise and was fully herself, beautiful, ageless, and hard. "My fate is a prison. It's the one thing humanity and I have in common. You were the only one of us who didn't need to inhabit one. I took responsibility for these souls for you, even though their deaths are your fault. You should be forced to feel what it's like for someone to be imprisoned."

Anguished, she disappeared. Love knew he was meant to follow, even though she had not told him where to find her. In the distance, a police siren wailed. And in a sickening moment of clarity, Love knew where to go.

Death waited for Love on the wind-scraped peak of the Presidio, looking over the hazy water toward Alcatraz. In the setting sun, the island darkened like a bruise on the horizon. It was the worst of prisons, and it's what she wanted him to see. A eucalyptus breeze lifted her hair. Then a foghorn blew, and she sensed his presence.

"Is it really inescapable?" he asked, closing the distance between them.

"What, the prison?" Given the circumstances, she had to ask.

He nodded. "Has anyone tried?"

"So far, just the one. A little over a year ago." She searched her memory. "His name was Joe. One day he tried to kill himself by breaking his glasses and sawing through his own throat."

"Was he insane?"

"Consider where it occurred," she said. "Also, he steered clear of his carotid artery. He didn't really want to die. He was sending a message in blood." The wind blew her hair again, and she pushed it back.

"What else of Joe?" Love asked. "Did he have friends?"

"No. There was no one. Even among outcasts, he was considered a freak."

"Why was he in prison?"

"He stole sixteen dollars and thirty-eight cents in a post office robbery. Twenty-five years to life."

"He would have stolen more if there had been more to take," Love said. "It's not the amount. It's the act."

"He was hungry." Death raised her voice so she'd be heard over the cold scream of wind off the bay. "He was hungry and couldn't find work. Care to guess the last image he offered me?"

Love shook his head.

"It was his own face. Unlooked at. Unseen. Unloved. In his life, there was one moment of great resolve: the moment he chose to climb the stone wall and escape. And then the guard's bullet found his back."

Love swallowed. "And you know this from a touch? How do you remember it all?"

"How do you remember your own hands?" Death said.

Love reached into his pocket and removed a chocolate bar. He broke off a square and handed it to her. She put it in her mouth, where it began to melt.

"Bittersweet," she said.

"It seemed the thing. Chocolate contains some of the same chemicals the human brain produces when it's in love. I'm surprised you have any taste for it."

She stared at him. "Condescension does not become you."

They finished the chocolate as stars emerged in the endless cage of sky, a few at a time, beautiful unblinking monsters.

"I'm sorry about what happened," Love said.

Death squeezed his hand. "Play as yourself. Not as me. Trust me on that."

Love nodded. Had any human eyes been on them that moment, they would have seen what looked like a couple in love standing beneath a sky pinned in place by a fishhook moon.

Chapter 27

HENRY MADE A DEAL WITH HIMSELF. IF HE READ FIFTY PAGES IN his history textbook, he could go to the Domino. Never mind that he'd be out late again and would certainly be too tired afterward to finish his remaining calculus problem. Other calculations mattered more — as in how he might get Flora to change her mind about "someday."

Clutching a sheaf of unruly pink peonies from Mrs. Thorne's garden, Henry hastened toward the club. He was sheepish and excited and had a million things to say. Mostly he wanted to be in his seat, watching Flora sing. He wouldn't press for more, but he had to be near her.

It was strangely quiet on the street outside the club. Usually, snatches of music leaked out of the building. Or couples on their way inside chattered with each other and called out greetings to their friends. Maybe it was just a slow night. Or maybe — he picked up his pace — a police raid had shut the place down. The bulb above the door was dark. The bouncer wasn't standing at his post. Something was wrong.

Henry pounded on the door until his knuckles hurt. Eventually, as he was about to give up, it opened. Flora's uncle emerged from the shadows.

"Club's closed," he said.

"Closed?" Henry felt stupid for saying it.

"Now I know you don't got a hearing problem, son. Otherwise, you wouldn't come here so often. So don't make me say it again."

Henry could hardly feel his limbs. "Closed . . . closed for good? What happened?"

"For now, kid," the man said, his voice bitter. "Bass player got shot and killed, not that it's any of your concern."

Henry felt ill, as if his antipathy for the man had caused his death. "But Flora, she's all right?"

The man did not answer. "Go home, son. You look like something a cat coughed up." Then he closed the door.

Chapter 28

Saturday, May 15, 1937

THREE DAYS LATER, THE BAND GATHERED AFTER GRADY'S MEMO-
rial service for a backyard picnic at Flora's. Several of the players,
still wearing their funeral suits, were distracting themselves with a
game of croquet using an entirely unorthodox set of rules. The core
of the band — Harlan Payne, the drummer, and Palmer Ross, their
pianist — sat around the table, arguing with Sherman about
whether Jack Johnson would've beat the stuffing out of Joe Louis if
they'd been the same age.

Despite the weight of the occasion, it was a fine day to be outside — warm and sunny, the air filled with the sweetness of cut grass
and wisteria blossoms. If anything, though, it made the guilt worse.
The last time Flora had seen Grady was after she'd been with Henry.
Grady had dropped her at home without a word, which at the time
had felt like a relief. Now it sharpened the feeling inside her that his
death had been her fault. She wanted to get in Captain Girard's plane
and leave town, start over somewhere else as someone else. She'd
never do it, not with Nana depending on her. But the urge was there.

Flora, who knew better than to stick up for Joe Louis in front
of Sherman, changed the topic before an amateur backyard boxing
match could break out. "A month off won't hurt the club," she said.
"That gives us time to find a new bass player and do it right —

work on our sets, learn some new numbers. Don't you boys want to take a vacation?"

"Music *is* my vacation," Harlan said. "I get bored without something to do." He drummed the table with a spare pair of sticks.

"So we practice," she said. "We just don't perform."

"You know who's good?" Palmer said, rubbing his whiskery chin. "That new fellow they have at the Majestic. What's his name? You know, Peaches Hopson. I say we try to recruit him."

Sherman clinked ice tea glasses with Palmer. "Now you're talkin'."

Something brushed against Flora's ankles. The cat, looking for a handout. She dropped a scrap of chicken. The cat's teeth made a wet grinding noise against the meat.

"That animal is playing you for a sucker," Sherman said.

In no mood to be conciliatory, Flora reached for an entire leg. She dangled it between her thumb and forefinger.

"Don't!" Sherman said. "That's my favorite part."

Flora tossed it beneath the table. "I can't believe you're talking about stealing Peaches from the Majestic. They're our friends," she said. "How'd you feel —"

"They're the competition," Sherman said. "It's business. Doc'll understand. And I thought we'd agreed after that tax situation that you'd focus on the music, and I'd focus on everything else."

Flora was in no mood to be reminded of what had happened with Mr. Potts. "The union might have something to say about the scheme you're cooking up." They were all members of the Local 493. "We'd do better to take out an ad. We could put one in papers from here to Los Angeles. Bound to find someone who wants a new gig. And then we could use that as a reason to draw people in. Besides, the bass player is the music."

"Girl has a point," Harlan said. "I wouldn't like it much if Doc tried to pirate Palmer or one of the Barker twins."

Palmer laughed. "No one but us would take Chet and Rhett." Chet and the trombonist, Sid Works, had pinned Rhett to the lawn with croquet wickets around his ankles, wrists, and neck. "Not Sid either."

On the street, someone killed a car engine. A door slammed. The cat scrambled away.

"Rotten thing didn't even eat the whole leg," Sherman said. "What a waste of tasty."

Flora smiled despite herself and took a sip of ice tea. "So we take out an ad, then. Do a search in Seattle, San Francisco, Los Angeles, New Orleans. We could look in Chicago and New York too."

Sherman rubbed his face with his palm. "Sounds as much fun as clipping my toenails with an ice pick. I still think we ought to just liberate someone from another club. Be done and open again by next week."

The screen door leading to the backyard slapped open, and Nana poked her head out.

"Sherman," she said. "Can you step inside?"

Behind her stood a figure silhouetted in the afternoon light. Sherman let the screen door bang behind him. Flora cocked an ear — it sounded like he was giving the heave-ho to a traveling salesman. They were always trying to get Nana to buy their encyclopedias, knives, brushes. Nana hated saying no, and she made Sherman do it whenever he was around.

There was a bit of chatter and then Sherman's voice. "More likely to find an Eskimo Pie in hell."

"Oh, Sherman." It was Nana's voice. "Are you certain? What would it harm?"

"You know what he's probably really after, don't you?"

"Don't be silly, Sherman."

Flora wondered what the salesman was offering.

More murmuring, and then, "Talk to her?" Sherman's voice

carried. "How'd you say you knew her? Say, aren't you that boy who's been sniffin' around the club? I didn't recognize you in the daylight. Now you get going before I take out my foul mood on you."

"Sherman!" Flora realized who was standing in her house. She didn't want to face Henry just then, but she didn't want her uncle being rude to him either. She raced up the steps. Henry didn't seem like the sort who'd sell things door-to-door. He might have come calling for a different reason entirely, a reason that made everything worse.

Red-faced, she pulled open the screen door. He wore a clean shirt and had just shaved — there was a tiny cut on his chin still red with blood. He'd combed his hair until it shined. And by his side, in its case, was a bass.

"Henry," she said.

"This slice of white bread here says he wants to be our new bass player," Sherman said.

Since when did he play music? And since when could someone like him play her kind of music?

"I — I just heard you were looking," Henry said. "You are, aren't you?"

"As it happens," she said, "we are. But —"

"I'm interested in the job," Henry said. "Baseball's nearly over. I could rehearse after school. And then I graduate next month and will be looking for work." He turned to unlatch his case.

The black cat slipped through the open screen door and brushed Flora's ankles. She put a hand on her chest, feeling dizzy. Probably from too much chicken and sunshine and not enough ice tea. She shooed the cat away, and it entangled itself in Nana's ankles.

"There's that creature again," Nana said. "I swear it will be the death of me."

Flora shook her head. The idea of Henry in her band was madness. And yet she was surprised to find she wanted it. Without knowing why, and with the certainty of knowing she'd never want anything else nearly as much. This was why she had to say no, and firmly. It would only hurt them both when he played and was terrible. She'd never be able to face him after that.

"I'm sorry," she said. "It's just —"

"Just what?" Henry said. "Do you think I can't play or something?" His eyes challenged her. Flora wanted to take a half step back.

"It's not that."

"What she's saying," Sherman said, "is that is the *least* of your problems. There's also the matter of your age. If you're over eighteen, I'm a juggling nun. I'm gonna have to talk to Bathtub about who he's lettin' in the place."

"Flora isn't eighteen," Henry said.

"Flora owns the club. The rules don't apply to her. Go on home, boy."

"Flora." Henry loosened the knot on his tie. "May I at least audition?"

The way he said her name sank into her core. Terrified people would guess her feelings, she stepped backward and smashed the cat's tail beneath her shoe. The creature hissed and zipped outside.

Then she said the last words she wanted to say. "I don't — you're not the one for us. I'm sorry." She turned away. As she walked down the steps and outside again, she heard Nana's voice.

"Can we at least offer you a bit of chicken? I fried it up myself."

Henry declined politely, and his silhouette disappeared from the screen door.

He hurried out, trying not to hit his bass on the edges of the doorway. She wouldn't even listen, a possibility he hadn't imagined, couldn't believe. It had been audacious to want to audition. But he had talent, and he'd been playing her songs almost since the moment he'd first seen her onstage. He'd practiced so much his fingertips were raw. She'd dismissed him without so much as an explanation.

He thought there had been something between them. The way they'd met as children. The way their paths crossed again at the airstrip and the park, as though fate were guiding them toward each other. How they both understood the language of music. The way she felt in his arms as they waltzed on the rooftop under a sky that had no moon and no stars but still felt full of light.

The difference between that and how he felt at the Thorne family dinner table with Helen was enormous. Helen was the right choice in many ways, but wrong in all the ones that mattered. And then a space had opened up for him onstage with Flora — in a terrible way, yes. But he was ready to step into it. He'd offered himself up. And she'd said no. How could he have been so stupid?

If that was the way she wanted it, he'd respect it. He'd let her go. Give Helen another chance. Maybe he'd been mistaken about love. Maybe Helen could teach him another way.

He set his bass next to Ethan's car. He popped open the back door and was just about to slide in the bass when a sparrow sang a lick exactly like the one Henry had been working to master. Coincidence, maybe. Or maybe just a trick of his reeling mind. Either way, a twitch started in his fingertips. It rose through his arms and across his chest, and there was only one way he could still it.

He closed the car door, removed his bass from its case, tightened the hair on his bow, and found a divot in the sidewalk that would hold the endpin steady. He would walk away from her, but not without giving her something to remember him by. He faced the fence surrounding Flora's backyard, tilted the bass against his heart, and checked to see that the strings were in tune.

He began the first movement of a Bach suite that had been written for the cello, but could be played on the bass by someone with enough skill. It was a good warm-up piece, sweet and smooth. He eased into his own rendition of "Summertime," constructing a bridge of notes that joined the two songs. He took his time traveling over it, like he was a man unweighted. And then, nearly there, he dropped his bow and bent himself entirely toward the pizzicato jazz style.

His playing took on urgency. His impulse had been to make Flora hear him and realize her mistake. But the music swallowed him. He didn't want to hurt her. He just wanted to play.

Time slowed down enough that he could turn what he was feeling into notes. A lock of hair slipped onto his forehead and his skin grew hot, but his hands stayed light and fast. He played as if he could not go wrong, as if he were meant to be right there, doing the thing he'd been born to do. The ground and his body and the sky were no longer separate, but as related as three notes could be in an infinite variety of chords.

Henry didn't notice when faces appeared over the fence. Flora's band. As they listened, the men removed their hats. Eventually, they ventured glances at one another. No one spoke.

Henry played until he'd said his piece. His shirt stuck to his back and a drop of sweat from his forehead fell to the sidewalk. He looked up and acknowledged his audience. Flora stood atop the porch steps. She held one hand on her chest, clutching her dress.

"Henry, wait," she said, her voice roughed up.

She started down the steps. Henry wouldn't wait. He put his bass and bow back in its case, snapping it shut. Then he turned, opened the back door of the Cadillac, eased his instrument inside, and closed the door. He did not look back as he stepped into the driver's seat, started the engine, and headed home.

Chapter 29
Saturday, June 5, 1937

HENRY'S BASS SAT UNTOUCHED IN THE CARPORT FOR THREE weeks. Having called a temporary cease-fire with calculus, he was lying on his mattress with his hands beneath his head, studying a hairline crack in the ceiling, when Ethan knocked. Henry didn't bother replying; Ethan would walk in anyway.

"What do you think?" Henry asked. "Old man or bear's ass?"

Ethan looked puzzled, so Henry pointed up.

"Bear's ass, definitely." Ethan closed Henry's textbook and moved it aside so he could sit on the desk. "You're going to have to get up someday."

Henry grunted. *Someday.* That word had grown tainted. There was no such thing.

In the weeks since Flora had refused him, Helen had been kind. She'd taken to making him plates of food and keeping him company while he ate, and he found her interest in him and his life and his thoughts on important topics to be flattering. He had no complaints about her sandwiches. He didn't feel like kissing her yet, but maybe that would come eventually.

He'd forced himself to go through the motions at school and baseball. He'd be lucky to pass his upcoming finals, and he'd already been moved off the starting lineup and onto the bench with the underclassmen. When he walked down the halls, rumpled and unfocused, students steered clear, as though heartbreak were catching.

The headmaster had pulled him aside the day before, just as he was leaving the chapel. "I'm hearing troubling things," Dr. Sloane said, scratching at a few stray hairs on his chin with nicotine-tinged fingertips. "We've come to expect more out of you than we're seeing in the classroom and on the field."

Henry's stomach twisted. "I'm sorry, sir. I'll do better."

"'How high a pitch his resolution soars.'" Dr. Sloane had a Shakespeare quotation for every situation. He coughed into his hand and clapped Henry on the arm. "You'll let me know if something is amiss? If you need any assistance? A new razor, perhaps?"

"Of course." Henry resolved to mow down his meager crop of whiskers.

"Not too much time left in this institution, Mr. Bishop. I know uncertainty can be hard to face, but let's not lose focus before crossing the finish line." D r. Sloane squared his shoulders and offered his hand.

Henry shook it. "I won't, sir. Thank you, sir." He couldn't imagine asking Dr. Sloane for help with heartache. *Well, you see . . . there's this girl who sings in a jazz band and I wanted to be her bass player, but we are the wrong color for each other, and she said no, and it gave me a burned-out hole in the center of my chest that the rest of me is slowly being sucked into.*

Dr. Sloane's expertise was literature, not life. In any case, it was impossible to imagine an old person with a broken heart.

"Good to hear, Henry. Good to hear. Because the last thing we want is for you to lose your scholarship this close to graduation."

The warning made Henry feel bad all over again. He was behind in school, perhaps hopelessly so. He'd managed to help

Ethan with his written work, but his own was unfinished, doodled on, scattered in stacks and tucked into books.

Ethan crumpled an expensive sheet of onionskin paper and pitched it to Henry.

"See?" Ethan said when Henry grabbed it. "You're fine. You might as well get up now. Besides . . . I heard of a new club. Jazz, even."

Henry pulled his pillow over his face.

"Don't tell me you're giving up on music," Ethan said. "Just because the raggedy old Domino is closed doesn't mean you can't hear jazz. James says this one's just as good." There was always a pause in Ethan's voice when he mentioned his source in Hooverville.

Henry moved the pillow away from his face and pushed himself up on his elbow.

"So James says it?"

Ethan's features shifted. Henry couldn't make out what emotion his friend was hiding.

"The article has turned out to be more complicated than I thought. Father doesn't want to give me any more extensions, but I want to get this one right. So I've interviewed him a few times, and we've gotten to know each other a bit. As people." Ethan walked to the window and looked out. Henry could swear the edges of his friend's ears were red.

Henry hadn't much considered Ethan's absences at night these past few weeks. He figured he'd gone to Guthrie's, or some late-night diner like the Golden Coin. Ethan was clearly slaving away, and Henry felt even guiltier for the labor he'd shirked.

"I can't go," he said. "I'm so far behind."

"Look." Ethan faced Henry. "You haven't told me what's eating you, so I can't help with that. But you haven't played music or listened to it in weeks, and that's like a plant going without water."

"Fine," Henry said. "I miss it. But what makes you interested in music now? I've had to drag you out to listen."

Ethan looked at his feet and scratched the back of his head, as if he wanted to buy time before answering. "You know I've always enjoyed music. Maybe I don't play it like you, but I listen to the wireless constantly." He smoothed his hair. "And I have been talking about it with James a bit, you know, as part of working on that article. He said he'd like to hear some, so I invited him along. I hope you don't mind."

"Of course I don't." Henry paused. He couldn't fathom why Ethan seemed to be so embarrassed about bringing a friend. Maybe because James Booth lived in Hooverville. A thought struck. "Do we have a suit to lend?"

"Oh, that." Ethan looked out the window again. "James said he had proper clothes. But let's don't tell Helen, all right?"

The floorboards outside Henry's room creaked.

"Let's don't tell me what?" Helen leaned against the doorframe, working an emery board around her index fingernail. "I thought I heard you two plotting something. You've both been as dull as a cemetery for weeks. If I have to polish another candlestick with your mother, Ethan, I'm going to kill someone." She held out her finger as if to appraise her work.

Ethan shot Henry a look. "We want to make sure it's the kind of place you'd enjoy before dragging you along."

If Henry didn't know better, he'd have believed Ethan. There was something happening, something that exposed a vulnerability. Henry picked up the ball of paper. He opened it and started to smooth the wrinkles. It would have been gallant for him to extend an invitation, but he chose friendship and the illusion of chivalry over the thing itself. He continued to work on the paper, even as he knew it was a lost cause.

Helen rolled her eyes. "I'm not afraid of anything. You should know that about me by now." She turned her attention to another nail, and for a moment, there was no sound other than the slow rasp of the file.

Ethan brushed his hands together, as if to wipe them clean. "Then it's settled. We'll go together. Sound about right, Henry?"

Henry nodded. It surprised him that Ethan had flinched, but Ethan always was a gentleman.

"Oh, goody." Helen turned to leave, looking at the boys over her shoulder. "This will be fun."

When he was alone, Henry laid the wrinkled paper back on his desk, understanding it was beyond saving, but unable to throw it away. He placed it between the pages of his book, knowing it wouldn't help. But at least he wouldn't have to look at it anymore.

Chapter 30

LATER THAT EVENING, AFTER HE HAD WRESTLED DOWN HIS LAST calculus proof and finished a paper comparing Athens and Sparta to the North and South during the Civil War, Henry shaved for the first time in three days. He took his time mixing the soap, brushing it along his jaw, and scraping it with the straight razor. His jugular throbbed in the mirror. So little flesh between that and the blade. The right cut would be lethal. And yet there wasn't a chance he'd do it. It was one thing to be sad enough to want to die, but an entirely other thing to be mad enough to kill one's self. The thought, dark as it was, made him feel better — and the prospect of hearing music again was proof that he very much wanted to be among the living, that in this regard, he was not his father's son.

He finished shaving, rinsed bits of soap from his earlobes and neck, and splashed aftershave against his cheeks. Then he dressed, straightened the books and papers on his desk, and glanced out the window. It had been a cloudy afternoon, and as a result, sunset was a slow fade to black. The quarter moon was little more than a pale dimple behind a curtain of clouds. Rain was on the way, but that was common in Seattle. The sky could hang heavy with moisture for days.

Ethan paced at the base of the stairs, fussing with his cuff links.

"Need a hand?" Henry said.

"What? No." Ethan looked up. "Just burning off energy."

"Don't burn it all off." Helen appeared in a white dress that hit her in the best of places. She wore a pair of black satin elbow gloves and a mink stole around her shoulders, the sort where they left the animal's head on. A hidden clasp fed its tail into its mouth, and its eyes sparkled cruelly. Henry was glad he'd cleaned himself. He offered his arm. As they walked down the stairs together, he caught a whiff of her perfume, and he remembered why he despised that scent. Lilies made up the sole arrangement of flowers at his father's sparsely attended funeral. Henry never knew whether it was the sudden poverty or the suicide that had driven away all of his family's former friends. Ever since, lilies had reminded him of despair.

It would simplify so much if he wanted Helen. But while her skin was pale and creamy, and her elegant collarbones were visible over the neckline of her dress, the sight only reminded him that she had a skeleton beneath her flesh. He wanted love, and when he looked at her, he could only think of death.

"The Majestic isn't far," Ethan said. "We could walk, even. But there's someone we have to pick up first."

"A girl?" Helen said. "Does Ethan have a steady?"

Ethan shook his head and smirked. "Don't you wish I could give you something to gossip about with my mother? But no. This is business. Something related to the newspaper. You couldn't possibly understand. It's an assignment from my father. You can ask him about it, if you'd like."

"It's not that I wouldn't be able to understand. It's that I couldn't possibly be *interested*." Helen unclasped her pocketbook and removed a cigarette from a silver case.

"Not in here," Ethan said. "You know what Mother would say."

"And Ethan would never do something that would cost him the approval of one of his parents." Helen removed the unlit cigarette from her lips. "Ethan is a perfect puppet. Sit up, Ethan. Walk this way, Ethan. Bow to us, Ethan."

"Not in the car either," Ethan said, pointedly ignoring her remark. "You'll burn holes in the seats."

Helen rolled her eyes and put the cigarette back in its case. Its tip had been stained red by her lips, and Henry found the sight of it both repellent and fascinating.

The night air was cool and damp, and made Henry feel somewhat more himself. In the cloud-filtered moonlight Helen looked like a figure in a painting. He could not tell if the sensation it gave him was pleasant or troubling.

"Anything else I'm not allowed to do tonight?" she said.

"An entire list," Ethan said. "Use your imagination."

"Oh, I am." She waited for Henry and reached for his arm, but Ethan swooped between them and guided her to the backseat.

"Henry, you don't mind riding up front, do you?"

"Not at all." Henry appreciated that Ethan was trying to spare him, but he wasn't sure he wanted to be spared anymore. In the backseat, Helen played with her lighter, making flames appear and disappear. Henry expected her to light a cigarette, but she didn't.

She wouldn't leave Ethan alone. "Who are we picking up? Is it anyone I know?"

"No." Ethan turned on the radio, which was broadcasting news about Neville Chamberlain's election as prime minister of the United Kingdom.

Helen objected. "Ugh, how impossibly dull."

"It's international news, Helen. It's good to care about events that shape the future of humanity."

"Please," Helen said. "I've had enough for a thousand lifetimes."

Henry looked out the window, eager to avoid the cross fire. Ethan switched off the radio. Hooverville was just ahead, lit with smudgy campfire light that gave the air a thick, sad smell. Ethan pulled over. From the darkness, James Booth appeared in a clean gray suit, looking as if he might be one of their classmates. Perhaps his fortunes had improved; Henry could certainly imagine where he'd made some money. Ethan got out, and the pair shook hands. He opened the back door, and James slid in beside Helen, grinning more broadly than seemed possible.

"Is this some sort of joke?" Helen looked at James as though he were a smelly dog.

"Don't be a snob, Helen," Ethan said. "This is the mayor of Hooverville. Had he been born into money, he might even be the mayor of the city itself in a few years. He's a terrific political talent. Full of smart ideas."

Henry watched in the rearview mirror as she lit a cigarette and exhaled in James's face.

"Helen." James extended his hand. "Ethan's said so much about you."

"Funny. He hasn't said a thing about you." Helen barely squeezed his fingertips. Her lit cigarette threatened to drop ash on the back of his hand.

"History has a famous Helen," James said. "Her face launched a thousand ships. You have a face that might launch a solid dozen, which I mean as a compliment on the grandest scale. The warships today are much bigger." He plucked the cigarette from her fingers and stubbed it in the ashtray. "There, now. We wouldn't want to set anything on fire."

Helen laughed. "We'll see about that."

Henry glanced at Ethan, wondering if Helen and James could possibly have met before. Their antipathy had such familiarity.

"Helen," Ethan said. "Mind your manners. James might not come from money, but he's got ideas and a gift for persuasion. You might even call that the wealth of the modern era."

"Oh, there's a lot I'd call the likes of him," she said.

"Go on." James leaned against the seat, cradling his head in his hands, as if he enjoyed being abused. "I'm all ears."

She raked her eyes over him. "The Helen in your story was a home wrecker, for starters."

"As I understand my mythology, she was the daughter of a god who was abducted from her husband."

"She didn't mind in the least."

"You have firsthand knowledge?"

"And what if I did?"

"Then I'd say you were remarkably well preserved."

"How lovely of you to notice," she said, looking more amused than anything. "As the story goes, she did not survive long after her husband reclaimed her. Death is cruel to lovers, is it not?"

"Love is a bad thing if it starts a ten-year war," Ethan said. "Home-wrecking aside."

Henry wished he knew more about the story. Mythology and philosophy were always more Ethan's thing. He had to hand it to his friend, though. He wasn't kidding about James's intelligence.

"There is no such thing as terrible love," James argued, leaning close to Helen.

"It's all terrible," Helen said, leaning right back.

"I can think of something worse," James practically spat at her.

The pair pulled apart when Ethan coughed politely, and Henry was relieved when his friend switched on the radio again. The news program had ended and the announcer was telling the story of a woman, her maid, a love made possible through the magic of Ivory soap.

"They're playing your commercial, Helen," Ethan said. He quoted the jingle: " 'Hilda will never get a Grecian nose by using a beauty soap, but we do hope she gets Henry.' "

"Hilda!" Helen said. "I'll have to write a stern letter correcting their pronunciation. Either that, or Henry has some explaining to do."

They arrived at the Majestic. Henry expected to escort Helen inside, but Ethan and James flanked her instead, leaving Henry to walk by himself into the club.

It was just as well. It gave him a chance to catch his breath, to take in the lighted marquee, the thump of the band, the weight of the clouds. There was no bouncer, so Helen, James, and Ethan walked in while Henry stood on the sidewalk, relieved to have a moment alone. The air around him pulsed with energy, and if he'd still been a little kid, he would have wanted to run up and down the street yelling at the top of his lungs, just to release the feeling. As unsettling as it was, it beat the sadness.

The rain started. As the first drops soaked his skin, the atmosphere shifted. He dabbed the water away with his handkerchief and breathed deeply, savoring the mysterious scent the drops had drummed from the soil. Light footsteps tapped the sidewalk behind him. He turned and saw her.

"Flora." He took a half step toward her before he remembered himself. She stood alone, a black umbrella hooked over her arm.

"Henry. I —" She pressed her lips together. She looked as though she'd rather be anywhere else.

After a moment, she looked away, and Henry realized he would let Flora break his heart a million times, if he could look at her face every day.

"What's keeping you, Henry?" Helen stood in the open doorway of the Majestic. She stroked the head of her mink. "We're all waiting."

He swallowed. "Excuse me," he said to Flora.

He walked into the club, knowing she was behind him, knowing she was watching. But he wouldn't let himself turn around or speak to her again. He was here with Helen. He'd honor that. He'd also keep Flora away from Helen, who could be a pill and a half. Besides, Flora didn't want him anyway. He owed it to his pride to steer clear.

Henry had wanted to lose himself inside the music, a complicated song being played in 5/4 time, a polyrhythm that felt murderously hard to pull off. But Helen and James had started in again about the Trojan War and the many other victims of the other Helen's treachery: the deaths of Achilles and his lover Patroclus, the isolation of Ajax, the endless journey of Odysseus. They shouted at each other to be heard over the music, with a glum-looking Ethan interjecting to referee.

"Love killed all those people," Helen said.

"The war did that. War." James finished his drink. "War is the machinery of death."

"The machinery was started by love." Helen slipped a cigarette between her lips and leaned toward Ethan to light it.

"You talk about love as though it's the root of all evil," James said.

"And you've failed to prove that it isn't." The look on her face surprised Henry: hurt and angry and scared. What had happened to Helen to make her turn out this way?

Ethan signaled to the waiter for another round of drinks, but Helen shook her head. "I've had enough of this." She stood.

"Helen, don't be that way," Ethan said. Henry wanted to echo the sentiment, but couldn't.

"Be what way?" she said. "It's just a friendly debate. Mr. Booth here thinks there is something magical about love; I say it's one of the swifter routes to ruin."

"I'm glad you and your cousin are not of the same mind," James said.

Ethan stammered. "Let's — let's just listen to the music."

Helen wasn't swayed. "I've enjoyed meeting your friend." She reached for her clutch. "What a charmer. But I really must be getting home."

Ethan stood. James put his hand on Ethan's forearm. "I'll take care of her," he said. "I feel responsible for the unpleasantness."

"Let me." Henry stood.

"No, I'll do it," Ethan said. The waiter rushed forward, as if concerned they were going to skip out on their bill.

"Sit," Helen said. "Both of you. Mr. Booth can walk me out, although I doubt he can pay for my cab."

"I can, believe it or not," James said.

Henry tried to step away from the table to escort Helen, but he found himself feeling rooted to the floor. It was the most curious sensation. He glanced at Ethan, who shrugged, then sat and sipped his drink. Helen and James walked out together, still arguing.

"Forget them," Ethan said. "What a bust this has been. She's the kiss of death to good times. Always has been. Sorry, pal."

Henry, dazed, fell into the chair next to him. He gulped his drink. What a strange evening, strange and terrible.

Across the room, he spotted Flora. She'd just set down her empty glass of champagne. She looked back at him, but as he smiled and lifted his hand to wave, she closed her eyes. As much as he wanted to be able to look at her and have it mean something to her, he didn't mind. She was beautiful lit up with song. So beautiful. And never to be his.

Chapter 31

STUCK AS ETERNAL COMPANIONS, LOVE AND DEATH NEVER worked as allies. But in that moment they left the Majestic, they worked toward a shared goal of keeping the humans inside the club, each for reasons of their own. Death slowed time, and Love dimmed the hearts of Henry and Ethan so they would stay complacently in their seats. This accomplished, their antagonism returned.

"What you're doing to that boy," Death said. "It's vicious. Irresponsible."

"Henry? You're the one toying with him."

"I meant Ethan," she hissed. "He's a little close, don't you think?"

"I'm playing the Game. Ethan loved Henry. Now he loves me. You, though — you're going straight for the kill. It's appalling. Never in the history of the Game —"

She interrupted. "I don't think you're entitled to make accusations along those lines. I carried those deaths to spare you that. You're not strong enough."

The words silenced Love.

She spoke again, more softly this time. "I, however, have not yet succeeded at love. Henry hardly looks at me. And to think that I've made him at least thirty-seven sandwiches."

Her confession made Love laugh. Death laughed too. Around them, the rain thickened. Steam rose from their shoulders, tangling with the mists of night. Love put his arm around Death's shoulder. "Go home. Dry off. Drink something warm."

"Home," she said. "Which do you mean?"

"Ethan's, of course. If you were to disappear now, James Booth would swing from the gallows."

"Don't tempt me." Her glee pleased Love, even though it was at his expense. "But I can't go home just yet. Business to attend to." Her eyes darkened. She was gone before he could ask what she meant.

Setting aside his anxiety about her swift departure, he approached Flora's car. He considered opening its hood and removing some necessary part, some greasy cog, or one of those little sparking wonders that made the beast roar. But for his plan to work best, his vandalism had to be visible.

To guard against witnesses, he shifted his guise. His pants and coat were now black, as was the cap that covered his golden hair. He pulled a folding knife from his pocket — every man in Hooverville had some sort of blade — and drove its tip into each tire. He stood in the cobblestone street, watching the car sink. As the rain spiraled down, he turned his face to the stars, the stars that always hung there, even when they could not be seen. Stars that burned their eternities in the cold solitude of space, piercing the darkness for as long as they could.

Chapter 32

FLORA HAD HEARD WHAT SHE NEEDED TO HEAR. PEACHES WAS fine, but not good enough for the Domino, at least not long term. They might be able to work with Doc to borrow him temporarily while they advertised as planned. She resolved to work on it the next day, and felt better than she had since Grady died. The clarity of the decision combined with the buzz of the bubbly filled her with a streak of daring — the same compulsion she felt flying loop the loops over Lake Washington.

On her way out, she veered past Henry's table. The girl he was with had gone, probably to the powder room. Flora pretended not to notice Henry until the last moment. Then, when he looked up at her, she stopped and bent her lips to his ear, resting one gloved hand on his shoulder.

"He's good," she whispered. "But nothing compared to you."

Her lips brushed down Henry's earlobe. She wanted to stay there, inhaling him, or even turning his perfectly curved chin toward her so she could kiss his lips, just once. But she didn't. That sort of thing . . . it couldn't happen. Ever.

She fetched her things from the coat check and stepped outside. The rain was coming down furiously, so she popped her umbrella and held it overhead. She'd nearly reached her car when she noticed something awful: all of her tires were flat. She stood staring at them for several minutes, torn between calling for a cab and walking home. A walk would cost less money. Just as she was about to set off, she heard footsteps. Behind her stood Henry, Ethan, and a fellow about their age. The girl was nowhere to be seen.

"Looks as though you might have a flat tire," Henry said.

"Or four," she replied.

"We have a dry car," Henry said, "if you'd like a lift. It's no trouble."

"No, thank you," she said. "I could use the walk."

"Flora," Henry said. "It's almost midnight. It's raining. You'll get soaked."

"Nonsense." She lifted her umbrella overhead. She held her pocketbook close to her ribs. It wasn't much more than a mile. Even in her high-heeled shoes, it wouldn't take more than twenty minutes. And, after her disclosure, it felt safer.

"Let us take you." Henry pleaded with his eyes.

"Thank you, but no." She turned and headed toward home. Her shoes would be ruined and she'd probably catch her death of cold, but she'd have her pride intact. That felt like enough. Wanting a safer distance between them, she walked faster.

Chapter 33

DEATH DID NOT TRAVEL BACK TO ETHAN'S HOME. INSTEAD, SHE slipped inside her black cat guise and meowed piteously until the old woman let her in. Flora's grandmother tucked small, even stitches into a quilt. Game or no Game, it was this woman's time. No one, not even Love, could fault her for that. She'd almost finished with the quilt, which melted over the edges of a table in front of her. It was a riot of color and fabric that had been cut from remnants of flour sacks and Marion's own dresses over the years, reassembled into a blooming chrysanthemum pattern.

A part of Death that had given way to being a cat felt an urge to bat at the silver needle and its fluttering tail of thread as it arced and looped in the woman's fingertips. Death wouldn't give in to that desire, but she did move closer and gaze up at the woman with her strange black eyes.

"I see you there, watching me," Marion said. "Don't think I don't know that."

Death licked a paw and ran it behind her ear.

"When you get to my age," Marion said, tucking a stitch into the fabric, "you see things more for how they are."

Death lowered her paw.

"Of course, there's no sense in talking about them." Marion examined her work a moment, and then completed a line of stitches. "People would think you'd gone 'round the bend if you did. I didn't expect that's what you'd look like, though I was ready to bash in your skull if you did anything to my Flora. Bash your skull, you hear? I'd maybe even use that lamp over there."

She gestured at a heavy brass lamp shaped like a whistling boy.

Flicking her tail, Death walked to the armchair by the window where Marion often sat waiting for Flora to return home. The chair smelled like the old woman, powdery and sweet. With grace, Death transformed herself into a human guise, one she hoped would give pleasure to Marion.

The old woman dropped her needle. "Vivian?"

"No, just someone who remembers her." Death smoothed the folds of a dress that looked exactly like the one Marion's daughter, Vivian, Flora's mother, wore the night she died. "Think of this as my gift to you."

"It is a gift." Marion breathed the word out on a wobbly sigh. She lifted her spectacles and pushed at the welling tears. "I'm glad — I'm glad I'm not the only one who remembers. That's what makes it worse, of course. Your child dies and no one wants to disturb you by talking about her, and then before you realize it, time has passed and everyone's forgotten. Everyone but you." She removed her spectacles. Tears fell. "Let me just look at you a moment."

She found her needle and tucked it beneath the topmost layer of the fabric, holding her place. Then she wiped her face and covered her mouth to hold back a sob. After a long while, she spoke. "I've missed you, child."

Death held still, hating this part of it. *It won't be much more time now.*

"You'd be proud of your girl," Marion said. "Grown up. So independent. And she sings. Not like you, though. She has her own way. And she flies a plane and has this dream of going across the ocean, although I know that'll be the death of her." She caught herself, apparently remembering to whom she was talking. She put on her spectacles and picked up her quilt, scowling at it. "A practical question, if I may. Will I be able to finish this? There isn't all that much left."

Death was tempted to adjust her face so that she was no longer the spitting image of Vivian, but rather, someone who looked like she could be a sister. It felt strangely intrusive being in costume at such a moment. But she held the form, not wanting to kill the woman's hope. "Keep sewing," she said. "I won't stop you."

"Thank you. I never was one for unfinished business." Marion slid the needle into the cloth. She looked at Death again. "You know, you didn't quite get her eyes right."

"Yes, those." Death shrugged. "My task requires a certain sort of vision. I always keep my own."

The two women sat in companionable silence until the mantel clock's hands found another hour. Midnight. The first of twelve chimes rang out. Nana sighed. "A sensible woman would be in bed by now. But I knew I'd have to finish this tonight. I knew it." She made three more stitches, as the clock chimed on, then paused and put a hand over her heart. "I knew you were coming. Felt it right here."

"It's late," Death said on the third chime. She grabbed the arm-rests of the chair, readying herself to stand.

"I'm not going to be able to finish." Marion looked down at the spread of her quilt, millions of tiny stitches representing millions of moments that would never return.

Death shook her head. "A life with all of its business finished is a life too cautiously lived." She believed every word of that. She would never lie to someone, not at a time like this. "Come on, now."

Marion glanced toward the door, and Death made a scolding face. "Sherman isn't coming. Neither is Flora. And if you run, I will follow."

"That wasn't it," Marion said, almost smiling. "If I run . . . the thought of it! I was trying to imagine how this will look to Flora. Isn't there some way —"

"I'm sorry." And Death was, in her own fashion. She couldn't get rid of the woman's body. That would make Flora feel far worse.

At the ninth chime, she stood. Pausing time for everyone except herself and Marion, she walked across the cozy parlor in Vivian's form, and the memories of that life came rushing back, unbidden. Death felt a pang that Flora had been too young to know her mother. Marion ran her hands over the slightly puckered quilt fabric one last time. She made her way to the sofa and patted the space next to her.

"Come sit beside me awhile," she said.

Sitting next to Marion, she could smell the woman's soul, and it made her ravenous.

"How will this work?" Marion said.

Death took her hand. Marion's soft arm wrapped around her shoulder, and her forehead touched Death's as the two leaned into each other. At the moment of contact, there was an explosion of memories, Marion's and Vivian's, cut apart and stitched together . . .

. . . and then Death's eyes turned white as Marion's life flowed into her, feeding that endless hunger until she felt as though she might burst.

Marion said one last word: "Oh!"

Her body grew heavy. Death eased herself out from beneath the old woman's shoulder and arranged her on the davenport. She laid Marion's head on a needlepoint pillow, slipped her still-warm shoes off her feet, and placed them neatly on the floor. She removed Marion's spectacles, but left the old woman's eyes open.

Death looked from the quilt to the clock and back to the quilt again. She slipped the needle out from the top layer of fabric. Fascinating how such a small, pointed object could bind together so much. She inhaled, feeling comforted by a variety of scents: cotton, baby powder, the beeswax Marion had used to stiffen her thread.

Death worked the needle and thread through the fabric as well as she could, picking up speed as she grew used to the task. Then, as abruptly as she started, she stood and released time. The clock chimed once, twice, three more times — and Death was gone.

Chapter 34

Henry retrieved an umbrella from the Cadillac and waved Ethan and James ahead. He'd walk a few paces behind Flora and see to it she got home safely. If he timed his steps to match hers, she wouldn't even know.

He liked watching her walk. He liked the look of the umbrella resting on her shoulder, the way her dress swished around her calves with each step, and the smart way her shoes met the sidewalk. No hesitation. *Ka-tap, ka-tap, ka-tap.* A high-heeled heartbeat softened by the gentle hiss of rain.

Every so often, she seemed to speed up or slow down. Henry was long used to keeping time with other musicians, so he had no problem responding. But after several blocks she surprised him by stopping short. The scuff-click of his own footstep echoed off of someone's garage. Flora held still, as though she were listening, and Henry waited for her to turn around. She didn't.

As she resumed walking, Henry followed. But after a few strides, she tossed in a little dance step he could not hope to follow. This time, when his footfalls rang out, she stopped.

"I thought I heard a shadow." She turned toward him.

"The noisiest one in the history of shadows. I'm sorry if I alarmed you."

"You must have confused me with some other person who is frightened by a stroll."

"At midnight? In the rain?"

Flora peered out from under her umbrella. She pretended to be injured by the raindrops that hit her cheeks. "We could keep going like this," she said, "or you could walk beside me." She paused. "Even though I don't have any gingerbread this time."

She remembered that day from when they were children, the day Charles Lindbergh came to town. His pleasure at that left him unable to hold on to his hurt feelings. Not now, not when he was so close to her, thinking about her voice, dying to know what she'd thought of the show. There was no one in his life to talk to about what music meant. He didn't realize until that moment how much he hungered for such a thing.

Their umbrellas knocked against each other overhead as they walked, shaking down a net of raindrops, and Flora laughed. "There's room under mine. Here."

She raised her umbrella to make space, and Henry folded his away. She took his other arm. She wasn't as tall as he'd remembered. The top of her head came to an inch or two below his shoulder. Still, she was the perfect size. His arm would wrap around her waist just so. . . .

"Cat got your tongue?" She looked up at him.

"Cat? What?" Henry was glad she couldn't read his mind. "What did you think of the music tonight?"

"One of the better bass players I've heard," she said. "But not the best."

His heart beat faster and they turned onto Flora's street. Henry wanted her to say who the best was, and he wanted it to be him, and that need embarrassed him.

"Ooh, stop!" Flora said. "Listen — midnight."

Henry stood next to her, feeling the brim of her hat against his shoulder, her skirt against his calf, the rise and fall of her breathing. The bells of a faraway church pushed through the rain-drops. Time slowed so there was nothing but the vibration of the chimes against his skin. The bells stopped, and he resumed breathing.

Flora tilted her head and looked toward her house. "Strange. The parlor light's on. It's awfully late for Nana to be up."

When they reached the porch, she ducked out from beneath the umbrella and dashed up the steps. She found the key in her pocketbook and unfastened the lock. She burst inside, leaving the door ajar. Henry wondered whether he should follow. And then Flora cried out.

Henry followed, ready to fight an intruder. Instead, he found Flora on her knees by the davenport, sobbing. Her grandmother's mouth gaped and her lips had a bluish tinge, but it was her open eyes that made it clear she was gone.

Henry froze. It was too late for a doctor. There was nothing the police could do. He felt as if he were the intruder. But he couldn't leave her alone. Not like this. He sat beside her, silent until she turned toward him a while later.

"Is there anyone I can call for you?"

She shook her head. "My uncle — he doesn't have a telephone."

"No friends? No minister?"

"No one I'd call at this hour," she said.

"What about Ethan? I could call him and he could drive here." He'd have to hope none of the other Thornes picked up. They'd be full of questions he did not care to answer.

"And what then?"

Henry was momentarily silent. "We should at least call the coroner."

"Not yet," Flora said. "I want to sit with her awhile." She smoothed her grandmother's simple dress. Then she reached up and gently closed the woman's eyes.

Eventually she leaned against the davenport. She unpinned her hat and set it on the ground, and Henry realized what people would say if they knew he was with her like this, in her house after midnight, unchaperoned. If he cared about either of their reputations, he would leave. He swallowed hard. Some things were more important than the judgments of others.

Henry had seen death before. The swift departures of his mother and sister from influenza were first. They'd been fine one day, and then the next, both were feverish. In the days after that, the horrible agony of watching them worsen, their lips cracking, their eyes glazing with incoherence. At the end, his mother had hallucinated about the summer place she had visited as a little girl. It almost looked as if she were having a conversation with someone from beyond.

He'd learned what a truly sudden death was when his father left the house without his hat for reasons Henry, just a boy of ten, could not understand.

Father will be back when he realizes he doesn't have his hat, he thought. *I'll wait for him by the door and he'll be so glad I found it.*

Henry was sitting on the wooden chair in the foyer with his father's hat in his lap when the doorbell chimed. He jumped up, holding the hat, wondering why his father hadn't just walked in. He pulled open the door ready to say, "Father! Look what you forgot!"

But it wasn't his father. It was two police officers with serious faces, their own hats held close. The one with the curving mustache asked him to run and fetch his mother.

"I can't, sirs," he said.

"It's important," the other officer said.

"She's passed on, sirs," Henry answered. "So is my sister. It's just me and my father now. We had to let the servants go after the crash."

The police officers took him to the station in their big car. They sat him in front of a scuffed wooden desk. Someone brought a paper sack from the diner down the street, and as he was eating the greasy doughnut inside, the mustachioed police officer informed him that his father had died. Henry didn't learn how until years later, when he overheard the Thornes whispering about it. Ever since, heights had made him ill.

Henry remembered himself with a start. Flora was staring at the fireplace.

"Are you cold?" He felt eager for something useful to do.

"Cold?" Flora said. "Maybe."

He found kindling and matches. Before long, he had a fire roaring. It wasn't cold enough for such a thing, but the activity helped and the flames were comforting. He turned on more lights in the parlor, keeping the night away as best as he could. Then he sat by Flora again, close enough that he could feel her next to him.

"She made the best gingerbread," Flora said.

"I remember," Henry said.

She'd moved her hand next to his. "You should have tried her fried chicken. Now —" She couldn't get the rest of the sentence out without crying again.

"I wish I had," Henry said. "I wish —"

"I wish I hadn't said no," Flora said. "I didn't want to. I was surprised to see you there, with a bass no less, and I felt terrible about what we'd done, and Grady, and I just couldn't . . ." She looped her little finger over his, and Henry's pulse raced.

"Let's forget it," Henry said, as soon as he could speak. "I showed up uninvited. I can see why you thought it was strange.

And we're not, we have no . . . Let's just forget it." He wanted to say something about her not having obligations to him, how he understood why her people wouldn't want her with someone like him.

"No," Flora said. She covered her face with her hands. "I apologize. All of this. I can't explain it. I don't mean to be cruel. Something in me went haywire a long time ago. You're better off staying away."

Henry went numb. To want her like this and not be wanted in return: The razor's edge would hurt less. He stood. "Are you hungry? I could cook you eggs or something."

"I don't think I'll ever be able to eat again. But help yourself if you want something." She led him into the tiny kitchen. She sat at the table, keeping a safe distance, folding and unfolding a napkin while Henry set to work.

He found a cookie sheet, laid strips of bacon on it, and then slid the tray into the oven. As that cooked, he took eggs from the icebox and cracked a half-dozen into a bowl, scrambling them with a splash of cream. He poured the mixture into the pan over a low flame.

"Just how Nana used to cook them," Flora said.

"Is there any other way?" As he nudged the slowly cooking eggs with a wooden spoon, he thought about bringing up the subject of music again. There were a million questions he wanted to ask her, a million things he wanted her opinion on. But he held his tongue. It wasn't the time. It might be their last chance, but even so, he wanted to comfort her above all else.

Flora brought up the topic on her own. "Peaches was all right, you know. Your rhythm is better, and you're bolder on the riffs."

He tried not to show how much this pleased him. "Their singer — what was her name? She doesn't hold a candle to you. Even though —"

"Ruby? She was having an off night. She's marvelous." She twisted the napkins and started refolding them.

As the eggs finished, he looked for plates. Flora read him like a piece of sheet music. "Second cupboard from the sink."

He nodded, found the plates, spooned eggs onto them, and finished everything off with a couple of strips of bacon. It didn't look elegant, and he didn't include a sprig of parsley the way Gladys did at the Thornes', but everything smelled as it was supposed to.

"Even though what?" She fidgeted with the napkin in her lap.

He set a plate down in front of her. "Even though you have more in you. I can tell."

She eyed him warily. "Maybe." She looked at the food and sighed. "I probably should try to eat something. It's going to be a long day ahead and I don't think I'll be getting much sleep."

"Only if you want to," Henry said. "I needed a task. And I really, really like bacon."

The clock struck one. Flora raised a bite of eggs to her mouth. A tear trickled down her cheek. She swallowed and wiped it away. "I'm going to be all alone."

"That's not true." Henry wished he knew how to comfort her. "You have your uncle."

"Not the same," she said. "My nana raised me."

Henry wanted to promise that she'd have him too. But he couldn't speak those words. She had to want it.

"I'll stay with you as long as you need," he said.

"Till the coroner comes. That'd be a kindness." She sighed and pushed away her plate. "I'll call him now."

She walked to the niche where the telephone was kept. Then she dialed the operator, who connected the line. In a brief conversation, she quietly provided all the necessary information. Her voice cracked once, and Henry's eyes stung at the sound of that small break.

She returned to the table, scraped her dish, and began washing up. Henry followed.

"Tell me about your grandmother." He accepted a wet dish from her hand. As he dried, he thought about life after his mother and sister had passed on. His father wouldn't allow him to talk about them. Said it wouldn't change things.

And then, after his father's death, no one wanted to mention it because of the shame involved. The silence made him feel as if his family had never existed anywhere outside his memory. It had been so long he was beginning to doubt any of it had ever happened, that he ever had a family and a sister who loved him, that he was ever anybody's most important thing in the world.

"What do you want to know?" she asked.

"Whatever you want to remember."

As they tidied the kitchen, Flora told him story after funny story — her nana had once stored extra frosting in a mayonnaise jar, and Flora accidentally made frosted chicken sandwiches with it. Another time, Flora had used salt instead of sugar when she made corn bread. Her nana choked down an entire piece anyway and said it was the most delicious thing she'd ever eaten.

"And she made quilts," Flora said. "Whenever anyone had a new baby, whenever she had enough leftover material. She learned how from her grandmother, who made them to send secret communiqués to runaway slaves. They used to hide all sorts of messages in quilts and hang them in windows and over fences."

Henry glanced at the quilt on the table in the parlor. "Was there a message in that one?"

Flora glanced at it. "I'm sure of it. She always put a message in there somewhere, the same one, every time."

"What was it?"

"It's silly," Flora said.

"You don't have to say." Henry put the plates back in the cupboard and set to polishing a glass.

"Oh, it's nothing I can't say," Flora said. "It's just . . . well, she

used to tell me that she loved me in the quilts. She always sews —
sewed — a tiny heart in it somewhere."

"I like that. A secret message," Henry said. He didn't think it
was at all silly. He loved it, actually. Secret messages had been used
to win hearts and wars for centuries. A Spartan general named
Lysander used to send them in his belt. It was the only part of
Henry's study of the Peloponnesian War that had interested him.
"Let's find it."

"She wasn't finished with this one."

"Let's look," Henry said. "It couldn't hurt."

Flora held the fabric in her fingertips, examining it closely.
"My word."

"Did you find it?"

"No," Flora said. "She finished it. She's been working on this
one forever, and she finally finished."

There was a light knock on the door. Henry stepped into the
backyard as she went to greet the coroner. A break in the clouds
revealed a splinter of moon along with a scattering of stars. He tried
to read them as if they were notes, to see what sort of song the heavens held, but there were so many possibilities he gave up. He inhaled
the night, which smelled clean and hopeful. Despite everything,
Henry felt calm, as though he'd done what he was meant to do for
Flora.

After the coroner finished, she invited Henry inside again.
They sat in the kitchen; the parlor felt too strange. The couch even
bore the shape of the old woman's body, and Henry couldn't imagine disturbing it. Flora kept apologizing for her tears and Henry
wanted to tell her it was all right, that he understood, but he was
too unsure of what he was supposed to be doing.

"Are you tired?" he asked.

"Exhausted," she said. "But I'll never be able to sleep."

"Should I go? I —"

"Stay," she said. "Stay until it's not dark out anymore."

She put her hand on his. He wanted nothing more than to lean toward her, touch her face, and press his lips to hers. As he thought this, she blushed and looked down, her eyelashes making that fringe that affected him so. The sky flashed white and thunder boomed, and the rain fell once more, like letters tipped out of a liquid book.

He did not kiss her. He wanted to. But resisting was the gift he gave her.

They were too tired to talk, and instead moved their chairs side by side and leaned against each other, quietly sinking into a dreamless sleep.

When he awoke, the rain had stopped. The first pearly light of day was visible through the window. Flora was up already, percolating coffee. A stack of toast sat on a plate in the middle of the table, but he couldn't stay. He needed to be home before his absence was discovered — and certainly before any neighbors saw and Flora's reputation was ruined.

"Do you have someone to help you with your car?" he asked, remembering her flat tires.

Flora shrugged and pressed her fingertips against her eyelids. "I'll figure it out. I'll have to track down my uncle this morning. And I was scheduled to work at the airstrip this afternoon. That isn't going to happen."

"Please call on me if you need anything." He allowed himself one light touch on her arm. "I'm so sorry about your grandmother." He wrote his telephone number on a scrap of paper. Then he gulped scorching coffee, not minding the pain.

A few minutes later, as he stood in the doorway, Flora touched his arm the way he'd touched hers. "Can I ask you something?"

"Of course." He braced himself.

"Do you still want to play in the band? We could . . . we could use you."

He weighed his answer. She'd hurt his pride, terribly. What's more, it would be almost impossible to explain to the Thornes, and he didn't know how he would combine it with his schoolwork. To say yes was to say no to everything else, everything that gave him any sense of security in the world.

But he said it anyway. *Yes.* Knowing his life would never be the same.

Chapter 35

As Love suspected, Ethan had not been sad to see Henry walk off after Flora.

"He's like that," Ethan said. He held a hand over his head, trying to keep the rain from landing. "Always doing the right thing. Does it make us heels, driving off?" He opened his door and looked at Love sheepishly.

"Not at all," Love said. "Mind if I move to the front?"

Ethan cleared his throat. "Be my guest."

Ethan's voice quavered, not enough that a human would have noticed. But Love, who was considerably more sensitive to such things, felt Ethan's entire body spark. He wanted to lean across the seat, to be close to this spectacular young man, to help him understand that the love he wanted was nothing to fear or dread. If he was not allowed to fill Flora's heart with courage, perhaps he could do it for Ethan. And if Ethan felt all right about loving another man, he'd surely understand Henry's love for Flora. Maybe then they might stand together as brothers in this, even if the world around them was hostile.

But he did not reach for Ethan. Not just then. Instead, he turned on the radio, which was playing an advertisement for Bright Spark Batteries. Humans and their fear of the dark.

Welcome to another meeting of the Bright Young Men's Philosophy Club, sponsored by Bright Spark Batteries! It's time for our pledge of allegiance to decency and to philosophy!

"By golly, I'd love to have one of these at Hooverville," he said, tapping the dashboard. "Of course we have no electricity to run such a wireless. Still. So much better than listening to the men singing and playing the washbasin."

As all you bright philosophers know, every club has its rules for membership, along with secret business meant only for the ears of those who belong. Now take the Bright Young Men's Philosophy Club, for instance.

"Except for the stupid advertisements. Bright philosophers. Keeping secrets." He clicked off the radio. The awkwardness between them was palpable, and Love regretted their inevitable parting. It would break Ethan's heart. But such was the cost of the Game. It was sometimes more than a human could bear.

Love removed his book and Venetian pen. "I was thinking about that article you're working on," he said, making full use of James Booth's charisma. "And I recalled this bit of Greek philosophy."

He pretended to read the philosopher's words to Ethan. Had the boy been more observant, he would have realized there was not enough light in the car to read. But, as Love was well aware, Ethan's blood was screaming.

"'Homosexuality'" — he paused to let the word sink in — "'is regarded as shameful by barbarians and tyrants. These same barbarians, these same despots, also consider philosophy itself to be shameful.'" The boy was still, his eyes glued to the road. "'These rulers are afraid of ideas, they fear friendship, and they fear passion — three virtues homosexuality often generates. Because these virtues are not in the interests of the corrupt, they condemn their result.'"

Ethan gripped the steering wheel so hard his knuckles were white. "I don't see what that has to do with anything." He pulled over. "What we've been doing, it's not . . . it's not that. I'm not that."

Love touched Ethan's hand to fill him with calm. But he couldn't take away the sadness.

"Don't you see," Love said, "the same system that is wasting the gifts of all the men of Hooverville, who wish for nothing more than honest work, is the system that prefers obedience over thought and ideas. The powerful are happy to send men to the front lines of war and have their limbs shot off or worse. But should that man ask a question, he's a traitor. This same system could condemn injustice, but instead it chooses to condemn something as simple and as fundamental as the search for the second half. We are all born wanting this. Why does it matter what shape this second half takes, provided it is the thing both sides seek?"

Love turned Ethan's face toward his and wiped the boy's tears. "Why choose fear over love? In what world does that make sense?"

Ethan bent over the steering wheel and sobbed. "I would rather be dead than this."

"Don't say that." Ethan's death would devastate Henry. It could cost him the Game, which would mean that Flora would die too. Love couldn't bear these thoughts, never mind his fondness for Ethan. He put a hand on Ethan's back. He could feel his heartbeat, and he set his own to match, to be that second half as he always knew he would, consequences be damned.

"Breathe," he said. "Breathe." A lifetime of shame and sorrow leaked out of Ethan. Love absorbed it with one hand and cast it away as though it were as slight as a spider's web.

"Who are you?" Ethan lifted his head. He'd stopped crying and looked curious. "Who are you, really?"

"The one you've been looking for," Love said. "One who is here. One who sees you. One who is able to love you just as you are."

Ethan leaned in and kissed Love. Rain pummeled the car, but neither one felt anything but the thrill of the other.

———————————————————————

Afterward, Love watched Ethan sleep. He'd dressed himself in James Booth's shabby everyday suit and returned the Book of Love and Death to his pocket, where, for the first time, it felt like an encumbrance. Even though he had ways of making it appear small, it was in fact a huge collection of heartbreaking tales of love. He'd been writing in it for ages, a small act of defiance against Death, the great unraveler of stories. To record the details of how the players met, what they noticed about each other, what captured their imaginations: All of this was how Love showed his affection for humans and their strangely beautiful, optimistic hearts.

To be written into story. That was how even the lost lived on.

Love's need to write, his book, had never felt heavy to him before now. He wished to be relieved of the burden, but there was no one else to carry it.

Chapter 36
Sunday, June 6, 1937

THE SUN WAS NOT YET UP, BUT ALREADY, THE AIR SMELLED OF WISteria and lavender. This day would be warmer than the previous one, but not by much. Gentle weather was one of the things Henry most loved about his city. The drizzle was no friend to baseball — the rain washed out a good quarter of the season — but Henry had always played more for the rhythm and connection than the competition of it, and so it hadn't mattered.

Sunday morning. He had a French exam to take tomorrow. It seemed ridiculous that a day as nondescript as this, filled with such mundane things as French grammar, could follow a night like the one he'd had.

If the world made any sense, a new day of the week would be born, one that didn't require him to think about school, one in which he could lie on his back in the grass and look at the sky and imagine what it would be like to run away with her and do nothing but play music and eat fruit and walk down the street together for as long as they lived without feeling like the whole world would be staring and judging, or worse.

A small part of him wished he'd never met her. Wished he'd never heard her sing. Wished he'd never eaten eggs in her kitchen. If these things hadn't happened, his life would be school, music, and baseball. Scholarship. Graduation. College. Orderly, predictable, respectable, safe. Perhaps even marriage to Helen followed by a lifetime of breakfasts, lunches, and dinners. Routine, sustaining, nourishing things that wouldn't fill his chest with pain and dread. Life in 4/4 time.

But it was only a small part. The greater portion wouldn't trade the hope for anything. It was as though he'd started seeing for the first time. He couldn't go back to darkness no matter how much it stung to look at the light.

A car engine growled behind him. Henry glanced over his shoulder. He recognized Ethan's Cadillac coming not from home, but from the opposite direction. Downtown. Or — a notion struck him — Hooverville. He raised his hand in greeting and Ethan pulled over. His tie peeped out of the pocket of his jacket, and his shirt was partially unbuttoned. The strangest part, though, was how happy and relaxed he looked.

"You didn't make it home either, apparently," Ethan said.

Henry slid into the front seat, suddenly aware of his exhaustion. "Nope."

"Scoundrel," Ethan said. "But don't worry, I won't tell my parents."

"What? No," Henry countered. "It was nothing like that. Her grandmother — she passed away."

"No fooling?" Ethan grimaced. "That must have been a terrible thing to come home to. What happened?"

"Old age, it looked like. She was just lying on the couch."

There was silence between them for a moment. Then Ethan spoke, his voice thoughtful. "Life is a temporary condition, Henry. And it's uncertain. That's why you have to seize chances when you find them. Pursue what you want. Take risks. Live, love . . . all of it. Every last one of us is going to die, but if we don't live as we truly want, if we're not with the one we want to be with, we're dead already."

Henry turned in his seat to see if someone had secretly replaced his best friend with an identical impostor. "Since when has that been your philosophy?"

Ethan turned onto their street. He filled his cheeks with air and exhaled forcefully, as a trumpet player might. "I couldn't even begin to say," he said, looking over at Henry. "But something's happened to me. Just . . . It's something I can't talk about." He ran his fingers through his hair, smoothing his disheveled curls. "But I think it's probably something you can understand."

He looked at Henry again with earnestness, and Henry swallowed hard. How much did he want to say? And what, exactly, was Ethan telling him? They drove down the long, treelined avenue in silence.

Ethan turned into the driveway and shut off the engine. "So it's a good thing, then?" Henry asked.

"Honestly?" Ethan's eyes had a pained look. He exhaled deeply before he finished his thought. "It's all I've ever really wanted. But I don't know that I'd ever call it good."

He covered his face with his hands. Henry wondered if he should say something. Then Ethan opened the door, stepped out of the car, and slouched toward the house, his jacket over his shoulder. Henry followed him to the front door, which swung open when they were a few steps away.

Ethan's father filled the doorframe. "Out all night, boys?" His face was stern — the expression he wore before he lowered the boom.

"Yes, Father," Ethan said, crossing his arms over his chest. "All night. I watched the sunrise, in fact. Did you ever do that when you were young?"

Mr. Thorne paused and stroked his chin.

"Actually," he said, "I did. Which is why I am telling you to go in the back door and use the servants' stairs. Your mother is up, and if she hears you coming in at this hour, we'll all have headaches to last a week. Make this the last time this sort of thing happens, though. There are raids on the horizon, and it would complicate things if you're swept up in any of them. The consequences for both of you would be severe. We're a prominent family, Ethan. No embarrassments."

Ethan threw an arm over Henry's shoulder, and the two boys walked around the ivy-covered north side of the house and into the servants' entrance. It led into the butler's pantry and to a narrow staircase that opened onto the third floor, where Ethan and Henry had their bedrooms. They kicked off their shoes and hastened up the stairs in their socks. Ethan grinned at Henry. Henry couldn't return the look. Police raids could spell disaster for Flora.

Chapter 37

Monday, June 7, 1937

AFTER A DAY SPENT ANSWERING THE DOOR TO RECEIVE VISITORS and their gifts of food, Flora stood alone in the kitchen, her hands deep in the suds of a dirty pan. She'd done her best to keep busy. Once she fixed her tires, she'd have to go to the airfield and explain her absence to Captain Girard, but he'd understand. Her ambition there felt so out of reach it almost didn't matter, and even if she achieved the dream, Nana would never know.

The morning paper had carried a small bit about Amelia Earhart's around-the-world trip. The aviatrix had flown from the mouth of the Amazon River to Dakar, Senegal, setting a record crossing the South Atlantic in thirteen hours and twenty-two minutes. Not so long ago, these exotic names and places, this world record, would have filled her with a competitive rush. Now, though, they were letters on a page, black ink on cheap paper that would yellow and dry out in a blink of time's eye.

And what was the point? Flora still wanted what flight offered: solitude, good pay, a chance to see the world on her own terms. But she also wanted Henry. She could not have both things, be both things. The impossibility of it was paralyzing. But even if she did choose, she'd still someday end up like her grandmother. Everyone did.

185

She finished her coffee and pushed the troubling thoughts out of her mind. Except for the mantel clock, the house was entirely silent. The absence of sound would take some getting used to. Nana was always up and about. Cooking, shining the windows, polishing the woodwork, working on a quilt, listening to the wireless.

She thought about switching it on. But there was no music she could listen to without pain, and the thought of a radio drama or worse, a comedy . . . it just wouldn't do. She walked into the parlor and picked up her grandmother's last quilt, which she'd folded and set on the table. She breathed its scent and then spread it out on the floor, poring over every inch of it until she found it, stitched in red, in the final section her grandmother's hands had completed. When everything else was gone, there it was, sewn into memory.

She folded the quilt and tried to muster the energy to handle the tires. Sherman was busy with the funeral arrangements, and then he was heading north for business, so he'd be gone for the day. But it would at least occupy the rest of the morning. She washed up and reached for a black dress. She heard Nana's voice in her mind chiding her for wearing black. So she found a long polka-dot skirt and blouse instead. Then she donned a hat, shoes, and her mother's gloves and walked back toward the Majestic.

As unbearable as the silence in her house had been, the clamor of life outside was worse. The sun overhead seemed like an affront, as did the barking dogs and rumbling cars. If the world made any sense at all, time would stop when someone died. Just for a moment, just to mark the loss. The sidewalk ahead blurred, and Flora blinked away her tears.

At the club, she set to work on the tires straightaway, glad to have something to occupy her. She had two spares, but she'd have to patch the others. Four flats at once. Flat tires happened often enough, but not when a car was parked. Someone had obviously been up to no good. Flora wished for whoever had done it to walk beneath the business end of a sick pigeon.

She found the jack in the trunk. She'd just lifted one side of the car when she heard someone pull up behind her. A door opened and slammed shut, and she knew who was there without even turning around.

"Hello, Flora." Henry's voice was gentle and warm. "Need help?"

"Don't you have school?" She stood, feeling conscious of her hands, as if she couldn't remember what she was supposed to do with them.

He lifted his hat and scratched his head. "Nope. Not today." His face told another story, though.

She wondered what he was missing. Final exams, maybe, given the time of year. She decided not to press it, surprisingly grateful for the company. She didn't ask him how he'd known to come, because she already knew what his answer would be. He'd known she was there, just as she'd known he was on his way. It was as if they were playing a duet, but on a much bigger stage. "You any good at patching a tire?"

"I do it for Ethan all the time."

They crouched side by side, and she couldn't help but smell the lemon-and-spice scent of his skin all over again. She liked it, but for some reason, it made her deeply sad, more conscious than usual of inevitable loss.

"The patches are in the trunk." She tried to sound as business-like as possible. "Orange tin. I'm going to put the spares on, then we can fix the ones I'm taking off, all right?"

As they worked, she found herself humming, out of habit more than anything.

"What's that song?" Henry said.

"Billie Holiday. 'Easy Living.' Ever heard it?"

"Nope. But I like it."

She had a wild idea, one she hesitated to say out loud. "I can teach it to you afterward," she said. "If you want. It can be the first number you learn."

There was a long pause, and she wondered if she'd said something stupid.

"Yes, of course," Henry said. "What's the harm in that?"

After they'd repaired the tires and driven to the Domino, they made their way down the steps together.

"It's different during the daytime," Henry said, removing his hat.

At first Flora didn't know what he meant by "it" — them? The way they interacted? The strange ease of the night of Nana's death was gone.

She guessed he meant the club. "The crowds and music add a certain something." She moved ahead of him to find the switch for the main room.

"I like it better this way, actually. There's more of a sense of expectation." He paused at the base of the stairs, and she turned back to look at him. "This is a place that wants to be filled."

Flora was glad for the inadequate lighting. She set her gloves down on a table and climbed the staircase to the wings where Grady's bass remained. Henry put his hat next to her gloves and followed her.

"I'll get that." He picked up the bass, carrying it with practiced arms across the stage.

"So the first few chords —" She breathed in, the way a person does before diving beneath the surface of a lake. "I'm not warmed up, but they go like this." She sang the notes so that they'd correspond with where they fell in the melody. "A minor seventh, E diminished . . ."

Henry checked that the bass was in tune and started plucking along with her, as if he were getting the feel for things.

She sang carefully, quietly at first, taking her time to warm up, making sure he was following. He looked at her every so often, then returned his attention to the bass, sliding his left hand along the neck of it as he found the notes, coaxing sound out of it with his right.

"You're holding back," he said. "Why?"

"I'm warming up."

"No, I mean in general. I think you could give more when you're singing. Put your heart out there more." He smiled, as if to let her know it wasn't a judgment, more of an observation.

She held up a palm, as if to dismiss the notion. As they eased their way through the refrain, she gave in. Just to see. And then all the way, as she had once earlier at the Domino. It was different, singing without the full band. But Henry was good, so steady as he pulled sounds out of more than one string at a time. He was a natural. He knew how to connect. He improvised here and there, and for the first time since the day they'd met, she felt something inside herself open wide. The thing that surprised her most was that it was easier to sing this way when she was letting each note be what it wanted to be. She felt it in her chest, in her head, and finally everywhere.

As she came to the last line of the song, she heard footsteps. Someone was coming. More than one person, judging from the irregular tap of shoes on the treads. She cursed inwardly when she saw who it was: Mr. Potts and his crew. And they'd brought a police officer with them.

"I'm sorry, my uncle isn't here yet," she said. She rushed toward them, intending to usher them out before Henry realized who they were.

"We're not here for your uncle." Mr. Potts strode toward her.

They met in the middle of the room. The police officer moved forward and reached for the handcuffs dangling from his wide leather belt.

"We're here for you," Mr. Potts said. "On account of that bribe you offered us not too long ago. Turns out that sort of thing is against the law. You, my dear, are in a world of trouble."

Flora felt all the blood leave her body. They'd trapped her. The club would have been shut down if she hadn't paid a bribe. And now they were going to arrest her anyway for paying it. All while Henry watched.

"That isn't fair," she said, jerking her hands away from the police officer, realizing how stupid the words sounded. "Please." She took a half step back and felt Henry behind her.

She looked the officer in the eye, and then glanced down at the name on his badge. J. WALLACE JR. "Come on, Officer Wallace. This is a misunderstanding."

Mr. Potts interrupted. "Miss Saudade. We are acting in the interests of the law, and you are a public menace." He lunged for her.

"That's ridiculous!" she said. She dodged Mr. Potts, and Henry stepped between them.

"Isn't there something that can be done about this?" he said. "Please don't cart her off. I know some people. . . ." A look of uncertainty came over him.

"What are you saying, boy," Mr. Potts said. "Are you offering us a bribe? Making a threat? Because believe you me, that is not going to turn out nicely."

"No," Henry said. "It wasn't like that. I —" He reached for Flora's hand. She squeezed his fingers.

"Oh, I see how it is," Mr. Potts said. "A young man has needs and he sometimes finds ways to take care of those that society wouldn't like. It's not illegal in these parts, not yet, even if it is shameful. But you do not want to lose your head here. A colored whore like this one —"

Henry's fist was a white flash. There was a crack, and Mr. Potts put his hands to his nose. Blood oozed through his fingers. "You broke my nose!" he said. "You done broke it!"

The men restrained Henry. Officer Wallace, who said not a word, was at least gentle as he fastened the cuffs on Flora's wrists. Henry did not enjoy the same kind of treatment. By the time he was in the back of the police car next to her, he had a pair of black eyes and a split lip.

"Oh, Henry," she said. "I'm sorry."

"It's all right," he said. "Their aim was lousy. They missed my nose completely."

She couldn't bring herself to smile at his joke. The backseat was too wide for them to touch, but she wanted to hold ice to his swollen face. She wanted to clean the blood from his lip with a damp washcloth. She wanted to kiss his forehead and apologize for bringing him into her world this way, with the roughness and injustice and frequent humiliations. She turned her face to the window. Thick clouds had gathered. It was sure to rain again.

Henry hummed the first few bars of the song they had been playing. "We'll do it again. I promise. Someday."

Flora's forehead burned. Overwhelmed with anger at being set up, wondering what her next move would be, she flexed her fingers and strained against the handcuffs. With a start, she remembered her mother's gloves. She'd left them next to Henry's hat. *Dammit.* Her hands felt naked without them. It wasn't just that they covered her skin and made her fit to be seen in public. They represented so much more. She tried to tell herself that they were just a pair of gloves, not her mother, that her mother's hands hadn't been inside of them for ages, and that any bit of her that remained inside had surely been worn away. She willed herself to hold it together as she leaned against the seat.

"Sure," she said. "Someday."

When she looked over at Henry, she wished she'd been able to keep the bitterness out of her voice.

"Flora," Henry said. "Have a little faith."

They arrived at the police station. Officer Wallace guided Henry out of the car, then Flora. They walked past a group of hungry-looking children leaning against the side of the building.

"Run along," Officer Wallace said.

The children scattered like dry leaves.

"I'd like my telephone call," Henry said.

"All in good time." Officer Wallace led Flora to her cell first. He clicked open the cuffs. The return of circulation made her hands ache. The door slammed behind her. The space was small and dark and dirty, equipped with something that was more a hole than a toilet, and a bed that barely deserved the name.

It occurred to her, as she lowered herself onto the thin mattress, that no one had offered her a telephone call. Not that it mattered. Nana was dead. Sherman was halfway across the state, picking up a supply of alcohol from his inexpensive source, and he wouldn't be back for hours, and neither he nor anyone else in the band had a telephone, anyway. There was no one to come for her.

Chapter 38

First Nana. Now this. Flora wanted nothing more than to fall asleep, to temporarily shut out the sadness of the world, but she couldn't. The cell was dank and smelly: the opposite of the sky. Somewhere in the gloom, a fly buzzed. She did not want to think about what it might be dining on. She tried to imagine herself in her plane, leaving all of this behind, but she couldn't. She leaned against the rough, damp wall and willed herself not to feel anything at all.

And then she heard Henry's voice. Singing. It hadn't occurred to her before that he might be able to do this too. He sounded as if his voice had been shaped to fit her ears alone. She moved by the bars, so that she could hear better.

The song wasn't one she knew, although it was the sort that immediately felt as familiar as her own skin.

You are the moon
And I am the sea
Wherever you are
You've got pull over me

The whole of the sky
Wants to keep us apart

The distance is wearing
A hole in my heart

Someday your moonlight
Will blanket my skin
Someday my waves
Will pull all of you in

Someday I promise
The moon and the sea
Will be together
Forever you and me.

Someday. For as long as she could remember, Flora had linked thoughts of this word with the certainty of death: hers, and that of everyone she'd ever loved. Someday had always been a source of dread. But the sweetness of this song showed her a different way to look at it, a way that made it hurt less.

As she listened, her grief over Nana, her rage at her situation, her guilt over Henry faded. She could have listened to the song, been suspended in its magic, for ages. But it was not to be. Slow applause and the click of heels on the concrete broke the spell. Henry stopped mid-note.

"Don't stop on my account," a sharp voice said.

Flora peered through the bars. Her stomach clenched at the sight of the hard-looking girl who'd been with Henry at the Majestic. If she was the one he'd called when he needed rescuing, she must mean something to him. And it made sense. She was beautiful. She looked intelligent. She was the right color. She was everything he needed.

Flora understood this, and even though the match would provide a happy life for Henry, she envied the dark-haired girl for having what she could not have, for being who she could not be. Worse, the girl would know Henry's humiliation was Flora's fault. She'd look down on her, and rightfully so.

The girl stopped in front of Henry's cell. "Congratulations. After bail, you have twelve cents to your name. It's a good thing I was never interested in your money."

Henry replied, too softly for Flora to hear.

"You must be joking," the girl said.

More murmuring from Henry.

"You're a lunatic." The girl raised her voice. "You know what the Thornes are going to say, don't you?"

"Helen, please. Don't tell them why I'm here. I beg of you. And once you've finished, if you could please pick up Ethan at school, and take him to his car, then he can come back for me. He has the money, and he won't mind that I took the Cadillac. Please . . . I need you to do this for me."

Flora held her breath and wished she knew what they were talking about.

Helen shot back a reply. "It's an awfully queer way to ask me for a favor, Henry. What do I care about her? I'm certainly not going to promise my silence. Not without anything from you in return."

There was a long pause, and Flora still didn't dare breathe. Then a whisper from Henry and Helen spoke again, her voice flip and uncaring.

"Fine," she said. "It's your funeral."

Flora, no longer trying to mask her hate for Helen, wished a piano would fall from the sky and land on her. Death in the key of B-flat.

And then, just like that, the girl was in front of Flora, accompanied by a guard. "Don't just stand there like a lump," Helen said.

"Excuse me?" Flora tried to hide her contempt for Henry's sake. "What's happening?"

The guard jingled his keys, and Helen said, "Henry's being a fool. He had only enough money to get one of you out, and because he's a gentleman — a quality I truly admire — he's chosen you. But if you're comfortable here, I'd love to talk some sense into him."

Flora felt like an animal on display. The disgust was palpable.

"Someone else will come for me," Flora said.

"That's not what I've heard," Helen said. "It's now or never. Decide."

Too tired to think everything through, Flora agreed. "I have money for Henry at my club. So if you can take me there, I'll come back for him."

"Your plans fascinate me," Helen said. "Thank you for sharing."

Death in the key of B-flat. Her kingdom for a falling piano.

Henry's cell was the last she passed on her way out. He rushed against the bars, but the officer elbowed her forward.

"I'll be back for you," she called over her shoulder. "I promise."

But then that would be it. After that, it was good-bye. It didn't matter what she felt about him, how tied to him she felt. Carrying on would only lead to ruin, if it hadn't already.

As they left the building, Helen waved to the police officers as if this were a social call. "Catch you all later."

The angle of the sun told Flora it was afternoon already. She'd missed her morning shift at the airfield. She didn't feel herself when she wasn't near a plane, even if Captain Girard had been understanding about her absence. What's more, she hadn't set up the Domino for that evening's service, so she'd have to rush around in a lather. Things could not fall apart more.

"How much money do we need?" Flora asked.

Helen quoted a sum that made Flora blanch. That would clean out the safe, and explaining everything to Sherman . . . She dreaded the conversation more than anything.

"Short on funds?" Helen said.

Flora didn't answer. "Where did you say you'd parked?"

"I didn't. I also didn't offer you a ride anywhere, but maybe, if you ask very nicely . . ." She gave Flora a wooden nickel of a smile.

"Please," Flora said.

Helen looked back over her shoulder. "Follow me."

Chapter 39

HELEN SPED TOWARD THE DOMINO AS THOUGH SHE HAD A DEATH wish: too fast, with no regard for other automobiles. At one point, as she fished for a cigarette in her purse, she swerved into oncoming traffic, laughing hysterically. Flora hoped Helen would never take an interest in flying planes. It wouldn't last long.

When they arrived at the Domino, Helen uncapped a tube of crimson lipstick and applied it as if she hadn't a care in the world. "Shall we?"

"Shall we what?" Flora reached for the door latch.

"Go inside to fetch the bail money, of course." Helen pressed her lips together and examined herself in the rearview mirror.

"This is where we part ways," Flora said. "Thank you for the ride."

Helen wouldn't hear of it. "I'd love to go inside the club I've heard so much about."

Flora wanted to refuse her on principle, but she also wanted Helen to see the Domino was something special. Something her family had built. Something that had survived all sorts of hardships. Something Henry admired.

"Fine." She found her keys.

They headed into the club, past the portrait of her parents, down the stairs, and then turned left into the kitchen, where Charlie was already hard at work on the evening's food. The air smelled good, a mixture of slowly cooking meat and corn bread.

"I'd offer you something to eat," Flora said, "but I know you have other places to be."

Leaving Helen for a moment, Flora went into the storeroom, opened the safe, and removed all of the bills, hoping Charlie wouldn't ask what she was doing. When she returned to the kitchen, Helen was seated at the table, and Charlie was leaning against the countertop, a hand to his forehead.

His knees buckled, and he caught himself on the counter. Flora rushed to his side. She put an arm around his back and held him steady.

"I don't feel well, Miss Flora."

"You should go home, Charlie," she said. "I can take it from here."

"But Sherman isn't back yet. There ain't enough hands to get the work done, and if you don't mind my saying, you're a bit behind in the dining room already."

"Charlie, please. You get on home. I know all your recipes and I'll be back soon. I'll call in some of the girls. We'll take care of it. You can't cook if you're ill. And setting the tables is no trouble."

Charlie looked chalky around his edges, and Flora hoped whatever he had wasn't contagious.

"It came on so sudden," he said.

"It's all right, Charlie. You go on. Rest."

"I think I will," he said. "I appreciate your understanding." He shuffled out of the kitchen and up the stairs. He rented a room a half block away, or Flora would have escorted him.

"Well." Helen turned her head slowly to look at Flora. "How unfortunate for you. He looked fine when we walked in."

"These things happen," Flora said. "We'll manage."

Helen had removed her gloves. Apparently she'd planned to make herself at home. Too bad for her. Flora led her up the stairs, remembering as she did her own pair of gloves, sitting on a table next to Henry's hat. She made a note to retrieve them after she sent Helen on her way.

At the exit, Helen said, "What, no grand tour?"

"No time," Flora said. "I do apologize. Thank you again for the ride."

Helen offered Flora her hand. Flora took it, mostly to end the exchange. But when their bare palms touched, she felt a startling coldness. Her body felt strange, as though she were underwater and sinking deeper, the pressure growing every second. The world dimmed, and she was no longer standing on the sidewalk, but inside the Domino — or at least a version of it from long ago.

The floor of the club hummed with noise and motion. A mustachioed man in a striped shirt and suspenders banged out a rag tune. Dice thumped on felted tables. Highball glasses plinked against each other, and beaded dresses rustled and clicked as women with bobbed hair leaned into the arms of men in suits and turned their powdered faces to the electric chandeliers. Laughter. There was so much of it. But then, it was clearly another time.

Flora wanted to look around, but she wasn't in control of her gaze. It was as though she was inside someone else's head. A man's voice interrupted her thoughts. "What's a pretty lady like you doing by herself in a joint like this?"

The view shifted to the bartender, whose sleeves were rolled up over his wide forearms. He leaned toward her across the polished slab of wood. A set of fingers, white ones, were laced a few inches away from her drink. The hands pressed flat on the counter and

Flora felt something flow into her, something that felt strong and old and smelled like Douglas fir. It was almost as though she were sucking the life out of the bar.

Then there was a sudden lightness in the air, the way she felt when her airplane left the ground. The piano music stopped. People paused in their conversations, drinking, and gambling. The gaze turned to watch as the pianist began to speak.

"Ladies and gentlemen, I present . . . Miss Vivian Crane and the Starlight band."

Vivian Crane. Her mother. Alive. How on earth was this happening?

Applause crackled like fire. Flora watched her mother emerge from the shadows into the finger of spotlight in the center of the stage, pivoting so that her back was to the audience. Even from behind, she commanded a person's full attention. When her mother spun at last to face the audience, sparkling reflections of her filled every eye in the room. But she had eyes for only one person. The bass player. Flora's father. Her heart lurched to see him, to see them both together like this, alive.

The music began, a shimmer of the hi-hat, a cry from the clarinet, the steady walk of bass strings played by expert hands. Vivian's lips parted and the sound that emerged was more of a feeling than a voice, one that pressed love and longing into Flora's borrowed ears, along her wrists, down her throat, and straight into her center. It was hard to breathe.

The view changed. Flora was still inside the Domino, but now she was looking at a man shooting dice. Somehow, she knew there was a police dry squad uniform beneath his overcoat. She also knew his pockets were fat with payoff cash, which he was spending at the dice table as he sneaked pulls of gin from the flask at his hip.

And then she was outside in the snow, waiting in a long and elegant convertible with high, round headlights and a many-spoked spare tire riding on its hip. Through the window holes, winter air sharpened its claws on her skin as she sat in the passenger seat. Time passed. Snow piled up. People wandered out of the Domino. Then, finally, the dice-playing man staggered out, supported by a much younger version of Uncle Sherman.

"You sure you don't want a cup of coffee, sober up a bit?" Sherman asked.

The man shook his head. "Cold air'll do the same trick." He slapped at his own cheeks and walked toward his car just as her parents emerged from the alley. Her father pulled the collar of her mother's raccoon coat snug around her shoulders. The moonlight bounced off the snowy street and lit them from below. Her father leaned in for a kiss; Vivian laughed and met him halfway, lifting one heel behind her before she finally came up for air.

"Happy Valentine's Day, my love," she said.

No, no, no. Flora knew what had happened that night.

The white man slid into the car, reeking of gin. He turned the key. The car coughed. The engine caught. Trying to throw it into reverse, he cursed when the car bumped forward over the curb. Then he found his gear and accelerated backward into the darkness behind him, his tires sliding in the snow. He hunched over the steering wheel and gulped air. Flora tried to scream, but the mouth wouldn't respond.

Flora's parents stepped into the street. She tried to reach for the wheel, but the arm wouldn't move. The man's foot sank into the accelerator. Her parents heard its engine and turned to face the car, still holding hands. The headlights caught bright pieces of them: eyes, teeth, jewelry that twinkled like falling stars in the blackness ahead.

The man stomped, aiming for the brake, but his sluggish foot found only the gas pedal. And then Flora was outside the car, holding her father. She felt his life flow out of him and into her: the glint of candlelight off the shoulders of his bass, the crack of a bat meeting a softball on Saturday mornings, the smell of corn bread baking in the oven on Sunday afternoons. In a bleak moment, she saw the jagged silver blasts of explosions in the night, smelled the gunpowder, fear and blood, the flash of Captain Girard's face lit up by a midnight firefight. And then a return to soft light, to the satiny patch of her mother's skin between her ear and collarbone, the feeling of lips against it. And then her own baby-girl face, all brown eyes and pink gums and fat cheeks.

The arms released her father and gathered up her mother, and Flora drew in memories of trimmed Christmas trees, of steam curling from oven-hot pies, of spring tulips and green summer lakes, of the feeling of music rising from the tender space where her feet connected with the curving earth, soaring upward through her body and out her mouth. In each of those, even when Vivian was a girl, the small face of the baby was there. Flora's own face, as though she'd been the one her mother always wanted, the love she carried with her until the day she was able to summon it forth in the form of a child.

And then she was dead.

The white man staggered out, tripping and flailing and breathing fists of clouds into the frozen night air. His hat fell off, revealing a pale, fragile-looking scalp covered with a few strands of silver hair. He knelt between the bodies and sobbed. Snow melted into his knees, darkening his pants. He put his hands over his face, revealing an inch of bare flesh and a leather-banded, gold-faced wristwatch that he'd forgotten to wind.

Then Flora was on her knees beside the man in the snow.

"Please," he said, peering at her through his fingers. He'd bloodied a knuckle somehow and a knot was rising on his head. "I don't know what to do. I can't live with myself anymore."

"You don't have to do anything," the mouth said. "It won't be long now."

"Thank God," he said, lowering his hands to his lap.

The hand reached for the killer's own. The images at first came in a jumble: the man himself in an undershirt and braces planting trees in a garden, wiping sweat from his tanned brow; him in a police officer's uniform, giving a rag doll to a weeping, soot-covered child sitting alone in the station; the same man, younger, at his wedding, the stainless steel flask of gin just a bulge in the pocket of his Sunday best suit. The flask of gin that turned into tumblers and entire bottles . . . what had transformed the laughing man with the straight black hair and clean-shaven jaw into the bleary-eyed mess in front of her.

"What's happening?" he said. "I'm seeing —"

"You're seeing what I'm seeing," the mouth said. The whole of her hand sank over his, and Flora was sick with sorrow and loss. The man's eyes widened. There he was, an infant in a white linen christening gown. And there, walking across an emerald lawn, wobbly on year-old bare feet. Then he was a five-year-old boy riding a pony at the county fair. Then, ten years older, hiking up a snow-covered volcano. That boy, sixteen, on a twilit country road on a summer night, leaning in to kiss a girl who locked her fingers in his hair. And five years after that, marrying the same girl, the love of his life . . .

. . . unless you counted the gin in the bottle, which even the Prohibition hadn't kept him from drinking.

"I did love her, you know," he said. "Like breathing, almost." The words had space between them, as though it was costing him the last of his strength to pull them out of his mouth.

"I know. But that's the thing with love. It isn't as strong as they say."

"Not afraid," he said. "Glad — glad you're here."

The voice replied: "Life is far more terrifying than its opposite."

He grabbed her hands. "Wait. Don't want to see all," he said. "Not the last part —" His stomach heaved, costing him his last drink of gin.

"They didn't suffer." The gaze shifted to her parents' bodies, their skin sugared with the lightest dusting of snow. "What's more, I'm letting you carry that part with you when you go."

"I'd carry it for the rest of time if . . . if it would make things turn out . . . different."

"You will," she said, closing her eyes for a moment. "But it won't. Everybody dies. Everybody. That is the only ending for every true story."

The sentence . . . Flora had heard something like it before. She fought her way back to herself. The skin on her face felt tight, as though it were being pressed against the bones beneath. She pulled her hand from Helen's, opened her eyes, and was back at the entrance of the Domino, utterly wrecked. What had happened to her? How had she seen her parents' last moments this way?

Helen stood next to her, even as she checked her watch. "Are you all right? You look as if you've caught whatever your cook had."

"I'm fine." Flora didn't want to give Helen the satisfaction of seeing her like this. "Henry's waiting for me."

"We don't always get what we want," Helen said. "We play the roles we're cast."

"What are you saying, that I'm trying to be something I'm not?"

A look of confusion flashed across Helen's face, then understanding. "I can see how you'd say that."

"Henry's waiting for me," Flora said again. "So if you'll excuse me."

"What makes you think he's still there?"

"Who would have paid his bail?"

"I might have left a note for the Thornes," Helen said.

Flora thought she might be ill. That would make things infinitely worse for Henry. She'd have to reach him first.

"Don't tell me you love him," Helen said.

"I said no such thing."

"I'm sure you've considered the cost," Helen said. "How much it could hurt him."

"I wouldn't dream of hurting him."

"But" — Helen paused, as if she were choosing her words carefully — "would you choose him if you could?"

"Choose him for what?"

"I think you know," Helen said.

"And I think you know this is none of your concern."

"Come now. Don't look so angry. In different circumstances, we might have been friends. There isn't so very much that separates you and me."

"Everything separates us," Flora said. "You can go where you want. Do what you want. Eat where you want. The world belongs to you and yours. My kind, we're here to be your mules. Your world rests on our backs. We even have to pay you off for the privilege of entertaining you. And then you arrest us anyway."

"So bitter," Helen said. "And I love it."

"We're finished here," Flora said.

"Here, perhaps," Helen said.

Flora had made it halfway up the precinct stairs when Henry walked through the door, his bruised face downcast, flanked on either side by two distraught-looking white people. The woman wore a fur coat and hat; the man, a forehead-splitting scowl.

"Henry," Flora said. "I'm sorry. I came as quickly as I could." She'd come in such a rush she'd left her gloves and his hat behind. This, she realized as she noticed his uncovered curls.

Henry looked up, his eyes wide.

"Who might this be?" the woman asked, looking horrified. "How does she know your name? Is she the reason you were in this place? Is she — tell me she's not — someone you hired?" She began to weep.

The man pulled Henry down the stairs past Flora, who had to take a step backward to let them by. Flora dropped her pocketbook, and its flimsy clasp popped open. The bills she'd gathered fluttered out.

The hungry children in ratty clothes who'd been skulking against the side of the building rushed forward and snatched most of it up before she could, but Flora didn't have the strength to care. Henry's guardians shoved him into the back of the car, which pulled away from the sidewalk with an angry squeal.

Chapter 40

DEATH WATCHED FLORA LEAVE THE DOMINO, NO DOUBT HEADED to the jail with her sad little wad of bills in hand. She drove a short distance away from the club and parked. It was late afternoon, a virtual dead zone for the neighborhood. No one was there to watch the intense, dark-eyed girl in the red dress walk up to the club and slip inside its locked door, which she opened with a single touch. Thus unobserved, she hastened down the stairs, knowing exactly where she'd start, hoping that the end would be as she intended: to take the last thing from Flora that was keeping her in Seattle.

Death lit a candle and placed it on the bar, inhaling the scent of burning wax as the glow of the lone flame found the edges of the room. Grady's bass, still tinged with the essence of Henry's touch, lay in the shadows. Though it was the size of a grown man, the instrument felt light in her arms as she moved it offstage, across the floor, and onto the bar. She placed it on its back, an echo of human sacrifices that had occurred over the millennia, gifts offered in the name of various gods, and every one a death that seeped into her endless hollows instead.

She materialized on the other side of the bar, filling her arms with clinking bottles: rum, vodka, bourbon, Scotch. Death set each one down. She uncapped the first of the bottles and emptied it over the instrument as one would anoint a corpse. Then the second and the third and the fourth. The wood groaned at the assault. Its pores drank in the booze; puddles of ruin trickled into the F-shaped holes on its face, drumming its back, scenting the air with dust and spirits.

She rested her hands on top of the bar, remembering the life she'd pulled from the wood the night she'd taken Flora's parents. There was even less life remaining, less to fight the flames. The sight would be spectacular. She took the candle and held it inside the curved opening.

A claw of smoke rose; the edges of the wood reddened, then charred. And then, as if the fire had discovered its own thirst, the wood exploded into flame. It lapped up the ooze of liquor that had leaked down the countertop. It flowed like a red river over the edges of the bar, finding places to bite the floor, the shelves, the velvet curtains.

Death picked up the gloves she'd once left in the small green house. They were hers, after all, and she always took what was hers. Then she turned to leave, feeling the smoke and the heat on her back, knowing it was true what Love said about fire. This one was its own sort of creature, a singular soul.

Long may it burn.

Chapter 41

FLORA LEFT THE JAIL AND HEADED TO THE DOMINO, WHERE SHE intended to finish with the food preparations as best she could before the show. She'd retrieve her gloves and set Henry's hat aside. She'd find a way to get it to him later, and then leave him to his life.

In the distance, a dark finger of smoke touched the sky. She wanted to believe it was not her club in flames, not her livelihood being consumed, but she could feel the ruin of it in her depths, as if a part of her very self was being reduced to ash.

She stopped the car a short distance away and ran toward the burning building. The heat pressed against her face and arms, and the smoke smelled oily and toxic, no doubt fed by the well-stocked bar and kitchen, the curtains, the wooden stairs . . . everything familiar to her, the last bits of her parents' legacy. The painting of them. When she realized that was lost too, along with the gloves she'd treasured, she could not hold back the tears. She stopped running.

Behind her, the bells of fire engines clanged, not that they would be able to do anything but keep the fire from spreading. Flora's shoulders heaved. Next door, the Miyashitos were frantically pouring buckets of water on their business. They cried out to each other in Japanese, and she felt even worse. It would be everything they had too.

A police car was parked across the street. When the officers inside saw Flora approach, they stepped out. One held a sheet of paper in his hand.

"You're the owner of this establishment?" the officer asked.

Flora nodded, not trusting herself to speak.

He handed her the paper. "Seems a shame to deliver this right now, but I'm legally required to."

Flora scanned the document. An order from the city, shutting the club down on corruption charges. A flake of ash settled on Flora's cheek, but she ignored the sudden prick of pain. She turned away from the police officer, crumpled the paper into a ball, and hurled it into the fire.

Words echoed in her mind, in a familiar voice she could not quite place.

Someday, everyone you love will die. Everything you love will crumble to ruin. This is the price of life. This is the price of love.

Someday had arrived.

Chapter 42

Mr. Thorne's mouth twitched as he sat behind his desk and ticked off the many ways Henry had failed.

"You stole Ethan's car —"

"I would have lent it to him," Ethan said.

"Don't interrupt. You stole the car, you left school during a day you had a final examination to take, you fraternized with . . . with . . . a colored *nightclub* performer, whom you then had cousin Helen bail out of jail, exposing her to Lord knows what kind of seaminess."

Henry blanched. He hadn't expected the Thornes to discover all that; Helen's betrayal there surprised and wounded him. It was possible, he realized, that this was her retaliation for his choosing Flora over her. The rest of the accusation — that Helen was the fragile type who could be harmed by helping out someone their age — was nonsense. But Henry kept his mouth shut.

"Does that about sum it up?" Mr. Thorne said. "Or are there more things you'd like to disclose?"

He glanced at Ethan. Henry interpreted the pleading look on his face as a request to say nothing about visiting Hooverville or socializing with James afterward. And Henry was certainly not going to confess how much time he'd spent at the Domino, or how far his grades had fallen.

"I believe that sums it up, sir."

Mr. Thorne's mouth twitched again. He pressed his hands against his desk and stood. His bulk blocked much of the light from the window, and his shadow crossed Henry's face as if it were a thing of substance. "You've put me in a terrible spot. A terrible spot."

"I know." Henry's voice hardly felt like his own.

"Do you? Do you know how it feels to have someone you've raised — almost as a son — commit an act of violence against a man whose job it is to uphold the law?"

"But he'd framed —"

"Don't even say her name. I don't want to hear another word about her. Please tell me there hasn't been any" — he waved his hand dismissively — "congress."

"No," Henry whispered, mortified even to be talking about such things in front of other people.

"Small blessings. It means this isn't a permanent disaster." Mr. Thorne lowered himself into his chair again, rubbing his hand along his bare scalp as he leaned back. "The newspaper will have to cover the attack and the arrest. Because you're under eighteen, you're not an adult. Your name won't be used. But your link to my family will be disclosed. Journalistic ethics require it. It's an embarrassment, an enormous embarrassment."

Henry swallowed. He'd considered this already and it only made him feel worse to hear Mr. Thorne spell it all out.

"And it goes without saying that you will not graduate with your class. We spoke with them already. They told us about your plummeting grades, and with today's escapade, you've been expelled."

Henry felt ill.

"And you have lost your scholarship to the university." Mr. Thorne leaned forward again on his elbows. "Obviously."

The scholarship was his future, or it had been. And now that was gone. The loss horrified him, but in a way, he felt like he'd been expecting such a thing his entire life. As hard as he'd tried to make himself useful, to follow the rules, to earn his place, a part of him knew he was an impostor in this world. A part of him was always waiting to be cast out.

But he knew this too: There was a future he'd rather have. One he'd always wanted more. And that was one with the possibility of love.

"Father —" Ethan put his hands on the desk, pleading.

Mr. Thorne spun toward him, his index finger raised. "Not a word out of you, Ethan. So far, you seem blameless, but you don't want to provoke me to dig below the surface and become aware of any shenanigans on your part, do you?"

"No, sir." Ethan stepped back, shoving his hands into his pockets.

"Out of consideration for the friendship I had with your father, and the pleasure I've had seeing you grow up under my roof, I'm not going to cast you out entirely," Mr. Thorne said. He pulled a cigar out of the humidor and lit it, exhaling a stream of blue smoke. "You may have a job, if you'd like, working on the press crew." He paused. "But you'll have to find another place to live. It won't do to have you here, particularly not with someone vulnerable like Helen being put at risk by your behavior and associates. And then there are Ethan and Annabel to consider. They have their own reputations that need protection."

Ethan sucked in his breath, and Henry felt sorrier for him than he did for himself.

"I understand," Henry said. "Thank you, sir."

Mr. Thorne lifted his cigar from the crystal ashtray whose edges gleamed like liquid in the soft library light. "You're welcome," he said, extending his other hand. "Stay out of trouble. And good luck."

Ethan followed him upstairs. "Henry, you have to reconsider."

"Reconsider?" Henry scanned the room to see what he should pack. Not much. A few items of clothing. Photographs of his parents and sister. His bass, which was still out in the carriage house. "There's not a chance of that. Could I trouble you for a ride, though?"

"A ride? Where will you go?" Ethan closed the door behind him. "Henry, this is insanity. If you take that job working the press, it's a dead end. You'll never get out. You'll never be able to afford a home, you'll —"

"It's not the only thing I'll be doing," he said. He opened a drawer and removed a small stack of folded undershirts, which he placed on the bed. "There's the Domino. Flora's asked me to join the band, and I said yes."

"But that's — beg for a second chance," Ethan said. His voice sounded strained, not like his own. "Promise you'll stay away from Flora and the Domino. Give up the music altogether. There's no security in that. You know it, I know it. It's time to face that."

Henry opened another drawer and pulled out his pants. The school uniform ones, he could leave behind. A good thing. They were itchy. He turned to look at his friend. "Ethan, I don't believe a word that's coming out of your mouth. Weren't you the one telling me to seize the day? Live the life I dreamed of living?"

"I know, I know," Ethan said quietly. He took the undershirts off the bed and moved to put them back in the drawer, but Henry blocked him. "And I still believe it, I suppose, in the abstract. But this . . . finding a rented room in a boarding house somewhere, and working inside a noisy pressroom until your hands are permanently stained black and you're crippled and deaf? I've seen those pressmen. I know what happens. And how can you possibly do that and then play music at night? Can't you please just see if there's a way for you to finish school? Graduate? You're days away from it, and I — I'll —"

"A diploma isn't going to get me where I want to be," Henry said. "And this job, it's a place to start." He held out his hands for the undershirts. Ethan relinquished them, and Henry set them on top of his bureau and pulled his father's old suitcase from beneath his bed. It still bore stickers of his travels. Italy, France, England, Brazil — all places that seemed forever out of reach.

He walked to his closet for his one suit. "Don't count me out just yet," he said. "Though I don't have any money for a room. I spent all but twelve cents on bail. What if I look up James in Hooverville? Do you suppose he'd help?" Ethan's face reddened as he nodded.

"Don't worry," Henry said. "Just until the first paycheck comes in. How's that story coming, by the way? Do you need my help with the writing yet? And what did James think of the music? We never had a chance to talk about it."

"No — it's fine, I — here, let me at least make myself useful." He wrapped the photographs of Henry's family in a wool sweater and laid them across the top of all the other items in the case. Then he walked to the closet for the borrowed tuxedo Henry had been wearing to the Domino. "You're going to need this," he said. "And I'll give you a ride if you'd like. Of course."

"I'm not taking that," Henry said, looking at the tuxedo. "It's your father's."

As he folded his life into a suitcase, he felt as he sometimes did in dreams, wanting to run but feeling as though his legs had turned to cement. But maybe that was what it meant to grow up and have the seemingly infinite possibility of childhood vanish in an instant.

You had to press on, no matter how dark and narrow the path ahead seemed.

Ethan slipped the tuxedo and white shirt off the hanger. "Look, I want you to stay. To ask my parents for one more chance. You just can't leave now. You can't." He put the clothing down and sat on Henry's desk, resting his forehead on his palm. "I don't know what I'm going to do without you, Henry."

"We'll still see each other," Henry said. "Your parents haven't forbidden that. And once you're running the newspaper, you can give me a promotion."

Ethan laughed, but it wasn't a happy sound. "Here this is your misfortune, and I'm making it seem as though it's mine. I'm sorry. You and I both know I'm doomed when it comes to the paper. It's just a matter of time before my father learns the truth. I knew it was coming eventually."

"I can still help," Henry said. "Let's write that Hooverville story together."

"I can't." Ethan paused to catch his breath. "If I can't read and write competently on my own, I have no business running the paper. It's strange, but I used to think that was the worst thing in the world. Now I know it isn't, and I'm almost eager for the inevitable. I might be asking you for a spot on the floor of your new place once you've got one."

Henry snapped the suitcase shut and moved it off the bed. "What if we did leave together? As soon as I have the money to pay my share?"

Ethan looked up at him. "My father would never permit it."

Henry immediately felt guilty. "I'm sorry. I know. And I'd never want for you to leave all this. You're lucky, you know."

"It doesn't feel that way most of the time."

Henry lifted his suitcase. Everything he had, minus his bass, he could carry in one hand. "You'll come visit me. I won't be far. And

I can help you with anything you need. Your father — he never needs to know."

"Henry," Ethan said, his voice growing strained. "I admire your courage. You should have your music. But you must look the part, if you're to play." He opened Henry's suitcase and slipped the tuxedo inside. Then he picked up the case. "You get your bass. Hang my father and whatever he has to say about it."

Annabel burst in. She crashed into Henry, her face pink and wet from crying. "Henry! You can't leave! I won't let you!"

He squatted so they were eye to eye with each other.

"I won't be going far," he said. "We'll ride bicycles together in the park."

"Promise?" she said.

"I promise. And I'll send you loads of letters. Now where's your handkerchief? Let's get you cleaned up." She took Flora's hankie out of her pinafore and Henry pressed it against her cheeks, his fingers touching the letters of the name sewn into the fabric. He wondered what Flora was doing, whether she was thinking of him. He'd had no time to contact her since that awful moment at the jail, and he didn't know when he'd next be near a telephone or able to walk to her house.

He folded Annabel into his arms. She smelled like grass and peanut butter, and the thought of not hearing her noise every morning and answering her annoying questions and watching her grow up in slow motion . . . He exhaled quickly, released her, and stood.

Ethan was waiting outside the door with his suitcase.

"Ready?" he said.

"As I'll ever be."

Helen waited at the bottom of the stairs. She wore a white skirt and sweater set, and a rope of pearls, which she held between her teeth. She spit them out to ask him a question. "Where are you two going with that suitcase?"

"None of your business," Ethan said. "I'm sure you already know, anyway."

Henry felt embarrassed by his situation. Not that he'd ever seriously considered Helen. But this would mean he'd never be with a girl like her, one with pearls and a soft sweater and shining hair. In the most superficial way, she reminded him of his mother, although without the warmth that suffused his memories. He couldn't tell what he felt about her, or anything else. The numbness went all the way through. Knowing she'd find out at some point, he opted for the truth. A quick drop of the guillotine, forever severing his life from hers.

"I'm moving to Hooverville," he said.

The look on her face was puzzling. Dismay and then anger.

"Excuse me," she said. Her breath and the air around her smelled of smoke. She started up the stairs, pausing halfway. "I'll be seeing you again. Soon. That's a promise."

He doubted that. He doubted it very much. He lifted his suitcase. On their way to his car, Ethan tried to talk Henry out of staying in Hooverville. "I have some money saved up. That place isn't fit for any man."

"James lives there," Henry said, putting his suitcase in the trunk.

"James — he's different." Ethan grabbed Henry's arm, as if he could physically keep him from leaving. "Things don't seem to bother him as much."

He slipped out of Ethan's grip and walked to the carriage house to get his bass, hoping it wouldn't be stolen or turned into kindling the second he turned his back on it in the shantytown. "It won't be long before I have enough saved up for a room somewhere. Hooverville isn't my destiny."

The drive to the encampment was short and silent. Hooverville looked much smaller than the first time Henry had seen it.

"At least take some money for food," Ethan said.

Henry tucked the money into his billfold. "I'll pay you back." He hated owing Ethan any more than he already owed.

"Not on your life." Ethan looked around in dismay. "Why aren't you at least asking for another chance?"

Henry didn't answer. He didn't want to say the truth, that it was almost a relief that what he'd feared most had finally come to pass. As long as there was still Flora, as long as there was the Domino, then nothing else could hurt him.

Chapter 43
Tuesday, June 8, 1937

HENRY ADJUSTED TO THE RATTLE AND HEAT OF THE PRESSROOM in less than a day. The chaos kept him from most of his own thoughts as he loaded rolls of newsprint into the oily flatbed press. The spinning, the noise, the flying of paper: All of it helped distract him from everything else. So much loss. For Flora, her grandmother. For himself, his home. It felt as though some unseen blade were slicing off the edges of their world, leaving them with little ground to stand on.

He'd set up temporarily at Hooverville, where at least James had been helpful. Almost too helpful, really. He'd clung to Henry like a shadow, even giving him a small shack that smelled of sawdust and tar. In those moments when Henry did stop and listen and breathe, he felt a certain shiver in the air, as though everything solid were about to crumble.

"Heads up, Bishop!"

Henry jumped out of the way of his supervisor, Carl Watters, who was pulling a barrel of ink on a dolly past the chugging press. "No wonder you got those black eyes. You're a klutz."

Henry, embarrassed, pushed a sweaty chunk of hair off his forehead and returned to the machine he was supposed to be oiling.

He put the rag back in his pocket and tightened a pair of bolts that had come loose.

Shouts came from behind. Henry turned. A sparrow had flown into the pressroom from one of the waxy windows that had been left open to siphon some heat out of the room. The bird wasn't enough to stop the presses, but if it got pulled into the webbing, there'd be blood and feathers on the afternoon edition, the sort of thing that would get taken out of the crew's paychecks.

He found the hook-ended wooden pole they used to open and close the windows and did his best to shoo the creature out, but it flitted away and dropped out of sight where the day's editions were being folded and bound. Henry followed, ducking behind a column. The way things had been going, the stupid creature would crap on top of the afternoon extra.

There. Sitting on the ledge above the day's paper. And then, just as if Henry had asked politely, the bird flew up and out a nearby open window. Feeling lucky for the first time in ages, Henry leaned the pole against the column and wiped his forehead with a dirty handkerchief. A headline caught his eye.

NEGRO NIGHTCLUB BURNS.

He recognized the Domino straightaway from the picture, which had been shot during daylight hours. It was a total loss. He scanned the text, the paper shaking in his hands. No mention had been made of Flora. He stood in a stupor until Mr. Watters bellowed more insults in his ear. Henry dropped the paper and looked at the clock. Ninety-seven minutes until the end of his shift. Well, hang that. They could fire him if they wanted. He pulled off his canvas apron and dropped it on the floor.

"I'm going to report you for this," Mr. Watters yelled after him. "I don't care who recommended you."

Outside, he turned toward Flora's neighborhood and had taken three steps when he heard a voice call his name. It was Helen. From across the street, she leaned her head out of Mr. Thorne's car, smiling as though nothing had changed. "Need a ride?"

Henry looked at his rumpled pants and his ink-stained hands. He was aware of his bruised face and the dried sweat on his back and in his armpits, and he would have known he reeked even if his nose had been snipped off. He crossed the street to avoid having to shout, but stood away from her automobile so that she couldn't get too close a look — or smell.

"This is a surprise." He didn't want to give her the idea he was happy about it.

"I was in the neighborhood," she said, tucking her hair behind her ear. "Ouch. Stupid hatpin." She pulled her glove off and held her finger out to Henry. A bead of blood had welled up. "Come closer so you can kiss it and make it better."

"Er," Henry stammered.

"Don't care for the sight of blood?" She stuck her finger in her mouth and sucked it clean. Then she slipped her hand back inside her glove and set her fingers on the steering wheel. "Where to?"

Henry hesitated. He hadn't any money for a cable car, and he was almost too tired to walk. But he didn't want Flora to see him anywhere near Helen — or for Helen to know where he was going. It was none of her business.

"How about something to eat? I'm awfully hungry."

Henry grimaced. Even if he'd wanted to, he wouldn't have enough money to take her anyplace. He could barely feed himself.

"My treat," she said, patting her pocketbook. "I have more money than I know what to do with."

A hot meal. There was almost nothing in the world that he wanted more. Almost. "That's all right. Thank you anyway."

"Just get in the car, Henry," Helen said. She looked angry, almost dangerous. "We haven't all day to waste."

From behind him, another familiar voice called out, "Henry!"

Henry turned. James Booth stood a few feet away, holding a sign that read A HAND UP, NOT A HANDOUT.

"This is quite the reunion," James said.

"What a coincidence," Helen said. "My goodness."

"Yes," James said. "The world and its mysterious ways and all." He looked every bit as hostile as Helen.

Henry wished he could disappear. "On second thought, I can walk. It's not far."

"Don't be ridiculous, Henry," Helen said. "Let me feed you. You look halfway dead already."

"As long as you're being generous," James said, "I'll take you up on that offer."

"I don't think that's wise," Helen said. "I'm just an innocent girl, after all."

"Then we'll miss you," James said, stepping between the car and Henry. Helen looked at James, as if she was calculating the best reply. Then, without another word, she reached over, slammed her door, and drove off.

"Where are we going?" James said, giving him a grin that suggested he hadn't been affected at all by the strange interlude.

Henry wasn't in the mood for company, and he didn't like the way James and Helen made him feel, as if he was some sort of plaything for the two of them to fight over. "I'm afraid I've got personal business to attend to."

"Personal business," James said. "Sounds intriguing."

"I'm sorry, James. You've been such a help lately, but I really can't stay. And this isn't the sort of business that requires company."

He was surprised at the look on James's face. Rather than looking disappointed, he looked relieved. Maybe even happy.

"I wish you luck with it," he said. "Truly."

And Henry found that he believed him, even as he wished James would leave him be.

Chapter 44

FLORA HAD TO STOP THINKING OF HENRY. THEY BOTH NEEDED TO rebuild their lives with as few scars as possible in the aftermath of the recent disasters. She'd kept busy planning Nana's memorial service, which would happen the next afternoon. And she'd received a note from Doc Henderson, inviting her to meet with him about picking up a performance or two at the Majestic. She was glad to have something to focus on besides the misery of losing her grandmother and her club and the uselessness of wondering where Henry was, what he was doing, how he was feeling.

"I love you," she said, just to see how the words she'd never give him felt in her mouth.

As she picked up a broom and started sweeping the kitchen, there was a knock on the door. Annoyed, she opened it, expecting some well-meaning person to be bringing her a casserole. She already had many more than she'd ever be able to eat. But it wasn't anyone bearing food. It was Henry.

Despite her desire to see him, she panicked at his actual presence. "What are you doing here? You shouldn't have come."

He stepped back. The sun was setting and silhouetted his face, but she could see how hurt he was, even through the shadow.

"That's not how I meant it to sound." She touched his forearm.

He swallowed. "I heard about the club. I — I wanted to say I was sorry."

"Well." She exhaled and looked past his shoulder, welcoming the sting of the sun on her eyes. Henry moved closer, and she could see the exhaustion on his face, and she was torn between inviting him inside for a glass of water and sending him home so she wouldn't say anything that would cause more hurt or trouble. She heard her grandmother's voice in her head. *Manners, Flora! Invite the boy inside!*

"Are you thirsty?" she asked.

"Like a camel," Henry said.

She led him to a chair by the window. Then she went to the kitchen, wishing she had something better than water to serve. She filled a glass.

"Are you hungry?" Food, she had.

"Like a camel that hasn't eaten anything in days."

"Ham or casserole?"

"No self-respecting camel eats casserole. It could contain a relative."

Laughing, Flora made a ham and cheese sandwich and set it on a tray next to the glass of water. These, she put on a side table next to his chair. He reached for the glass with ink-stained fingertips.

"You look like you lost a fight with a fountain pen."

"The pen is mightier than the sword." Henry picked up his sandwich. "It's a wonder I survived." He took a bite, chewed, swallowed. "Truly, though, it's a long story."

"I have time," she said, sinking into a nearby ottoman. She looked up at him, feeling finally at ease. "Tell me."

He did between bites, although she suspected he made Hooverville sound like a nicer place to live than it was.

"I'm sorry," she said. "This is my fault."

Henry moved off the chair and sat on the floor next to her, taking her hand in his. "Shh," he said. He touched her cheek with an inky finger. Her heart drumrolled in her chest.

"Henry, we shouldn't do this. There's no future with you and me in it."

"Shouldn't isn't the same as can't," he said. "Besides, there's no future for me without you in it."

"You're white," she said. "In case you hadn't noticed."

"I can't help that. I'd change it if I could, but I can't. This is it."

"You come from money," she said.

"Not anymore. Not for a long time. I never belonged with the Thornes. But I belong with you."

"It's my fault you went to jail."

"It wasn't, and I've forgotten that already." He kissed the back of her hand and she leaned into him, resting her head on his shoulder. "I love you. We are meant to be a pair. It's that simple."

The words and the weight behind them weren't simple. She knew he meant them. But their lives were not their own, not when it came to this. There were too many other people, with too many other thoughts on the matter. There was also the truth of love, that its end was nothing but pain.

"The world is against this sort of thing. Surely you can feel it," she said.

"If it's us versus the world, my money's on us."

She moved away from Henry, to lighten the mood. "Easy for you to say. Last I heard, you had twelve cents. You're ridiculous. You know that, right?"

"When it comes to being ridiculous, I am very ambitious."

Amused, she let herself rest her cheek against his chest, listening to his heart, inhaling his scent before she sat up with a start. "Henry?"

"Yes?" He held her hands and looked into her eyes, so sweetly serious.

"You smell terrible." It was the best kind of terrible, but he'd feel better if he was clean. "The bathroom's down the hall. Wash up. I've got some clothes that ought to fit you."

He laughed. "And then what?"

"Then I'm calling Sherman," she said. "And we're maybe stopping by the Majestic if we can get things together quickly enough."

"The Majestic? But I don't have any money, and all my other clothes are at my tar-paper castle. It's almost two weeks before I get my first paycheck —"

"Shh. Doc's going to pay us," Flora said, touching his lips. "So are a bunch of the other clubs in town. They will. I know it. So clean yourself up. We have work to do. And I have to keep moving, or I'll start thinking about everything else and fall apart."

"I'm sorry for what's going to happen," Henry said.

"What?" she said, her shoulders stiffening. "What's going to happen this time?"

He didn't answer.

Not with words. Instead, he wrapped his arms around her and kissed her as if it would have killed him to do anything else. And she was glad, because if he hadn't, she might have died. His mouth was soft on hers. Soft, and warm, and those lips she'd studied so intently tasted salty and sweet, and they moved against hers as if they'd been made for no other purpose. They would never be the couple he wanted them to be; but at least they would always have this moment, this secret sliver of joy that could live on in memory, if no place else.

———

By the time Henry was clean and dressed, the rest of the band had arrived. Voices, laughter, warm-up notes from trumpets . . . a world of sound he thought he'd always stand at the periphery of, never getting to dive in. He listened from the short, narrow hallway, keeping himself in the shadows.

"We talked to Doc already," a man said. "We've just been waiting for you to come around."

Flora replied: "You know I'm only singing until I have enough money for my flight."

"You keep saying that," the voice said. "But you don't ever got to be just one thing. Life isn't divided up like that, where you're one thing at the cost of another. And it's not just the Majestic. Plenty of places for us to play as featured guests."

"And he's all right if Henry —"

"He wants to hear him, obviously," the voice said, "but we vouched. Henry's in."

Henry, feeling bad about eavesdropping, cleared his throat and loudly entered the room. He felt painfully aware of his wet hair and white skin and the fact he was wearing clothing that must have belonged to Flora's father.

"Look what the cat dragged in — our bass player." It had been Palmer, the pianist, talking.

"Really?" Henry replied, not having to pretend to sound excited and disbelieving.

Palmer pointed at Henry. "That one's dimmer than a new moon. We been trying to get her to sign you up since that day at her house. And now she tells us you wrote a hit song. Let's hear it."

The slow smile that worked its way across Flora's face was about the best thing he'd seen. He looked around the room. The band filled chairs, windowsills, the davenport. The ones who'd been having private conversations stopped. They were waiting. For him.

"But I don't have my bass," he said.

"Flora," Sherman said. "You still have your daddy's, right?"

"Still do," she said. "The strings are going to be ancient, though — I don't know."

"Better than nothing," Palmer said. "Need a hand in fetching it?"

"I've got it," she said.

"I'll help," Henry said.

"Just don't help yourself to *too* much," one of the trumpet players said. Henry made a mental note to throttle the guy later. He followed Flora into a bedroom that clearly had been her grandmother's. In the corner, looking like an old soldier, stood a bass with dusty shoulders.

"Here," he said, reaching for it. "Let me."

"Wait," Flora said. She took one hand, then the other, so they stood facing each other. "This is it. Are you ready?"

"Someday," he said, making it sound like a promise.

"You mean the song, right?" Her forehead wrinkled, as if something worried her. "Because now would be a good time to be ready to play."

"That's not what I meant," he said.

"I know." She dropped his hands and her tone changed. "Nervous?"

"Petrified," Henry said. God, he wanted to kiss her again.

Flora laughed. "They'll love it. I —" She stopped and smoothed her hair, and Henry wished they had more time. It felt as though he'd never have enough. "Shall we?"

Henry nodded. He followed her into the parlor and set up the bass. Then he walked the band through the chords and the chorus and the verse. He played it, hoping they'd feel what he put into the song.

There was a long moment of silence after they finished.

"That song's gonna change your life, son," Sherman said.

"Darn tootin'," Palmer added.

It didn't feel like that to Henry, though. It wasn't so much about changing his life as much as it was about him stepping into the one he was meant to live. And, after all of this, he'd arrived.

Chapter 45
Friday, June 25, 1937

MORE THAN TWO WEEKS PASSED. DURING THIS TIME, HENRY, Flora, and the rest of the band rehearsed and set up shows in clubs around town at night, while Henry worked at the paper during the day. Love and Ethan continued their assignations, which had become as much about philosophical discussions as physical interactions. Death, meanwhile, had been quietly observing. Her relative silence terrified Love.

When the night came for Flora and Henry's debut at the Majestic, Ethan breathlessly invited James to join him, and Love, eager to hear what the players would create, agreed. He wished he truly were human so he could embrace the evening as a man in love should, wearing a cloud-white shirt of crisp cotton, a fine tuxedo of black wool, and a carefully knotted tie of cerulean silk.

He wanted to scrub the dirt of life from his fingernails. He wanted to steam his face, soap his chin, shave with a new blade — or better, have the practiced hands of a barber perform the duties. He thought of frosted bottles of champagne. Tender rib-eye steaks dripping juice onto bone china. Rich wine. A stunning, audacious dessert: perhaps a cream-filled swan made of dark chocolate, its feathers edged in edible gold.

He'd had these pleasures before. And in previous Games, where he had developed no direct attachments to the players or their friends, he'd indulged himself when the urge struck. But this wouldn't be the way of James Booth, and so Love would have to forgo such things in favor of humbler clothing, humbler fare.

There was beauty enough in the Majestic, where the musicians had gathered. Candlelight from the table illuminated Ethan's carved cheekbones, his blue irises, his straight white teeth. Game or no, Love might not have been able to resist this one at any point in history. Ethan was like no other: smart, creative, passionate, handsome. The world was his to inherit.

As the show began, the curtains that covered the stage billowed and split, and the smallish audience that had gathered for the opening act began to applaud politely, though most continued with their conversations as if the music wouldn't matter. There was a pop of brightness as the lights came on, then the *rat-puh-puh-tat* of the drum. The Majestic wasn't set up the same way as the Domino, and it didn't have that club's history as an underground speakeasy to lend it an air of danger and intrigue. It was closer to a regular restaurant, so the stage was simpler. But it was lovely, all the same.

The band launched into the Gershwin hit "Summertime" — an appropriate choice, as the days had peaked in length and were growing warmer every night. Flora made a straightforward entrance from the left side of the stage, and the look she gave Henry as she walked past him and toward the microphone, her arms swinging languidly, could have lit a city block.

The humans, who did not know what they had before them, scraped their forks against their plates and chattered to each other over the sound of the band, until Flora opened her mouth. When the first note emerged, a few people put down their drinks and watched. Conversations ended. The girl was no longer holding back.

The tune had a meaty bass part for Henry, a sort of slow, sad, wistful walk up the strings that reminded Love of his favorite part of summer, when the heat of the day broke and the light turned a soft purple, and the world was womb-warm and just as safe. Henry gave everything to the song, his hands a blur on the strings, creating a counterpoint to Flora's melody and a rhythm for her to follow. As Love listened, certain details mesmerized: the way the spotlight burnished the edges of the musicians; the scent of the melting wax from the candles; the occasional, purposeful break in Flora's voice, turning it from satin to velvet.

The first set ended. Ethan leaned to whisper in Love's ear: "This is aces, isn't it?"

Love nodded in agreement, just as the young man's face took on a stricken look. Death, in her guise as Helen, approached the table in a red dress: hard, modern, impossible to ignore. It was the color she wore when she was in the mood to kill. Love regretted letting himself get so swept away that he'd missed her presence until it was too late to prepare.

The hi-hat shimmered and a new song began. Death crossed her arms and made a face that looked as if she were smuggling a lemon wedge in her mouth. She pulled off her glove and reached for Ethan bare-handed. Love gasped. She stopped short of touching him, as if reminding Love that she held Ethan's life in her hands too.

She pulled out a chair between the two of them and sat. "What's in your pocket?" She tapped the spot where he kept his book of notes and observations about the players and their progress in the Game. "Is it a book? Some sort of journal where you write down your James Boothian exploits? What I wouldn't give for a look inside of it."

Love glanced at Ethan to see if the boy had noticed. He had. His face colored as he turned toward the stage and pretended to be transfixed by the music.

What was her aim? The book was merely a record of the Game, a record of things that had happened and could not be changed. He turned his focus to the music, and he turned his affection for Ethan outward, so that every heart in the audience would swell with the joy of it. The effort was exhausting, but he had reached the point in the Game where he could save nothing.

Chapter 46

HENRY AND FLORA MADE EXCUSES TO LINGER AFTER THE SHOW. A sudden summer rainstorm had descended, and they hid from it under the red awning in front of the Majestic.

"I'm starved," Flora said, wrapping her arms around herself.

Henry draped his jacket around her shoulders. "Our stomachs have so much in common. Where would you like to go?"

"Go?"

"There's the Sterling Cup, there's Guthrie's —"

"Henry," she said. "Neither of those places will let us in."

"No, they're open," he said. "Ethan and I eat there all the . . ." His voice trailed off as he understood her meaning. These were white restaurants that would serve colored people through the back windows during the day, at best.

"You might go there," she said. "*We* don't."

"I'm sorry," he said. "I never thought about it. It was more that you have your places and we have ours."

Flora shrugged out of the jacket and returned it to him. "Yes, like the lovely Coon Clucker Inn."

"What, that place?" he said, refusing the coat. "No one goes there. It's —" He stopped himself. It was a place for low-class whites. Ethan's family considered themselves above rubbing elbows with that sort. He thought about the restaurant's sign: a huge cartoon character with black skin, red, rubbery lips, and a winking eye. It was grotesque, and he'd never given it a second thought. He'd never had to. He was so used to being able to go where he wanted, and so unused to thinking of Flora as anyone other than the girl he loved, that the idea of their not being welcome at a restaurant — or anywhere — hadn't entered his mind.

"If no one goes there," she said, "why does every third automobile in the city have a Coon Clucker tire cover?"

Henry had no answer. He stood holding his jacket open for her, not knowing what else to do. "Flora, I'm truly sorry. Please. Wear it. Your dress will get soaked, and you'll catch your death of cold. I'll go anywhere with you."

"Exactly." She accepted the coat. "That's part of the problem. You'll go anywhere. The world is yours."

"I didn't mean it that way. I meant I'd go anywhere you'd like."

Rain hissed on the pavement, and every so often, cars honked and doors slammed. It was otherwise quiet.

"There's one place," she said after a moment. "It's called the Yellow House. On Yesler. Open twenty-four hours and they do a pretty mean omelet."

Henry smiled. "I don't suppose there's any way of doing this without getting soaked."

"You should have worn a jacket," Flora said. "Dummy." She lifted Henry's coat overhead to keep the rain away.

"What can I say," he replied. "School dropout and all."

"On the count of three," she said. "Let's make a run for it."

"I'm not in any hurry," he said. "Let's get soaked."

"You *are* a dummy," she said. "Here's to turning ourselves into human dishrags."

"To dishes."

The restaurant's windows glowed gold on the sidewalk ahead, lighting their way. A bell dinged as they opened the door. Conversations ceased when the diners caught a glimpse of Henry. He pushed his hair off his forehead with his free hand. With his other, he held tight to Flora. They were both drenched.

"You all right, hon?" the waitress asked Flora, who'd tried to slip out of Henry's arm. One of the diners lurched as if he was going to stand. Henry's pulse raced. He didn't want trouble, just a spot out of the rain and darkness and something to eat. And someplace to spend time with the person he loved.

"I'm fine, Miss Hattie," Flora said. "Just a little wet." The man sat, but did not resume eating. Henry looked away.

Hattie inspected them both. "Hmmph." She shrugged, smoothed her white apron, and took them to a booth by the restroom door. She laid two menus on the table. "Coffee or juice?"

"Coffee, please," Flora said. "Cream and sugar."

"I'll also have a coffee, if that's all right," Henry said.

"How dark do you like yours?" Miss Hattie asked. The men at a nearby table snickered.

Henry studied Miss Hattie's expression, which reminded him of his long-departed grandmother. She'd always sounded crabby, but she also invariably sneaked him peppermint candies. He had plenty of room in his heart for cranky old ladies. "I like mine the way she likes hers."

"Hmmph," Miss Hattie said. "Cream and three sugars. Be back in a minute with your coffee. You best be ready to order then too."

Henry looked at Flora over the top of her menu. "What's good here? I mean, besides the mean omelet and the cranky coffee?"

Flora laughed. "Everything except the oatmeal." She laid her menu down. "That's like eating marbles."

He folded his paper napkin into a boat and pretended to sail it through rough seas toward her, trying to recapture that easy connection they had when they played music together.

"What are you doing?" she asked.

He put the napkin down. "I don't know. Making an ark?"

Miss Hattie returned with their coffee. "What's it gonna be?"

"Two eggs," Flora said. "Side by side. And two pieces of toast."

Henry scanned the menu, looking for something that could build on Flora's ark joke, but he couldn't find anything. "Eggs, scrambled, with sausage and a biscuit."

"Fine," Miss Hattie said. "Anything else?"

"No, thank you, ma'am," Flora said.

Miss Hattie sighed and headed for the kitchen.

"I think you meant Noah thanks," Henry joked.

Flora rolled her eyes over the top of her coffee mug.

"See, we're finding a place," he said.

"One of us might be," she said. "I'll never belong in your world."

"Flora." Henry's voice caught in his throat. "You are my world." He wrapped his hands around his cup of coffee, wishing its warmth would reach the rest of him.

Miss Hattie returned with their food.

As she ate, Flora looked at him with pitying eyes. "I like you. Against my better judgment, I do. The way you play music. Your decency. Even your stupid jokes. But I want other things. If I do what Amelia Earhart is doing, but faster —"

Henry interrupted. "I get it." His eggs tasted like paste. He pushed the plate away. If she didn't want him, what else could he do?

Flora lowered her voice. "For now, can't we just focus on the music? Everything else can wait."

They sat in silence as the rest of the customers cleared out. Hattie, looking exhausted, leaned against a wall and closed her eyes. Eventually, the first rays of morning sun began to bend through the foggy windows. Henry's clothes had dried, and he felt a rumpled and weary mess.

"I don't understand," he said, trying to choose his words carefully, knowing his exhaustion made him likely to say the wrong thing. "I don't see how we could go from everything good that's happened to this."

"It's safer this way," Flora said. "Trust me."

Henry reached across the table, but Flora wouldn't take his hand.

"What do you dream of?" Henry said. "What do you dream of if it isn't this? You, me, music. We could build a life out of that. I know it."

"Look at your fingers," she said. "Covered in ink."

"Please don't change the subject," Henry said. "But it's not just ink." He turned his left palm up and showed her the fingertips he'd played to shreds. "See? Blood."

"Ink by day, blood by night. Days of ink, nights of blood," she said. "Sounds like a song."

"You should write it," he said.

"Don't be ridiculous."

"I'm not the one being ridiculous," he said.

"Henry."

"Look how far we've come. I don't want to give up. Not now. Because someday —"

She yawned and rubbed her temples, as though her head ached. "We can think about that sort of thing another day. But not now."

Miss Hattie shuffled to their table. "Heat up your coffee?"

Henry glanced at his empty cup. "No, thank you."

"Then you'll be wanting to settle the check," Miss Hattie said.

Henry took the hint. He pulled out one of the bills Doc had paid him the previous night and laid it on the table.

"Keep the change." It was twice the money he needed to leave. But he wasn't above buying an ally.

"Flora?" He held out his arm.

She hesitated. "We should walk away from it now, before it gets worse. It's what Captain Girard says about flying. 'Only a fool goes into a storm.'"

"The rain has stopped," he said.

"You know what I mean. This won't end well."

"Who says it has to end at all?" he said.

She took his arm at last, and together, they walked out into the fragile morning light.

Chapter 47
Saturday, June 26, 1937

DEATH WISHED SHE NEEDED TO SLEEP. HOW FORTUNATE HUMANS were, to spend a third of their lives unaware. She never had a moment to forget who she was. Never a moment to pretend she was anything but a scourge. It felt better to glean souls as she did it. But then afterward, the pain, the hunger for more, was worse.

Death wrapped herself in a silk robe. She inserted her pale, soft feet into slippers. Surely Ethan was asleep. Surely she could be quiet enough. . . .

She blinked and rematerialized in his room, not wanting to chance that someone else in the house was awake. His breathing was slow and warm and even. Through a gap in his curtains, light from the nearly full moon seeped in. She inched toward him. He lay on his back, one arm flung over his head while the other clutched his sheets, his skin indigo in moonlight. She knew exactly how his life would taste. She leaned in and inhaled his skin. His heat warmed her lips. She willed him to remain still. And then she whispered soft things into his ear, words to shape his dreams.

When morning came, he would rise full of urgent desire. Not for Love, but for what Love kept tucked in a pocket over his heart. The book. The book and its secrets. In its pages, Ethan would learn he was a pawn, and that Henry was in even more danger. However he dealt with that information, she'd have the advantage. And all of it was in accordance with the rules.

In another blink, Death was back in Helen's room. Numb. Alone. Waiting for the light of day to wash over her.

Chapter 48
Sunday, June 27, 1937

ETHAN GASPED HIMSELF AWAKE, SWEATY AND SHAKING. IT WAS too early even for birds. He heard nothing but his own rushing blood. His dream had felt like a murky pond with something vital beneath its surface. The edges of the memory felt just beyond his fingertips. Something about a book. A book, open in James's hand. A book in which James was writing.

Ethan sat up.

What did James write in his little book?

He swung his legs over the edge of the bed. His pulse was everywhere: in his ears, in his hands, boiling beneath his skin. If the book contained stories about what they'd done, if it listed his name . . . Ethan threw open the window. Somewhere in the distance, a bird opened its beak and sang a few lonely notes.

The book contained Ethan's ruin. He knew it as surely as he knew the feeling of a line drive hitting his glove. It made him wish not for death but for something beyond, to have his existence erased so thoroughly that it would not even echo in memory.

Someone knocked. He stood still. Please let whomever it was think him asleep.

"Knock knock." Helen opened the door.

She was dressed for the day already in a red frock with black polka dots, and she carried a tray of breakfast offerings. Coffee. Buttered toast. A wedge of flesh-colored melon. Juice from a fresh-squeezed blood orange.

"What's all this?" Ethan sneered at her to hide his worry.

"I had an inkling you'd be up," she said. "Can't a girl bring her favorite cousin breakfast?"

Ethan sat on the deep windowsill. "Henry isn't here anymore."

"You and your self-loathing. Besides, Henry and I aren't blood cousins," she said. "Careful there. You might fall out the window."

"Yes, and then who would you have to torment?" It was a rude remark, but he couldn't summon the grace to apologize. Instead, he slid off the sill and picked up the toast, smearing it with jam. "Thank you for breakfast."

"My pleasure. Let's spend time together soon, all right?" She smiled as she left the room, her dress swishing around her calves.

Ethan ate in silence. There was something he had to do. He just had to figure out when.

Chapter 49

Monday, June 28, 1937

Death sat at a rolltop desk in Helen's room. A sheet of creamy stationery lay on a red blotter, by a bottle of ink and a fine fountain pen. She closed her eyes, willing the tears to rise. One was almost certainly enough. But to ensure the job was thorough, she produced three. These, she transferred to the bottle with a trembling fingertip. The tremor — that was new. No doubt a sign of strain. This Game, unlike the rest, felt slippery, a fish pulled with a bare hand out of a swift and frigid river.

The tears hissed as they fell into the bottle. And there was an odor: sharp, tinged with decay. The blank page before her contained infinite possibilities. But not for long. The moment she set the pen to the flesh of the page, certainty would return. Certainty. It was her kingdom.

She dipped the pen. Her fingers shook again — damn them. A spot of ink made a fierce little shape on the page. She rocked the blotter against the wayward ink. She'd gotten ink in the space between her second and third fingers too. And on her dress, another drop. The lack of control it indicated thrilled her, as if in this body she'd finally become someone else, someone unpredictable.

She did not wad up the page, but put her pen to it again. The words flowed. *Scandalous. Reckless music. Dangerous mixing of the races. Not what God intended.* She would send this letter to the editor of the newspaper — Ethan's father, Henry's employer. It would reach the eyes and hearts of concerned citizens, moving them to close the Majestic, to end the spectacle of a white boy singing a love song to a dark-skinned girl. Flora and Henry would lose it all: their livelihood, their hope, their friends. Their love would die. Flora would run from him. Or, more likely, fly.

It was a shame, really. Most humans laid waste their hours to the superficial, to the transitory. Great oceans of passion poured over smoke, while the actual fire burned elsewhere. Henry was one of the rare men with a firm grasp on the important. She set down the pen and blew on the glistening ink. Ah, well.

She sealed the letter in an envelope and sensed a presence behind her. Annabel.

"What are you doing?" the girl asked.

"Writing a letter." She showed Annabel the envelope. "Would you like to learn how to send one?"

"Yes," Annabel said. She set down her doll. "Yes, I would."

Death taught her.

Chapter 50
Tuesday, June 29, 1937

With the money from his first paycheck, Henry had moved into a boarding house on Capitol Hill. The room was simple, in an old Victorian run by a tiny tyrant named Mrs. Kosinski. Henry shared a bathroom with eight other residents, but the room itself was his own and infinitely better than Hooverville. It came furnished with a bureau, a twin bed, and a narrow closet. His bass was the most beautiful thing about the place, kept by the west-facing window where the light would grace it during the late-afternoon gap between work at the printing press and performing.

His new life felt full and right. Flora's band had picked up other gigs here and there. But it was their opening act at the Majestic that shined. The crowd loved "Someday," as Flora's uncle had predicted. It had become a duet featuring the two of them.

Ever since Henry had moved into the boarding house, Ethan had been stopping by every afternoon for help with his article about Hooverville. Something was amiss; Henry could tell. Since graduation, Ethan had lost weight, and he looked exhausted. Henry had asked Ethan once or twice what was the matter, but Ethan waved him off. For certain, though, the Hooverville story was part of it.

"Father's going to blow a gasket at this, isn't he?" Ethan lay on the bed and looked at the ceiling.

"It's true, right? You've managed to take some notes documenting everything?"

"Yes, but I also know these facts inside and out." Ethan rubbed his eyes and yawned. "Would you read me that last part again?"

"Certainly." Henry cleared his throat.

" 'Hooverville is the abode of the forgotten man. By this journalist's count, six hundred thirty-nine live here, each one with a story worth hearing — far too many to include in these humble columns. They are the modern melting pot, counting among their ranks Filipinos, Scandinavians, Africans, Mexicans, Indians, South Americans, and Japanese, along with Caucasians who fell down on their luck during the Crash of '29.

" 'Some men had wives and children. Some owned homes. Some worked as laborers and craftsmen. Others helped tame the forests surrounding the city, providing the lumber for houses and businesses. Others still were maimed in the Great War and cannot work. They have come together in shabby camaraderie to form an ethnic rainbow, dreaming not of a pot of gold at the end, but a pot of soup and respectable employment.

" 'It is not so different, really, than what any man wants. Respectability, repast, and a roof over his head. Or so says James Booth, a charismatic and handsome twenty-year-old fellow who calls himself the mayor of Hooverville.

" ' "If people could see us for who we were," Mr. Booth said, "the better angels of their nature would respond." ' "

Ethan sat up. "That bit," he said, "was it too much?"

"The part about James being handsome and charismatic?" Henry said. "You could perhaps leave that out."

Ethan's expression shifted and Henry stopped himself. In that instant, he understood something. Something that made his stomach fall, though not with horror, as it might have before he and Flora had found each other. The feeling was sadness and compassion. It made Henry want to confide his own secret to Ethan, to let this person who was like a brother to him know that he understood. But he could not betray Flora in the process. Even if she had not consented to be with him, not yet, their bond felt sacred, secret.

The situation worried Henry. Ethan would soon be occupied with college. Henry, who had not graduated from high school, would not be able to help. These secrets, this distance . . . the natural thing might be to drift apart.

But he would fight that.

"Never mind," he said. "It's good. It's the truth. What does the Bible say about truth? *Veritas vos liberabit?*"

"The truth shall set you free," Ethan said, looking out the window. "The older I get, the more I hope it's true, but the less I believe it."

Chapter 51
Thursday, July 1, 1937

PROTESTORS STOOD IN FRONT OF THE MAJESTIC carrying pieces of painted cardboard.

YOU CAN'T SPELL SINGER WITHOUT SIN.

MISCEGUNATION: AGAINST GODS PLAN FOR MAN.

Flora hated walking past them on her way into the club, hated the way they'd block the sidewalk and make her step around them, hated their bad spelling and punctuation. The worst of them hissed and spit at her. As Flora arrived, a car carrying even more pulled up. The passengers, four large white men, reeked of trouble.

Inside, Doc's wife, Glo, was painting the window trim.

"Don't mind them," she said when she saw Flora's expression. "You'd think they'd find something better to do with their days." She stepped back to inspect her work. "In my opinion, anyone who claims to speak for God is probably talking out of the wrong end, anyway."

Flora laughed. "Amen."

Glo dipped her brush. "It's a good problem if it can be fixed with a bit of paint, and even better if I can get it done with a snifter of gin. I've been wanting to spruce this place up for years. Thanks to the business you're bringing in, I can."

Flora didn't have a chance to respond before shadows filled the window. She shoved Glo out of the way. There was a burst of breaking glass as something hard sailed through the window. A car squealed off.

They lay on the floor a moment, panting. When it felt safe, Flora looked up. A newspaper-wrapped brick lay inches away.

"Oh, Glo," she said.

Glo was on her knees. "My windows, my beautiful windows. And oh, Lord, no. The paint is all over the floor." A puddle of it spread across the linoleum, mixing with shards of glass.

Flora fetched rags and mopped up as much paint and glass as she could. "Turpentine might help. Do you have any?"

"Doc's got that in the back," Glo said. "I'll fetch it." She knocked back the rest of her gin.

Flora wiped up the bulk of the paint. She folded the rags over on each other until the mess had been contained inside, and she dropped the bundle in the trash. Then, fingertips sticky, she bent to pick up the brick. She untied the string and unwrapped the paper, a letter to the editor about the music they'd been performing. The writer called their show a crime against humanity, a sign of moral decay, and any number of things that twisted Flora's insides. The voice of the letter, which had been signed *A Concerned Citizen*, felt like a living creature in her mind, a sharp-toothed shrew, a gnawing rat.

She spread the newsprint on the ground and used it to wipe the rest of the paint off of her hands. It was somehow worse that Henry's own people had published it, that Henry's hands had been on the press that joined ink and page. Surely he'd seen it. Surely he would lose his job if he continued playing. And then how would he pay his rent — especially if the city shut down the Majestic next?

"What is it, baby?" Glo returned with Doc, who carried turpentine and more rags.

"Nothing," Flora said, wadding the paper.

"Don't seem like that."

"It's a letter to the editor. Stupid and vile. Nothing worth thinking about, Glo. Really."

As Glo swept the glass, Flora went outside with the brick, halfway wishing whoever had thrown it had stayed around. She wanted to toss it back. See how he liked it. She checked her watch. The set would start in a few hours. But it would have to be without Henry.

She'd send word, or better, let him know in person. It had been foolish to let down her guard and let him get that close. As if it hadn't been embarrassing enough in the diner, now Henry's people and everyone else in town was turning against them. Worse, Glo and Doc were suffering too. Flora knew better. She'd known better. She wouldn't let herself make that same mistake again.

Chapter 52

ETHAN PARKED NEAR THE STONE INQUIRER BUILDING. THE WORLD around him felt sharp, as if someone had cranked up the sun a notch. He noticed everything: cracks in the sidewalk, the missing toes on the pigeon hunting food scraps, the dot of mustard on the leg of the doorman's pants.

"Afternoon, Mr. Thorne." The doorman tipped his hat.

"Afternoon, Mr. Bowles," Ethan said, remembering the man's name just in time.

In his briefcase, he carried his article on Hooverville. Words that had found the page only because of Henry's help. Never again. It wasn't that he wanted the world to know he struggled to write. He no longer had the strength for the charade. With Henry out of the house, with college just a few months away, the strategy that had worked thus far felt like a road that ended in a cliff.

The air inside the building was a warm accumulation of breath and body heat. It smelled of sandwiches, stale coffee, and cigarette smoke, three scents he'd always associated with his destiny. Now, though, he wasn't so certain. He could not see beyond the present.

He rode the elevator accompanied only by the operator, aware of his damp palm on the handle of the briefcase. He licked his lips, wishing for a cold glass of water. The elevator dinged, the doors opened, and the sounds of the newsroom burst forth: jangling telephones, shouting men, the clatter of typewriter keys.

"What've you got for me?" The city editor, Roger Gunner, wasn't much for small talk.

"The piece on Hooverville."

Gunner adjusted his green visor and rubbed his palms together. "Finally. And you found proof they've been brewing liquor without paying taxes?"

"Nothing to that rumor. I found a different angle," he said, surprised at how smooth and calm his lie sounded. But then, he'd had years to practice.

"Oh?" Gunner leaned back in his chair, removed his visor, and wiped his forehead with the back of his hand. "Let's have a look."

Ethan snapped open his briefcase and removed the sheets of onionskin. He'd charmed a girl in the steno pool into typing up Henry's handwriting. It was amazing what you could get a person to do with a compliment and a smile. If his father had ever tried the technique, perhaps his mother wouldn't have turned into such a brittle thing.

Gunner snatched the pages, and Ethan considered leaving. Going for a malt. He never liked watching someone read his work, not just because he feared their opinion but also because it reminded him how easily other people could make sense of words. Watching someone's eyes move over a page was like poking a wound.

Gunner looked up before he made it to the second page. "This is what you want to run with?"

Ethan knew what he was really asking. *Are you sure you want to pick this fight with your father?*

"Yes." How little this all seemed to matter now.

"It's good," Gunner said. "Your old man will hate it, but it's good stuff, kid. Important."

Gunner's praise meant everything. "Thank you."

The editor had already returned his attention to the pages, scribbling notes in the margins with a red pencil. After a moment, he paused. "Scram, Thorne. Make yourself useful. You're blocking my light."

Ethan smiled as he walked toward the elevator, taking one last good look at the shabby wreck of the place, the men in their rolled-up shirtsleeves, dropping ashes from their cigarettes all over their desks. It was a messy wonder, the most exciting place in the world sometimes. A place where men shouted and pounded the table, and ferreted the truth out from where it liked to hide. A place where history was written on the fly, along with a fair share of heartbreak.

Ethan had never belonged there, or in the thickly carpeted executive offices upstairs, where his father and other brokers of power nudged the world where they wanted it to go. They'd always made Ethan feel like a chip of glass: small, transparent. He belonged nowhere, to no one. If it hadn't been for Henry's loyalty and discretion, Ethan would have been written off by his family long before. He knew it, but he was not ready for the reality of it. He had to get James's book before anybody else did. He had to find out what was inside, and, if necessary, to destroy it before his sham of a life was laid bare.

Now that Ethan no longer had a professional reason to be at Hooverville, he wanted his visit to be private. The men there wouldn't judge. They were as far from that sort as he'd ever met, and he and James weren't the only ones there to have come to an understanding. Even so, he felt watched all the time.

He stood on the edge of the encampment. A light breeze had its way with the dust, smudging the horizon, giving the angled columns of light that pierced the clouds an otherworldly definition. Something compelled him to turn his head, and there, leaning against the Hooverville chapel, his face half in shadow, was James, as still as a man in a photograph.

James pushed himself away from the wall and turned toward his shack. He looked back over his shoulder, as if to ensure Ethan was following. The glance was unnecessary. Ethan careered after him.

James kicked the door closed. Light and shadow merged into the half darkness. The men embraced, and Ethan felt the outline of the book. He helped James out of his jacket, making note of where it landed. And then both their shirts were off, and Ethan wished he could melt into the muscles of James's chest, to be pummeled by the beating heart beneath.

"Slow down," James whispered in his ear. "We have time."

Ethan couldn't. What time they had was nearly out. Or it would be, as soon as he could find the courage to break it off.

"You hungry?" James said, gently easing back.

The question struck him as funny, and soon, they were both laughing until their eyes watered.

"I handed in the story," Ethan said.

"And?"

"My editor liked it all right. My father's going to hate it."

"What do you think?" James turned up the wick on the lantern.

"What do I think?" Ethan never considered his own opinion. It was everyone else's that mattered.

"What we create must be something that we love. That's how we know it's true." James moved the lantern aside. The way they were together was everything Ethan wanted and needed, everything that terrified and grieved him. Afterward, James held him on his makeshift bed, whispering soothing words that made Ethan's eyelids grow heavy. He fought sleep in vain.

When Ethan woke, he was alone. He pulled his bare legs to his heart, trying to persuade himself that he was the same person he'd been before any of this happened, before he had faced the truth.

He stepped into his pants, pulled his shirt on, found his socks, his shoes. He smoothed his hair as well as he could. James's coat lay in the corner. Ethan closed his fingers around the book. He hesitated. Then he pulled it out, marveling at the intricate detail on the leather cover. He did not open it, as he had no hope he'd be able to read it. It was enough to prevent anyone else from seeing it. He wished he could discover what James had written, to know whether James had felt the same things, or if even in this, he was alone.

Ethan stole away from Hooverville. It occurred to him later that he might just have asked James what was in the book. But, as with everything else, that realization came too late.

Chapter 53

From the peak of the cross on the Hooverville chapel, Love watched Ethan leave. His sparrow guise felt cramped and limited after all the time he'd spent as James Booth, despite the ease of flight, despite the sharpness of his vision.

There are deeper ways to see than with eyes.

He'd forgotten the truth of this.

Love had felt the human's desire for the book when they were with each other. The agony of it made Love wish for death. Ethan's every nerve ending had been set alight with pleasure and recapped in pain. That he was able to breathe, to stand, to walk, to converse with others despite this . . . perhaps mortals weren't as fragile as he'd thought.

It was good that Ethan had not asked for the book. Now, whatever happened was not Love's responsibility. He would have read the stories to him, of course. Stories of love, held like handfuls of water, for the shortest and sweetest of moments. He might not have stopped when he came to the part about Henry and Flora. Of all the stories, theirs was his favorite. He could have shared this with Ethan. But if Ethan told the players, Love could not protect him. And Ethan would tell them. The knowledge could be useful to Henry and Flora, and Ethan was a loyal friend.

Regret seeped into Love's heart. It rose and swelled and became birdsong. Below, the men of Hooverville stopped their conversations, their cooking. They listened, and they stood, mesmerized, as the planet spun them from lightness to darkness. These men understood that melody. Afterward, the men returned to their activities, their misery softened only by the knowledge they were not alone in the world.

Chapter 54

Henry had been looking for Ethan's article. He knew every word, but he still hoped to see the story in print with Ethan's byline. Maybe they were holding it for the big Sunday edition. Ethan hadn't stopped by in a couple of days; Henry would ask the next time he did.

He noticed a letter on the editorial page as he sat at the table in the break room eating a thin sandwich of mustard and bread. Unable to swallow the bit of sandwich in his mouth, he forced himself to slow down as he read. The letter was about him. Him and Flora.

"Amen to that."

Henry looked up. His supervisor sat next to him, tucking into his lunch. Henry forced himself to swallow. "Excuse me, Mr. Watters?"

"Someone finally taking on those dirty colored jazz clubs. They're nothing but bad news. Wheels on the handbasket that's rolling straight to hell."

"Have you ever been inside one?" Henry moved his hands beneath the table so his boss wouldn't see his fists.

"Don't need to. Not in a handbasket, not in a colored club," the man said, taking the waxed paper off of a thick corned beef sandwich that smelled so good Henry's mouth watered.

"How do you know they're trouble, then?"

The man sank his teeth into the sandwich. Then he shifted the bite to the side of his mouth. "How can you *not* know? That sort of music is bad enough. But to have the different colors onstage at the same time? It's not what God intended. He meant for there to be separation, which is why the Negro races are in Africa. I'm telling you, this sort of thing will spell the end of society as we know it. They need to nip it in the bud." He ate more sandwich, glancing at Henry's lunch. "Ha! Looks like you forgot to put anything between the bread, son."

A year earlier, Henry might have considered this argument. Now that he knew Flora, he couldn't understand how something that felt so normal, so essential, could be wrong. But he couldn't live in both worlds. He pushed his plate away, brushing a few crumbs from his apron as he stood.

He stood and tossed his napkin on the counter. "Mr. Watters," he said, "I've found employment elsewhere. I quit."

Mr. Watters held up a finger. He took another bite of sandwich. He wiped a bit of mustard from the corner of his mouth. "I don't think so."

"Excuse me?"

"You can't quit," Mr. Watters said. "Direct orders from Bernie Thorne. Son of a gun was right about you trying." He laughed and finished his sandwich.

Henry tore off his apron, surprised at how much lighter he felt without it. Not allowed to quit, was he? He wasn't making much playing music, but it was enough to pay his room and board. He burst out laughing. Why had it taken him so long to realize he didn't have to do everything Ethan's father said?

"Bishop!" Mr. Watters yelled his name. "Mr. Thorne isn't going to like this."

Henry kept walking.

"I could lose my job if you walk."

Henry paused. He hated to think he might be responsible for someone else's hard times. There was only one way around that. Much as he didn't want to face Mr. Thorne, he knew he had to, to limit the damage the man could do to everyone around him. He chose the stairs over the elevator, knowing he'd be less likely to run into anyone on that route. At the sixth floor, he looked out the window to the street below, wishing he didn't feel that rush of fear. He took a deep breath and pushed through the double doors that separated the hallway and the carpeted antechamber where Ethan's father's secretary sat sentry.

"You can't be in here," she said, before giving Henry a double take. "Oh, I'm sorry, Henry. I didn't realize it was you. Mr. Thorne is on the telephone. Shall I tell him you stopped in?"

Henry walked past her and into Mr. Thorne's office. She followed, protesting that this interruption was not her fault. Mr. Thorne's padded leather chair faced the bank of windows that looked out over the city. He was in the midst of what sounded like a serious conversation — something involving a raid and arrests and how the newspaper might cover it.

"Mr. Thorne," Henry said. "Bernard."

Ethan's father spun in his chair, annoyed at the interruption. He pointed at the telephone.

Henry walked to the desk and pressed the button that would end the call.

"Henry!"

"I told him not to disturb you, Mr. Thorne," the secretary said. "He just barged in."

"I'm here to let you know that I quit," Henry said.

"You can't."

"I already have," he said. "It's a matter of conscience. I can't agree with your decision to print that letter to the editor."

"It's time you come to your senses." He put his hands behind his head and leaned back into his chair, which squeaked in protest. "Look at everything you're throwing away on her account. First, your education and home. Now, your job. I don't even want to hear that girl's name. And we print all manner of letters, not just ones we happen to agree with."

"Do you agree with that letter?"

Mr. Thorne paused. "Wholeheartedly. It's not in your job description to judge editorial calls. You're in the pressroom. You look after the ink and paper and the machinery. That's it." He reached for his phone again. "Now if you will excuse me."

"I quit," Henry said. "I don't want to be associated with this newspaper."

"That's the same thing Ethan said when I refused to print the garbage he brought me. I don't know what's wrong with you boys. In my day —"

"Good-bye, Mr. Thorne," Henry said.

"If you leave now, our association is done. You are not to have any contact with Ethan or Annabel or Mrs. Thorne. And don't come crawling to me when your money runs out and you find yourself on the streets with a tin cup. If I had known your music would turn into this, I would have set fire to that instrument years ago. Your father — this would kill him."

"My father's dead already," Henry said. "He killed himself."

He turned and walked out the door.

Chapter 55

FLORA HAD A FEW MORE TABLES TO SET BEFORE SHE COULD HEAD for the *Inquirer* offices. It seemed kinder to tell Henry in person. He'd surely find another band — every club in town knew his name now. It would devastate him. But there was no choice.

Doc snapped the last big shards of glass out of the frame. "I'd cover this," he said, "but it's such a nice day I hate to block our air."

"But what about security?" Glo laid cutlery on a neatly folded napkin. "The people who did this might like to come back and rob the place. Or worse."

Doc rubbed his chin. "Sure enough." He returned a few minutes later with a sheet of plywood, which he pounded into the frame.

"Such a shame," Glo said. "There goes our light."

"I'm sorry," Flora said. "I've brought this on you."

"You did no such thing. We'll call it atmosphere. Meanwhile, let's don't curse the darkness." She flicked a light switch so they could see well enough to keep working.

"As soon as I have some money," Flora said, "I'll pay you back."

Sherman walked in. "Who needs money? And please tell me one of our guys didn't do that."

"Brick through the window," Doc said. "Little gift from

someone who is not a fan of our opening act, apparently. Flora, show him what the newspaper said."

Flora fished the newspaper out of her pocket. It had stuck together in parts where she'd gotten paint on it, but there was enough legible for Sherman to get the gist.

He whistled low as he read.

"That's a terrible thing. Just terrible." He opened his wallet and offered Doc cash. "For a new window. Our insurance ship came in."

Doc waved away the money. "You got your own windows to buy."

Flora looked at Sherman, hoping the money would be enough to rebuild the club. He shook his head. Her stomach fell. He didn't need words to tell her the payment had been poor.

"We're not thinking about windows at the moment. New ventures, maybe," Sherman said. He laughed, but it wasn't a happy sound. "Let's just say the ship that came in was more of a canoe."

"You are always welcome here," Glo said. "I don't suppose there was enough for Flora to make her flight?"

Flora shook her head. Talking about this . . . she just couldn't.

"Time will tell." Sherman put his hand on Flora's shoulder. "Where there's a will, there's a way."

"Knock knock," a voice said. Flora bristled, recognizing it immediately.

Helen stepped inside. "I read the newspaper today and I had to see for myself what madness you and Henry have gotten yourselves into," she said. "I'm so concerned. How *are* you? Since your incident with the po —"

"Fine." Flora's tone was short. She hadn't told Glo anything about her arrest and didn't intend to. That was her private sorrow and Ethan's father had maneuvered to get the charges dropped against the both of them so there would be no further embarrassment to his family. "Unfortunately, we're not open yet." She slapped silverware down with more force than was necessary or wise.

"But I'd be happy to let you look at a menu," Glo said, layering her words with extra warmth. "You can come back tonight for the supper and show."

Helen accepted the menu but did not read it. "Your bad luck follows you like a tail follows a dog." She nodded toward the broken window. "Such a pity."

"Bad people, not bad luck. There's a difference." She had no need for Helen's condescension. "Is there something I can help you with?"

Helen laughed. "I was planning to help *you*."

Flora doubted that very much. But she didn't want Sherman, Glo, and Doc to think she was rude. "And what did you have in mind?"

"Pour me a drink," Helen said, "and I'll tell you."

Sherman nudged her from behind. "Don't keep the lady waiting," he said. "We need all the friends we can get."

Henry practically danced out of the Inquirer Building. Who needed that crummy job, anyway? Well, he did. But he'd make do. He took off his jacket, rolled up his sleeves, and hopped a cable car to Pike Place Market, where he planned to buy a peach for himself and a bouquet of roses for Flora.

The peach was easy. He found one from Frog Hollow Farm the size of a softball. He ate it standing in the middle of a crowded aisle, but for the first time in his life, he didn't care that he might be in the way. This was history's most perfect peach; this was the moment his life became his own. He finished the fruit, dropped its pit into a trash barrel, and then chose a bouquet of red roses.

"Robin Hoods," the flower girl said. "Everybody's favorite." She wrapped them in the previous day's paper. Henry shook his head to see it. So much sweat and stress and yelling over this dirty, flimsy newsprint. It was supposed to be his future, his and Ethan's. And invariably it was the next day's trash. That was no way to spend a life.

Henry cradled the bouquet and walked north and then west, past vegetable stalls and fishmongers. He fished a nickel out of his pocket and caught the Third Avenue cable car, which carried him past the Smith Tower. For the first time, he felt nothing as he passed through its shadow. The Majestic wasn't far from the Yesler stop. Flora stepped outside just as he arrived.

"Henry!" she said, surprised. "What are you — I thought you'd be at the paper."

"I quit!" he said. "I feel like a new man."

Her face fell.

"These are for you." He held the flowers out to her, puzzled at what made her look so unhappy. She glanced toward the windows. He noticed the plywood sheets and his stomach sank. "What happened? Are you all right?"

"I'm fine, but I have to tell you something." She paused, as if she were struggling to find the right words.

Henry swallowed. "I understand. It's because of the letter to the editor. Doc didn't like it. Bad press for the Majestic and all." He felt like a fool holding the flowers. What a lousy idea that had been.

"What we're doing, it riles people too much. Next time, it might be worse."

His mouth became dry. He knew what he had to do. "I'll quit, then. Don't you worry." He regretted the luxury of taking the cable car. He'd need those nickels.

Flora twisted her dress in her hands. "That was my first thought. That we might find you another band, maybe even get some help from the union finding you an uptown gig. But music is not my life. It's yours. You breathe it. I still want to do what Amelia Earhart is trying to do."

"But what about the money?" They'd gone over figures. She'd need a fortune to pull it off. Her music was half her income.

"I've found a sponsor. I'm out. Not you."

Her news stunned him. He tried to sound happy. "If I may ask, who?"

Flora's eyes widened, as if she expected him to know. "I'm surprised she hasn't told you." She pressed her lips together, looking uneasy. "It's Helen. She bought an airplane for me. It'll be ready in a week."

Chapter 56
Friday, July 2, 1937

DEATH HAD ALWAYS RATHER LIKED AMELIA EARHART, WHO reminded her of Flora in many ways. The auburn-haired pilot wasn't one to give her heart easily. Her husband had to propose six separate times to get her to agree, which she did only after writing him a letter asking for release if in a year's time she was miserable.

The letter read, *I may have to keep some place where I can go to be myself, now and then, for I cannot guarantee to endure at all times the confinements of even an attractive cage.*

Flora might have written the very same words to Henry. Oh, how she feared the attractive cage of love. The sky was her refuge. Death could make this refuge more appealing than ever. She could remove Flora's competition.

The aviatrix and her navigator were surprised to see Death on board their Lockheed Model 10 Electra. Even more surprised when their radio transmissions stopped working. Death had consumed them before the plane hit the water, her blood ringing with things she had not expected to feel as their lives drained into her. Humans and their secrets. Perhaps someday they would stop surprising her.

The next day, she was the black cat peering through the window of Flora's house, watching the girl read the morning newspaper.

Flora's reaction was another surprise. The girl did not look hopeful, or even thoughtful, as someone might when a new opportunity opens up.

Rather, she folded the newspaper, put her hands over her face, and wept.

Chapter 57
Sunday, July 4, 1937

Days after he'd taken the book, Ethan had still not decided what to do. It felt like a living thing in his pocket. The book gave off warmth, and occasionally it seemed to shudder, as if it were drawing breath. He touched it often, not because he wanted to check that it was still there, but because the feeling was so strange he had to be sure of it. He'd glanced inside a couple of times, but had closed it when he saw how ornate the script was.

In that time, he hadn't seen Henry once. Likewise, he'd stayed away from James. His father had returned his article with the word *Killed* written on every page. Ethan hadn't protested, lest his words give his father reason to believe his relationship with James had been any more significant than source to journalist.

Restless, he'd driven around the city until the sun was low in the sky. He did not want to go home, not if it meant he had to face his father and the absence of Henry. He had no interest in joining the crowds at the Seattle Tennis Club awaiting the fireworks display. He considered stopping for food, just to have a diversion. But he had no appetite, and so he headed home not long before sunset and parked beneath a silver maple by the carriage house. He pulled the book out of his pocket, determined to make sense of it. The text was the same inscrutable mess.

If it had been a baseball, he'd have pitched it through a window, just for the pleasure of smashing something. Instead, he put the book back in his pocket and slipped in the servants' entrance, risking that Gladys would see him as she cleaned up after dinner. But even if she did, she'd nod and look down as she'd been trained to do by his father. It struck Ethan, as he moved through the butler's pantry, that his father believed anything he didn't want to look at shouldn't be seen. Ethan had obliged with invisibility of his own for so long without realizing he was doing it.

The kitchen, blessedly, was empty. A bowl of bing cherries sat on the kitchen counter, their red-black flesh shining. Ethan had helped himself to a handful when someone whispered his name. He started and dropped the one he'd been about to consume. Helen stepped out of the shadows — the shadows he'd just examined and found empty.

"That seems a waste," she said.

"What are you doing in here?" Ethan picked up the fruit, which stained his shaking fingertips.

"Goodness, that looks like blood." She didn't look as though she minded.

"I was hungry." He was in no mood for teasing.

She walked closer, the heels of her shoes tapping like bones.

"Where've you been?" She lifted a cherry out of the bowl, popped it into her mouth, and pulled the curving stem between her lips. She closed her eyes as she stripped the pit of fruit before spitting it into her palm.

"Out," Ethan said. He crossed his arms and felt the edges of the book under his right hand.

"So mysterious." She stepped closer to Ethan, looking up at him through her eyelashes. Her voice cracked. "Come on, you can tell me. I'll take your secrets to the grave. I'm lonely here, Ethan. I could use a friend. Someone a bit more sophisticated than Annabel."

"We'll never be friends. I don't trust you." He uncrossed his arms.

"Whatever have I done that makes me seem untrustworthy?" She put a hand on his chest, right where the book was. "If only you knew the things I've done, you'd never worry about anyone's opinion of you again."

Ethan moved her hand away and ate a cherry. It was a good one: just the right amount of give between his teeth, its flavor balanced between sweet and tart. Simple and perfect, just as it was. He could not point to any specific untrustworthy thing Helen had done, and he felt himself softening toward her. If truth be told, his behavior — his predilections — were far more scandalous than anything in Helen's past. If people knew . . . The thought made him want to choke.

Ethan looked at Helen and recognized the lonely aspect of himself. "Put a few more cherries into the bowl," he said, offering her his arm. "We'll eat them in the library."

She smiled, and Ethan thought it a pity he could never love her, not in that way. It didn't mean that they couldn't be allies of a sort. The wiser part of him knew he should wait until Henry had time to read him the book. But Henry would be disappointed in Ethan if he knew what had happened with James. Worse than disappointed. It might end their friendship.

Helen caught his gaze. "We're going to be the best of friends, Ethan," she said. "For the rest of your life."

He pushed away the rising feeling of dread. "I found a book."

"Books are dull," she said. "Wouldn't you rather play a game?"

"It's an interesting one. I'd love to hear you read aloud from it." Such a thin request. Surely she'd see through it and realize his illiteracy. But he had to know what it said, and he could stop her if James had written anything too scandalous.

"Oh, all right," Helen said. "It has been a tedious evening. I'll read it — with feeling. But perhaps we should invite your parents to join us. Make a show of it."

"No! — That is to say, it would be much more fun if it were just the two of us, don't you think? If it's worth sharing, we can always do that later."

"Whatever you'd like, cousin," Helen said. "I'm all yours."

Chapter 58

FOR THOUSANDS OF YEARS, LOVE HAD FILLED THE BOOK. DEATH knew this, and yet she'd never been tempted to look inside for fear of what had been written about her. It was one thing to do what she had to do. It was another thing to see it on the page, especially through the eyes of her enemy.

"Where shall we sit?" She looked at Ethan's bare wrist. She could make him feel better, temporarily and then permanently, with a touch. She ached to show him his life so that he could see the beauty in it.

"How about there?" Ethan interrupted her thoughts, gesturing toward a hand-carved love seat covered in crimson velvet, the one style of furniture she found amusing above all others. On more than one occasion, she'd turned one into a death seat.

"The perfect choice." She fought her urge to kill Ethan on the spot. "And so cozy."

Ethan helped her sit. He reached into his pocket and produced the book. It was a lovely object.

"Where did you get this?" She traced the intricate cover. Love had an eye for beauty and a way of transforming the simple into the spectacular.

Ethan faced her, the barest bit of moonlight on his face. In the long, silent war with time, his beauty would give way. His skin, now smooth, would pucker and sag. Dark spots would mottle its edges. His clear eyes would grow rheumy, as yellow tinged the whites and cataracts muddied his irises. Wouldn't it be a gift to deliver his beauty whole, before time had done its damage?

He cleared his throat and looked away, the liar. "I — I found it."

"On the street?"

"Something like that." He blushed.

"And you haven't looked inside? Perhaps the owner wrote his name. Or hers. This is a fairly feminine cover, don't you think?" She took it from him.

"It is fancy. I wouldn't say feminine." Ethan swallowed. "I looked inside, but I didn't see a name."

"The curiosity is killing me." Death opened the book. "Hmm."

"What? What does it say?"

She'd only fed something to a mind a few times. And that was just a few memories, most recently the scene of Flora's parents' death. What would the entire book do? Possibly kill Ethan, or drive him mad. She closed her fingers around his wrist.

"Your fingernails. They're red." Ethan's voice slurred. His eyes rolled back and his limbs jerked as she poured the contents of the book into his mind. He fought back, trying to peel her fingers away. But even this perfect human specimen could no sooner escape her than the earth could unhitch itself from the sun.

If he lived, the boy would know the entire futile, messy history of the Game. He would watch the asp sink its fangs into Cleopatra, the castration of Abelard, the slow death of Lancelot, the suicide of Juliet, players all. Certain things she would keep from him. Her own identity, for example. She would also conceal the fact that the Game would end in three days. Should he tell Henry and Flora, that knowledge might risk her victory. Everything else, he would learn. And he would understand her gift: deliverance from pain. Real love was death. If he withstood the learning, he would welcome the gift.

And yet she could not end his life. Not yet. Not when they were so alike, Ethan and she. So she released his hands. Left him gasping on the love seat as she walked slowly from the room, taking the book with her.

The earth turned, dragging tracings of starlight across the velvet sky. Ethan stumbled into the hall. He climbed the stairs, one slow step at a time until he was at the top. Helen's room was near. He could hear her rustling about. What had happened? They'd sat down to read, and then she'd taken his hand, and then he knew all of these things that seemed impossible.

And yet, they explained so much. They explained the hold James had on Ethan. Why it felt like love when he'd first laid eyes on him, even if was he nothing more than a pawn.

Ethan closed his door. Looked at the space where he'd spent so much time: at his bed, at his desk, at the windows that looked out over the grounds below and gave a view of the booming finale of a fireworks display in the distance. If James Booth was someone else, someone who was not a human exactly . . . perhaps what Ethan had done with him didn't count.

Perhaps he wasn't one of *those*.

For a moment, Ethan felt relief so great he wanted to weep. To not be attracted to boys. He wanted this so much for himself. He'd spent hours in this room, trying to talk himself out of the wanting, the desire for Henry most of all.

And yet he could not continue to pretend. All of that attraction had happened before James. Even though he had never acted on it, it was who he was. There was no changing it. The Independence Day celebration outside had ended, and the open curtains revealed a crescent moon. Was it waxing or waning? He never could tell. But if it had a choice, would it shrink into complete darkness or make its journey bursting with reflected light?

Ethan picked up a pen and a sheet of paper. One slow letter, one hard-fought word at a time, he wrote to Henry, who needed to know what he and Flora were part of. Henry needed to know who James was, that he was an ally of sorts. Ethan wished he knew who Death was. One of the musicians? The person who had arrested Henry? That seemed the most likely thing of all.

He told Henry not to give up on Flora. *We do not choose whom we love*, he wrote. *We can only choose how well.*

The handwriting was atrocious. Entire sentences had been crossed out. Ethan was sure he'd spelled half of the words wrong. It wasn't good enough. He couldn't send it. Tired as he was, he copied the words on a new sheet. He threw the draft away. He sealed the letter and addressed it. Then he wrote a shorter note to his parents, explaining that he would be enlisting in the navy in the morning. He slipped it under their door. Then he packed a bag, left Henry's letter in the outgoing mail slot, and disappeared into the night. Ethan wanted to spend one last night as a free man, a free man who knew who he was and who he would never be. He wanted to watch the sun rise on that day his life began anew.

When the door closed behind him, Death slipped out of her room. She found the letter in the mail slot.

And then she burned it.

Chapter 59
Monday, July 5, 1937

AFTER THE WHOLE SORRY ETHAN BUSINESS, LOVE DEMANDED A
meeting. Death agreed, but insisted on choosing the location.
When Love arrived in the Chinese room of the Smith Tower, a few
floors down from where Henry's father had jumped, Death was
already there, lounging in a rosewood chair carved with a dragon
and a phoenix. She faced a small table with a glass of red wine and
a plate of escargots, and was tearing the snails out of their shells
with a tiny fork.

Love settled on a plain mahogany chair. The space over his
heart where the book had been felt empty. Nagging, like a missing
memory.

Death demolished a snail shell between her teeth. "That one
didn't want to come out." She spit the splintered remains into the
dish. A shard clung to her lips, and Love wanted nothing more
than to remove it.

"Soup?" she said, pointing to a tureen. "It's turtle."

Love declined.

"I don't know how the girls stand this chair." Her lips glistened
with butter. "It's uncomfortable."

The Wishing Chair had been a gift of the Chinese empress.
Any young woman who sat in it was guaranteed an engagement

within a year. The chair might have been uncomfortable, but it worked as promised. He felt a stab of compassion for his opponent, who had no capacity to feel hope. He shrugged it off. This was not his sadness to carry. He wanted his book back. Ethan too. But that, he feared, was a heart he dared not call again.

Behind him, the city of Seattle reached toward the water's edge. Electric lights burned in many of the buildings, hazing the bottom of the sky with their glow. Beside a nearly vanquished moon, stars hung overhead, the solitary recipients of infinite human wishes.

"You'll have to ask nicely," Death said. "I will also consider begging."

Damn her and the way she invaded his mind. If that was how she wanted to play, fine. He sent her images of things he'd witnessed without her as he followed Henry about town.

Here, the image of Henry fastening his tie around his neck; there, Henry combing the unruly curls from his forehead; the shine of lamplight on his shoe as he polished it; the gray ribbon of sidewalk unrolling itself at his feet. Leaves full of sunlight. The world seen through the eyes of someone in love with a woman, in love with life.

It took most of Love's concentration to send the images so purely, but he paused now and then to watch Death's expression change. She grew impatient and pawed through the rest of the memories as quickly as he could form them: of stolen kisses and swift touches, and most of all Henry and Flora as they played "Someday," every charged note of it, performance after performance ending with crashing waves of applause.

This magic had happened. Even if they never performed together again, they'd been altered by it. Irrevocably.

She pulled away, her eyes dark around the edges. He leaned in to dab her face with his handkerchief, but she grabbed his wrist. "Don't."

Then she shoved everything off the table — the wine, the empty snail shells, the soup. "And what of it? We have two days left in the Game, and still she refuses him."

His wrist stung where she'd grabbed it. "How are you faring in your attempts to lure Henry away?"

She arranged herself carelessly in the chair, draping one hand over its back. "I have two ways to win. You have but one. History and the odds are on my side."

Love could not argue either point.

But what were odds? The odds against any one human being born were tremendous. The chain of moments that led to it was long, a chain made of infinite human choices that each had to occur in sequence to lead to a particular birth. The odds of either Flora or Henry being here at all were one in four hundred trillion, give or take.

"Two days left." She held up a pair of fingers. As if Love could forget or would not understand the words. She tossed the book back at him. He caught it and felt immediately soothed by its warmth and familiarity.

Then Death gave him her awful Helen smile and faded like Lewis Carroll's Cheshire cat. As she did, Love thought of something he hadn't before. Where was the real Helen? The one Death was impersonating? It seemed a small matter, really. And yet, much could hinge on the minutiae. He sucked in his breath and stood, hoping there was still time.

It was the middle of the night when Love reached the human Helen. The place smelled of stale breath and antiseptic, and an acid light filled the hallways. The rooms, each a white rectangle behind a door with a square of reinforced glass in its middle, were for the most part dark. Almost all of their inhabitants were sleeping. Helen wasn't, and Love was glad, for he hated to disturb the rest of someone who'd been so wounded.

He materialized in the room not as James Booth or any other human, but as a creature Helen would welcome: a wiggling cocker spaniel puppy whose breath smelled of hay and summertime. He whimpered, and she sat up, looking left and right. Then, in the gray light, she spotted him on the floor and lifted him in bed with her. Love felt her heart. *Please tell me this is not another hallucination. They say I went mad, but I know that I didn't. I've forgotten, is all. I've just forgotten.*

Love kissed Helen on the chin and she giggled. She curled around him in bed, her heart pressed to his rounded back. Love sensed the spot where Death had taken the girl's memories. The edges around that hole in her mind were ragged, preventing her from reaching the ones that lay further back. Love repaired the tear. The form he'd chosen was perfect for this: soft, vulnerable, full of life and love.

Helen fell asleep around him as soon as he started. He was gone by the time she woke in the morning, and forever after, she thought of his visit as a dream, the sweetest of her life. The restoration of most of her memory caused great excitement with her physician, who telephoned her parents once he'd determined her recovery was indeed legitimate, that she was a person of consequence, and, most important, that someone would cover the bill for her care. By the time all of that was settled, Love had already returned to Seattle.

Chapter 60
Tuesday, July 6, 1937

WHISPERING. THERE HAD BEEN SO MUCH WHISPERING SINCE Ethan left the house. Annabel hated whispering. It was rude, rude, rude. And now, after the phone call, there was more of it, and when she asked what everyone was whispering about, she was sent from the room.

It wasn't fair.

First Henry, and then Ethan, and now Helen, who had disappeared not long after Mama had hung up the phone. Helen had been listening at the door, and Annabel had been hiding in the alcove behind her. It was very strange how Helen had left the house. First she was there, and then she wasn't. Annabel would have to ask about it once Mama calmed down.

Annabel crept into Ethan's room, which still had most of his things. His baseball uniform. His school pennant. All of his suits and ties and Oxfords. It still smelled like him too. Grass and perspiration and Lucky Tiger Bay Rum aftershave, Annabel's favorite.

There was a piece of paper in his wastebasket. She lifted it out and smoothed away the crumples. *Dear Henry,* it read. She started reading it, but it was about mushy, yucky things. Besides, she was excited to get to the part where she sealed it in an envelope, wrote an address, and licked a stamp. *That* was the fun of letters, not writing them.

Annabel sat at Ethan's desk. She found an envelope. She dipped his fountain pen in the ink and addressed it properly, as Helen had showed her. She'd memorized Henry's address from the letter he'd written to her asking about her bicycle riding. She attached the stamp and put it in the slot. The mailman would deliver it the next afternoon.

The whispering stopped, but no one came for Annabel, who fell asleep on Ethan's bed and dreamed about him. It wasn't a good dream. In it, Ethan was a sailor in a war, and he died. The dream made her cry. She woke when Mama called her down to supper, glad it was just a dream and not real life. She dried her face and went downstairs to eat. She couldn't remember being this hungry in her entire life.

Chapter 61
Wednesday, July 7, 1937

BEFORE LONG, HENRY WOULD HAVE TO LEAVE HIS RENTED ROOM for the Majestic to do his sound check for the night's show. A week ago, he'd have been out the door already, counting down the minutes until he could see Flora again. They hadn't replaced her since her departure, and she was spending all of her time at the airfield, breaking in the new Staggerwing Helen had purchased. Henry was now singing Flora's numbers, but he wouldn't perform "Someday," no matter how much Sherman and the audience begged. The audience, he ignored. Sherman and the band, he promised a new song as soon as the right idea struck.

He'd been trying to write one, but all that he'd produced were notes to Flora, notes he knew he'd never send.

Someday, we will climb the Eiffel Tower.

Someday, we will lie on the sand beneath an Italian sun.

Someday, we will play music in New York City.

Someday . . .

There were so many of them, each more vivid than the last. He'd torn the page into strips so there was one wish on each ribbon of paper. These, he slipped into his jacket pocket when Mrs. Kosinski knocked, because they were only meant for one set of eyes.

Henry opened his door.

"This came for you in the post." Mrs. Kosinski stood there in her housecoat, examining the letter. "Looks like little-girl handwriting, if you ask me."

He held out his hand. After a moment, Mrs. Kosinski relinquished the envelope. She waited in the doorway.

"Thank you," Henry said, ignoring the look of disappointment on her face.

He closed his door, leaned against it, and eased open the flap, expecting a letter from Annabel. But it was from Ethan. He read it twice, the second time sitting on his bed because the contents were so bewildering. On its surface, Ethan's tale made no sense. But below that, in the part of Henry that could feel the truth of things as easily as he felt music, as deeply as he felt bound to Flora, he knew everything Ethan had written was true. It was true, and it changed everything, for all of them.

He put the letter into his pocket next to the someday notes. For a moment, he wondered what he should do, because he did not want to look foolish in front of Flora. But only for a moment. And then he had his hat and his coat. And he was out the door, for he was not going to the Majestic.

"Musta been some letter!" Mrs. Kosinski called out after him.

He did not reply.

Chapter 62

GOING ON INSTINCT ALONE, HENRY TOOK A CAB TO THE AIRSTRIP. He spent the last of his money doing so. Had he guessed wrong, he'd have been stranded there, miles from home. It was a possibility he didn't let himself consider. And he found her exactly where he'd imagined she'd be, working alone on her new plane, a Staggerwing the color of a candied apple. Dressed in coveralls, she wiped her forehead with the back of her hand, as if it had been a long day with much to do. But she looked happy — so content Henry almost turned away and began the long walk back to the club.

He couldn't resist watching her a moment longer, taking in the way the slanting light found her, the way she seemed to know exactly what she was doing as she circled the red Staggerwing, studying it from every side. If he could have left her to this happiness, knowing he was leaving her free to do this thing she loved, he would've, without a second thought.

But if he could not persuade her to love him, she would die.

That was the end of the Game Ethan had spelled out in his letter. Henry wished it had been otherwise. Had he been the player cursed to die, that would be different. He would have hated such a fate, but not nearly so much, particularly since the Game had brought them together.

The sky darkened as Henry stood there, weighing his options. The ruin of the situation and the cruelty of the Game sank in fully. He saw two choices: He could keep the truth secret and make one last play for her, ask her one last time to love him. If she agreed, and did not know her life depended on it, then he would know she was telling the truth. Or he could tell Flora of the letter and use it as leverage. Surely loving him was preferable to death.

But to love someone in order to avoid death: This was no form of love at all. This was cowardice. Flora would never choose it.

As he stood, he realized a third option.

He'd tell her the truth. If she refused him, he would find Death, and he would offer his own life in trade. Would it be enough? It had to be. It was all he had left to give.

Flora finally noticed him. "Don't you have a show tonight?" She tucked a lock of stray hair behind her ear.

"I had something more important to do."

"Henry," she said, her voice full of warning.

"I won't take much of your time," he said, walking closer. "There's something . . . something you ought to know. Is there someplace we can go, someplace where we're not outside like this?"

She led him to the hangar. He handed her Ethan's letter, which she read in the light of a single bulb hanging down from the ceiling.

"Henry," Flora said afterward. "You can't tell me you believe this is true."

"I didn't want to believe it," he said. "But I can feel it. Can't you?"

Flora didn't reply for the longest time. Her teeth chattered. As ever, Henry gave her his jacket.

"Thank you," she said. "I'm not even cold. I don't know why I'm shaking like a wet cat."

"I can guess," Henry said.

More silence. Flora folded the letter and handed it back. "I don't want any part of this. Even if it's true, it's humiliating. We've been played. Tricked. Manipulated. I never consented to be owned like this. It's barbaric."

He looked at her in disbelief. "Is that what you really feel? That's all?"

"What do you mean *feel*?" she said. "I don't know anything about what I've ever felt. And neither do you. You can't. Everything you feel — everything you've felt — that was put inside of you by someone else for his own purposes."

"But I *can* know," he said. "I do." He reached for her hand, but she pulled hers away and hid them behind her back. "I don't care how I came to feel this way about you. I want it to continue forever. I want to give you everything —"

Flora held up her hand so he'd stop. "I knew better than this, Henry. I did. All along, I knew I wanted nothing to do with love. And it's madness for us to continue, knowing how it will end."

"You can't mean that," he said. "It doesn't have to end that way."

"I refuse to submit to it. I choose not to believe. Not in the Game. Not in the consequences. I'm going to live my life, by myself, as I choose, and I suggest you do the same."

"What if we ran away?" He hated how desperate his voice sounded.

"Henry." She looked up at him, her eyes glazed with tears. "They'd find us."

"Maybe not. Or at least maybe not right away. It's worth a try."

"I can't say yes to this, not this way," she said. "If only —"

"If only what? Just say the word. What do I need to do?"

She turned away from him. "There's nothing you can do. So now, before we hurt each other any more, let's say good-bye. I'm not going to live on anyone's terms but my own. With Helen's sponsorship, I'm going to make that trip. It's going to change everything for me."

"Why is she even doing that?" Henry moved so he was facing Flora again.

"Why do you think?" Flora let out a hard burst of laughter. "She's buying me off. Once I'm out of the picture, you're all hers."

"But —" The thought hadn't occurred to Henry. It made a certain sort of sense, even if it was appalling.

"The new airplane is ready to go. I'm taking Helen tomorrow for her first flight."

Henry was silent. He reached for Flora's hands, and she did not resist. "I have known my whole life that I wanted you. You and no one else. I have loved you from the first moment I saw you."

"We were children," she said.

"But don't you remember being a child?" he said. "How much simpler and clearer everything was? Sometimes I think they're smarter than any of us when it comes to love. They don't doubt it. Not for a second. And they don't doubt that they're loved in return. Something happens to us when we grow up. Misfortune tramples us. We forget how it feels to simply love without throwing the whole mess of life into the stew. We trade love for fear. I'm not willing to do that anymore."

"Something happened to you and me when we were infants," Flora said. "Something terrible. We never had a chance. And this was never love. It couldn't have been."

Henry didn't argue. He did not want to fight with her. But he would not dispute or deny the contents of his heart. Nothing would change the fact of his love. He didn't know what would happen to him after he died, but his heart's position was as fixed as the sun.

"You were somebody's plaything," she said. "Both of us were. This is a game we can't win. No matter what we choose, we lose. I die, you die, we both die . . . someday, whether it's soon or not, we're both going to die. The only thing we can do at this point is refuse to be part of a game that was never our choice to begin with. We refuse. And we live our lives."

He put his hands on her shoulders. "I'd choose you. Game or no, I'd choose you every time. *Please.*"

"There is no chance," she said. "There is no chance in this lifetime we will ever be together again." She wriggled out of his grasp. "The show. It starts" — she pushed his sleeve up and looked at her wristwatch — "it starts in twenty minutes. You should be dressed and getting tuned up. It's time for you to go."

"I'm not playing tonight," Henry said. He'd spent his entire life doing the right thing, being the person everyone else depended on. He was done with that.

"You can't quit before they find a replacement," Flora said. "I'll give you a ride."

Stunned and angry, Henry turned away and stepped into the twilit air, doing his best to breathe. She couldn't have said anything worse to him. After all of this, nothing about him meant anything to her. She thought he was replaceable, like a piece of furniture. He turned back to take his parting shots.

"You'd rather risk your life than love me?"

"It's not that simple," she said.

An avalanche of hurt made it impossible for him to speak. What was so unlovable about him? Why wouldn't she try?

"Henry!" Flora said. "I'm sorry."

"I'm not," he said. "But I don't know why you were so certain we would lose. I would have fought for you. For every second we had left."

Chapter 63

And so, Death won.

The moment Flora refused Henry, even knowing the cost, Death felt it. Her senses honed themselves beneath the cover of a moonless sky. Music, car horns, small bites of conversation, laughter . . . the din of humanity filled her ears. And the smells . . . smoke and wine and flowers exhaling the last of their perfume.

All she had to do was wait for midnight. And then the hour came.

It was a shame the Thornes had discovered the business with Helen. That was inelegant. But now that the Game was over, it hardly mattered. They'd never guess her real identity, and she had no plans to return to their mansion.

She'd been recalling Love's little book in a café, puzzling over it as victory arrived. Death was struck with the understanding that she and Love were every bit as different as she imagined and feared. It meant, as ever, that she was alone, the eternal villain.

Love inspired the stories. He wrote them down. She destroyed them and sucked them up. She was a monster. A monster with no choice. A monster who needed to feed. A monster no one wanted.

Ah, well. If she was cursed to be the monster, she would be the worst of them. The only question remaining was when she might claim her prize. She was entitled to it anytime. She was hungry for Flora, though she wanted to hold off. It would be even more satisfying to dine on the girl's life when the urge was sharper.

Unless . . .

Unless Henry chose Death.

If he did that, she could have them both. And she could prove beyond doubt the weakness of love.

And weak, it was. As often as not in Death's vast experience, people preferred the idea of love to the act of it. They wanted to pursue, but grew weary once they'd won the prize. If they were loved, they used it as proof of their worth. In the name of love, they manipulated each other. Out of cowardice, they lied, overtly and by omission. There were so many ways for love to decay. And unlike the decaying of a corpse, which fed worms and grew trees, what did rotting love ever feed?

Love believed Henry loved Flora. He believed in his player's perfect heart. Death believed no such thing. She suspected Henry loved the idea of being loved and the security that came with it. She would hold off consuming Flora until she'd won Henry as well.

She'd already won the Game as herself. There could be no greater victory than winning as Love too. She transformed her guise into something Henry would not be able to resist. And as she traveled toward him, she felt better than she had in ages.

Chapter 64

AFTER HENRY DISAPPEARED, FLORA REMEMBERED SHE WAS STILL wearing his coat. For the longest time, she waited in the column of light as the night closed in, expecting he'd return — if not for her, then for his jacket.

She'd even hoped he would, although she did not trust a single thing she felt. How could she, knowing Death had chosen her as a player when she was a baby in an apple crate? And of course she'd been Death's choice. That she would have been chosen by Love was unthinkable. Her parents had died on Valentine's Day, for God's sake. When it came to love, her entire line had been cursed.

Henry did not return. The night grew cool. She checked her watch. Just after midnight. The day had become another, without fanfare, unlike that other midnight she'd spent with Henry, when bells chimed and everything felt so magical. And then, moments later, she'd found Nana's body. The sadness rang in her bones once more, heartbreak's echo.

Suddenly cold, she put her hands in the pocket of his jacket. There was paper there. Torn strips of it. She pulled one out and read it.

Someday we will climb the Eiffel Tower.

With a pang, she recognized Henry's handwriting. Paris. She could go there on her own. It was where Bessie Coleman learned to fly.

Curious, she removed another strip. Another *someday*, this one about making Saturday breakfast in their small green house. She looked at her watch. The band would be in full swing right now, with or without Henry, because that was what happened in life. It went on.

She pulled out another note. She opened it and began to weep. She could not read about the children she would not have.

Flora read every note until she reached the last one, a series of secret messages that meant the same thing as the heart Nana had sewn into all those quilts.

Someday starts now, it read.

You couldn't write something and make it true, not on a piece of paper, not with a sheet of music. At best, it would just give you something to want that you couldn't have. The strength of a father. The warmth of a mother. The devotion of a grandmother. Love was loss. Flora had known that since . . .

She stopped herself midthought.

She'd known it her whole life. It was the one thing she was certain of. That someday, everyone she loved would die. Everything she loved would crumble to ruin. It was the price of life. It was the price of love. It was the only ending for every true story.

This was the certainty Death had given her. This. Not love.

The love she'd felt for music, for flying, for her parents, for her grandmother, and most of all for Henry? That was real, and it came from within, in whatever mysterious way love arrived.

Game or no, she would someday die, as all living beings did. But that wasn't the tragedy. Nor was there tragedy in being a pawn. All souls are, if not of eternal beings, then as pawns of their own bodies. The game, whatever shape it takes, lasts only as long as the body holds out. The tragedy, every time, is choosing something other than love.

That had been her whole life. And now it was too late for it to be anything different.

She ran out of the hangar, and, breathing hard beneath a sky missing its moon, she felt the words of the song he'd written for her rise in her chest. Without accompaniment, without audience, without caring about anything but feeling them to their depths, she sang out into the void, filling the darkness with everything she'd denied herself, sending the love she'd lost to the world beyond, knowing that nothing more could hurt her worse than she'd already hurt herself.

"You are the moon and I am the sea," she sang. "Wherever you are, you've got pull over me."

Even with the music, she had never felt more alone. The desolation was deep enough to drown in.

Henry would never want her back, not after what she'd said to him. She'd ruined them. She would put the notes back into his pockets, pretend she'd never seen them, and return his jacket to him tomorrow, just as soon as she'd taken Helen on her flight. Or, better. She'd ask Helen to give Henry what was his. Death could come for her now, or Death could come later. She would welcome him when he arrived. Surely what came next could not be worse than this.

Chapter 65
Thursday, July 8, 1937

IT TOOK HENRY HOURS TO WALK HOME. EVEN SO, HE COULDN'T sleep. He was folding laundry when someone knocked. For a moment, Henry hoped it was Flora. She'd changed her mind. Persuaded Mrs. Kosinski to let her up, even though it was well past the hour when visitors were permitted. He pushed his hair off his forehead and glanced around his room. He tucked the stack of folded clothes away. Everything else was fine. The bed was made. His bureau, clear. His bass, looking sharp in front of the window.

He opened the door.

Helen stood in front of him, wearing a black coat and heels over an admittedly fetching red dress. She walked into the room. She pulled off her hat, her gloves, and her purse, and laid them on the center of Henry's bed.

"Love what you've done with the place," she said. "Really homey."

He couldn't tell if she was being serious. It was far beneath the style of living she was accustomed to.

"Helen," he said, wondering how she'd gotten inside.

"Cat got your tongue?" She glanced at her purse and Henry knew she would walk over to it, snap it open, and pull out a cigarette. She did just that. In a way, it comforted him, knowing her so well.

"No," he said, "it's just that it's late, and this isn't the best neighborhood, and —"

"And what," she said, after she'd lit a match and taken a drag. "Blow this out, would you?" She held the match toward him. It burned close to her long white fingers.

Henry leaned forward and blew. The look in her eyes was strange, and she seemed nervous. "Are you all right?"

"I just wanted to see you," she said. "Tell me you've missed me. It's dull spending time with only Annabel."

He looked around the room, wishing he had a chair. "Would you like to sit? I can only offer you the bed, unfortunately."

She stretched out on it, kicking her shoes to the floor. Henry's pulse sped up. She looked down at the empty spot on the blanket next to her, patting it with her free hand.

"Let me get you something for the ashes," Henry said, pretending he hadn't noticed her invitation.

"Henry." Her voice was a warm purr. She exhaled smoke through her red lips. Despite himself, he felt something radiate from his center outward. Flora didn't want him. Not the way he wanted her. And here was Helen, the girl who'd once been intended for him, making herself astonishingly available. She'd even helped Flora on his behalf. Maybe choosing her made sense after all.

He had nothing for the ashes but a nearly empty drinking glass. He drained it and wiped his lips with the back of his hand. He offered Helen the glass. As she took it, their fingertips touched and Henry found himself on the bed next to her, trembling and dizzy. Her back was to the headboard and he faced her, his hand brushing the silk of her dress and the thigh it concealed. He looked down, blushing fiercely.

"Henry." Her voice was a lethal whisper. He froze in the sound of it. "I could talk to Ethan's father for you. Get him to give you a second chance."

A second chance. Would he receive a third? He knew what Helen was offering, what it would cost. There were worse bargains to be made. He leaned toward her, just an inch. He hoped she couldn't see that he was shaking. He caught a whiff of her perfume. Lilies. It brought him back to his father's funeral and the misery of it. He stood, feeling wobbly. Helen looked up at him, her eyes pleading.

"Henry." She said his name again. She reached for his hand. But he did not take hers.

"What is it?" she asked. "Why don't you want me?"

Henry felt sad for her. Her expression was one of open need, of hunger almost. He recognized himself in it. But she was not the one he wanted, and as much as he craved the touch of another, his heart had been built for Flora alone. The more time he spent with Flora, the more time he watched her sing, the more he understood the love she had for her airplane, the less he could imagine life with anyone else. If he could not have her, he did not want anyone.

For the longest time, he stood there, breathing and looking down at Helen, who had closed her eyes.

"I'm sorry," he said.

"Don't be," Helen said. Her tone changed suddenly, in a way he did not fully understand. There was a petulance to her, the sort he used to experience in elementary school with the kids who couldn't stand to lose at games. "The loss is yours."

She crushed her cigarette on the edge of the glass and dropped the smoking remains inside. She set the glass on the bureau, smoothed her dress, and stepped back into her shoes.

"Help me with my coat?"

Relieved to be giving her something she wanted, he slid it up her arms and over her shoulders. She stood close, and he knew that in refusing her now, he was refusing her forever. She would not be a path to reconciliation with his old life. She would not be the cornerstone of a respectable, plentiful future.

But this choice: It wasn't one he'd made in haste in the middle of the night. He'd made it long ago. It was Flora. It always had been. It always would be.

Even if she did not want him, she had to live. He would not let Death take her, not without a fight. At first light, he would visit James Booth, who might be able to help. At the very least, he might reveal Death's identity. The thought terrified him. But what choice did he have? If this Death character was not a man he could fight, perhaps he was someone who would consider taking Henry's life in trade.

Helen slipped her hands back inside her gloves and laid a hand on Henry's cheek, firmer than a gentle touch but something short of a slap.

"See you around, Henry," she said.

"Let me walk you to the door," he said.

"No need." She nudged the tumbler off the dresser. It shattered, sending fragments of glass and ash across his floor. "So sorry." Though she didn't sound it.

Henry went to his closet, where he kept a broom and dustpan. By the time he turned around, she was gone. Henry peered into the dimly lit hallway, puzzled at her disappearance. Exhaustion set in. He cleaned up the glass and staggered to his bed, which smelled of her. Nonetheless, he fell into a deep, dreamless sleep, the sort said to be enjoyed by the dead.

He woke with a start the next morning, anxious to find his way to Hooverville. But when he looked out the window to see what sort of day he faced, he spotted Mr. Thorne's car parked across the street from the boarding house. It was so early, and yet, how long had he been there?

The color drained from Henry's face, the feeling from his hands. This was the last thing he needed. He did not want to be berated about any of his choices. Nor did he know anything about what had made Ethan enlist; even the prospect of speculating about that felt disloyal at best.

If he used the back door, he might slip out undetected. He tried, but one of the risers squeaked, and Mrs. Kosinski met him at the bottom of the stairs.

"I've a bone to pick with you," she said. "No visitors before nine o'clock. The policy is as clear as day." She pointed to a framed cross-stitch on the wall. Henry found it impossible to argue with a policy that had been sewn in green thread. He wondered for a moment how Helen had made it in so late, but he didn't have time to puzzle that one through, not with Mr. Thorne waiting.

"I'm sorry," he said, realizing that Mr. Thorne had probably barged into the place and demanded to see him whenever he'd arrived. "It won't happen again."

"He won't tell me who he is or what he wants with you," she said. "And he refuses to leave. It's almost as if he doesn't give a whit about cross-stitch."

Henry started to apologize, but she wasn't finished.

"I think he's a gangster. Is he a gangster? What would a gangster want with you? I didn't offer him any coffee, because I don't want gangster lips on my good Haviland. Are you in trouble with gangsters, Henry? Because that is also against the rules, even though I haven't yet had time to work it up in thread."

"He isn't a gangster." Henry had to smile at that, just a bit. Mrs. Kosinski had closed the French doors, but through the lace curtains, Henry could see Mr. Thorne sitting on the edge of the couch, his hat in his lap. He had the sort of profile that should be carved in stone.

"Should I bring coffee, then? Made with fresh grounds?" She firmly believed you could use coffee two to three times before the beans were spent.

"That would be nice. Fresh grounds."

"I'll add it to your weekly bill," she said. "Coffee costs extra, of course. So does cream and sugar."

"Bring us everything," Henry said, mostly wanting her to be out of the blast zone when Ethan's father blew up.

"Biscuits? Because —"

"Everything," Henry said. He walked toward the French doors. Mr. Thorne rose, still holding his hat. When Henry noted the man's pallor, his heart lurched. He opened the door, knowing terrible news awaited.

"What is it?" he said. "What's happened? It's not Annabel, is it? She didn't fall off her bicycle —"

"It's Helen," he said. "Something terrible has happened. It seems we've all been fooled, and I thought it only right to warn you."

Chapter 66

THE TELEPHONE RANG AS FLORA WAS GETTING READY TO LEAVE. She'd dressed in something she rarely wore: a daring red dress with black buttons up its back. Too fancy for most days, not quite fancy enough for a performance, but perfect for a life-changing day like today. She had her sponsor. She'd make her flight. Her dream was coming true. She didn't feel quite the way she'd thought she would, but maybe a bit of tarnish was the price of reality.

The ringing continued. Strange. She could not imagine who might be calling her so early in the morning. Or at all, really. She considered answering it, but she had an appointment with Helen. That, and no desire to talk with anyone. No desire for any human connection at all.

Even as she knew that hunger for solitude was how Death had shaped her heart, she didn't see a need to change it. Ironically, it had served her well. Just as no one could hurt her if she did not form attachments, keeping to herself also meant she would not hurt anyone else, most especially Henry. The expression on his face when she turned him away was one she never wanted to see again, on anyone, as long as she lived.

She slung his coat over her arm and walked to the door. Her plan was to get to the airstrip at least two hours early to make sure the plane — and her nerves — were in fine shape. After their flight together, Helen could return Henry's coat. She tried to ignore the pang that image gave her.

Helen. She shuddered a bit to think of the girl. She appreciated what Helen had to offer her: a way out. Flora was to stay away from Henry, and Helen would fund her trip. In return, Henry would be loved. It made perfect sense. But it didn't mean Helen was someone she wanted to be around. The last time they'd been together, Flora had suffered that awful vision of her parents' death. She wasn't worried such a thing would happen again, as it had happened neither before nor since. But in the same way that certain scents evoke memories, the prospect of seeing Helen again, of being dependent on her in an even greater way, put Flora on edge.

The ringing continued. Flora locked the door behind her and walked down the steps to the street, and soon she was too far away to hear or care.

At least it was a beautiful day for a flight. Pale blue sky. No wind. Not a cloud to be seen, so no chance of thunderstorms, and it was the wrong time of year for ice. She couldn't have asked for better conditions.

She sat in the cockpit of the new plane, polishing the wood until it glowed. Helen wasn't due for another hour yet, and Flora had already checked everything she could off her list. Frustrating. She put her hands on the yoke and looked around, making sure everything was tidy. Something glinted underfoot. Flora bent to pick it up. A penny, and it was faceup. Lucky.

"I'm rich," she said, to no one in particular. *If only.*

What would it be like to live as Helen did, to pull thousands of dollars out of a bottomless trust fund at a moment's notice? To wear a dress only once before discarding it? To be considered a fair match for someone like —

Flora crushed the thought before it bloomed. She closed her hand around the penny. Flipped it in the air. Heads, she got a wish. Tails, she didn't. The coin crested its arc. She snatched it, holding it a moment in her closed fist.

What did she want?

She glanced at the sky, knowing that she was supposed to want the freedom of that blue beyond. Knowing that she wasn't so certain of that anymore. Knowing, in fact, that she wanted something else. Someone else.

What if it were Henry she was meeting? What if she could show him what it was like to own the sky? From above, one couldn't see the mess of life. Not the chipped paint on the houses. Not the cracks in the sidewalk. No signs of imperfection or decay. Everything was clean lines and vivid colors. What's more, the engine was too loud for idle conversation or even for much thought. The focus that flight required consumed her. It felt safe. And yet she wanted to share it, at least with him. As he had showed her that love was nothing to fear, she could show him the embrace of the beyond.

She wished on the penny until it felt warm, and then she opened her hand. Heads. She'd won. The ridiculousness of it made her laugh out loud. She dropped the penny into the pocket of her dress and decided to turn the props and check for oil. She'd have to do it once more before takeoff, but at least it would keep her hands busy.

Her boots had just touched ground when she heard his voice. Not wanting to believe it, Flora slowly turned around. And there he was, wearing the same clothes he'd been in the night before.

"Back for your jacket?" she said. "I have it with me. I was going to give it to Helen."

"My jacket?" He looked momentarily puzzled. And then: "Oh, of course. Very kind of you."

Something seemed strange about him, strange and formal, but she wasn't surprised, given how things had ended.

He stepped closer, and a lock of hair slid down his forehead. He didn't push it away. He looked as though he hadn't slept well. She knew the feeling.

"I'll just get it for you, then," she said.

"I want to fly," Henry said. He walked closer. "In the plane."

"You're sure about that?" Flora tilted her head, scarcely wanting to believe he'd had a change of heart about heights.

"Yes."

She smiled, tentatively. "I happen to know a pilot who doesn't have anything to do for the next hour."

Henry smiled back. It was pinched-looking, but it was better than nothing. She deeply regretted what had happened between them before. If she could take those words back, she would. It wasn't that she was ready to accept what he offered, ready to choose him. But love and a life together: Maybe it could be possible someday.

Her head began to throb. The best thing for that, though, was to take to the skies.

"Ready?" she asked. "The conditions are perfect."

She stopped herself before she started rambling. Best just to show him what she loved. Perhaps it could be the beginning of forgiveness.

Chapter 67

HENRY TRIED TELEPHONING FLORA AS SOON AS MR. THORNE departed. He had to warn her about Helen, about who she really was. The phone rang and rang, but she did not pick up, and Henry feared she'd already left to take Helen up in her airplane. He burst out the door and ran down the steps before he stopped on the sidewalk, not sure where to go: to Flora's house, to the airfield, to Hooverville to seek help from James, to confront the fake Helen wherever she might have run to.

Unable to decide, he stood paralyzed as cars zoomed by, kicking up clouds of dust on the cobbled streets. People hurried past him, giving him sidelong glances for his obvious distress. He decided to take his chances bargaining with Death. She'd as much as invited him to, only he hadn't realized it. What if he had kissed her? Would it have saved Flora? He would have done it a thousand times were that the case.

To think, he'd turned away from Helen because it felt like death to live without Flora. He'd been right about that. He just hadn't understood how right he was.

His pockets empty, he ran toward the airfield. He had miles to go, but already, his shirt stuck to his back and his lungs burned. He ran downhill on Twenty-Third Avenue, heading toward the bridge;

the barest hint of a breeze blew from behind. A car pulled up. It was James, only not the version he'd known earlier. This James Booth sat behind the wheel of a Cadillac even finer than Mr. Thorne's. His suit was new, finished with a gray silk tie worn over a snow-white shirt. It figured that Love was vain.

"Get in," James said.

Henry obeyed, relieved, yet angry for what Love had done to him, to Ethan, to all of them. "We have to hurry. They're at the airfield. If Helen gets there first . . ."

"I know." James's voice was quiet.

"You have to help me," Henry said. "I want to trade. I want to take Flora's place."

James did not reply, though he turned for a quick glance as he held the steering wheel with both hands.

Henry yelled, "Will she take me instead? Tell me!"

James did not answer right away. The street curved and they approached the Montlake Bridge, whose copper-topped turrets reminded Henry of Rapunzel's tower. Lights flashed and the guardrail dropped, signaling the bridge was to rise. The delay was agony. At last the bridge began to lower itself. They sped over the Montlake Cut past the University of Washington, veering toward Sand Point.

James finally spoke. "She's never said yes to such a thing."

"What else can we do?" Henry's stomach felt full of snakes. "There has to be something. Anything. It can't end like this."

"You've done nothing wrong." James's voice was reassuring but distant, as if he were a school administrator explaining some foul-up with a test packet. "You played as well as I had hoped. I'm proud of you."

Henry slammed his hands on the dashboard. "You're talking as though it's over. It's not."

"It is," James said. "It's over and we lost."

Henry's throat was so tight it hurt. "Then can nothing help? Can nothing save Flora? What about Death? What will kill her?"

"Nothing," James said. "She's immortal, as am I."

"Then what makes her suffer? I want to hurt her as she's hurt me."

"Waiting. She's been suffering all along, and she won't wait anymore. I could turn back, Henry. No one would blame you. This could be terrible to watch."

"Could be?"

"Depending on her method."

Henry curled his hands into fists. "Drive faster."

Chapter 68

DEATH LEANED BACK AS THE PLANE ROSE, FEELING THE COMFORT of victory in hand. And it could not come soon enough. Her hunger had peaked. It threatened to burst outside of her, to lick the world with a tongue of fire.

The shivering sky filled the windshield. Flora gripped the yoke. Death wanted to touch those hands, to take just a little, but she forced herself to hold off a moment longer. She'd waited so long for this. The perfect time would soon arrive.

The girl leveled the plane, and the sky slid upward until it shared the windshield with the silver of the lake and the green of the trees around it. She turned toward Death, her face vulnerable, full of hope. Death had to look away. Flora would find out soon enough, but Death still felt shame at the fundamental truth of her existence. She wanted to hide it as long as she could. And she wanted, just once, to have someone look at her with love in their eyes.

The earth rushed below them, a patchwork of color and shape, a view humans weren't meant to have but had somehow managed, through a combination of persistence and passion. Death would never understand the urge to fly. Why do something that was not your nature? Why waste time on a temporary thrill?

Flora pointed at something below. The lake, perhaps, as smooth as glass and sapphire blue. It was beautiful. And the girl had courage, Death realized. She knew about the Game. Knew about its end. Rather than choose Henry, she'd chosen something else, something that had no word, although integrity probably came close. That, or maybe truth. This quality seemed in increasingly short supply with humans. It was a shame that she was blind to how little time she had left. But that was the way with humans. They always thought there would be more days.

The moment arrived. Death exhaled, and as she did, her Henry guise melted away. She did not become Helen again, but rather, wore her true form. Flora deserved as much. The look on the girl's face when she noticed: It was one Death would remember for the ages, even though she'd seen variations on it for the entirety of her existence.

Blanching, Flora turned back toward the windshield. The plane dipped and banked, and Death understood the girl was trying to land, most likely to save anyone on the ground who would be killed by a falling hunk of burning wreckage. Ah, well. Everybody was to die someday, whether by accident or act of time. Death reached for Flora's hand, pushing away ill-timed memories of a Spanish flower seller and a German zeppelin pilot. One wanted to live for love; the other was willing to risk his life for his fellow man. She never should have spared these souls.

Chapter 69

HENRY AND JAMES ARRIVED AT THE AIRSTRIP AS FLORA BOARDED her plane with someone who looked exactly like Henry. Death had stolen his guise, from his rampant curls to his scuffed shoes. Henry yelled after her, but she did not hear. The pair climbed into the plane. Henry ran toward them, holding a hand up against his face to block the wind from the propellers. But Flora did not see him over her tail wheel, and soon, the plane was airborne, growing ever smaller as it climbed.

Henry stopped running. He turned to look back at James. Words would not come. His body felt scorched from the inside out. Exhausted. Wasted. As though it would never quite be right again.

"Why couldn't it have been me?" he said at last.

He stood there, staring at James, whose face was tipped toward the sky as his hands hung at his sides. After what seemed like an age, James turned to Henry. He shrugged. Then he disappeared.

Henry stood under the perfect blue sky, alone.

When he had most needed Love, Love had forsaken him. The feeling struck him like a cold wave. He couldn't breathe, couldn't see, and did not know how he could go on living in the face of it. He fell to his knees, not even noticing when the gravel tore his pants and cut his flesh.

Then he stood and looked to the sky. He didn't want to watch, but he could not bear for Flora to leave the world unseen. And so he waited. For what, he did not know. But he trusted this instinct, and he sent his love outward and upward, so that she might know he was there, answering her call, unto the end.

Chapter 70

ONE MOMENT, THE FIGURE NEXT TO HER IN THE PLANE WAS Henry. The next moment, it was not, and suddenly, Henry's strange behavior at the airfield made sense. It wasn't that he was angry with her, or fearing the flight. Rather, it wasn't Henry at all.

The figure sitting next to her, a woman of indeterminate age, was someone she'd never met. But Flora knew her. She knew her deep in her bones.

This was the woman who'd worn Helen's face. The one who'd chosen Flora for suffering when she was but a sleeping infant. The gloves this woman wore now, the ones Flora thought had been her mother's — they had belonged to this woman, this monster, all along. They were a small thing, the gloves. But sometimes the smallest thing is everything. Flora had believed these gloves brought her closer to her mother, that in wearing them, she was being blessed by her mother's touch.

Flora knew now this was nothing but a beautiful lie. The gloves hadn't protected her. They'd kept her from feeling the world. They'd kept her from living.

In that moment that Death came for her, Flora understood all of this. She understood the lessons Death had to teach. And she understood one last, worst thing: that these lessons had come too late. Had she known in time, Flora would have chosen differently. This is true for almost every human. Death is the finest teacher. The finest, and the most cruel.

She reached for Flora, who twisted away. First, Flora had to land the plane. She'd surrender afterward. To crash the plane would take the lives of innocents, and this she could not do. She banked and began to descend, determined to cheat Death out of everything she could. But Death unbuckled herself and moved in.

"NO!" Flora twisted out of reach. *Be brave*, she told herself. *Land the plane.*

They were speeding now toward the runway, faster than she would have liked. Her hands shook, and she wondered if there was any sort of deal she might make. She leaned as far away as she could while still keeping control of the yoke.

Death grabbed Flora's hand. The horizon tilted. The color of the sky changed, and the plane itself seemed to shudder, as if it were a body losing its hold on life. Her fingers froze, and the heat drained out of the rest of her. In a way, she was glad. It numbed her to what she knew would follow.

Then something cracked inside of her. Her fingers and toes hummed. A different feeling crept up her arms, up her legs. It was as if she were being filled with some substance other than blood. The feeling reached her chest, her neck, her face. She could not move. There was a shock, a moment of confusion, a transformation. Her body was no longer her own, not entirely.

But it was strange. It did not feel like death, or at least what she'd expected death to feel like. Death was an absence, a coldness. It was the bodies of her parents being covered by snow, erased by whiteness.

This was heat. It was fullness. And once she gave in to it, it was strength.

Flora, a voice said from somewhere so close it filled her skull.

The voice she had not yet heard, but knew nonetheless.

She responded. *What now?*

That's the thing, Love said. *I can't tell you the answer. I can only be here with you when you need me.*

Flora wanted to laugh. *Where were you before? Haven't I always needed you?*

It's true that I did not choose you as my player. I chose the best heart I could, knowing that Death was choosing the strongest player she could. But you were born of love, Flora. Your grandmother loved you. Your parents. Henry. In that way, I was with you all along.

The truth of it struck Flora like a blow.

There's no time to waste on regrets, Love said. *There is only time to live the way you would have, had you known the stakes from the start.*

What difference will that make? The plane's engine cut out.

All of the difference. The only difference.

I don't believe you! They were falling now, and the view through the windshield had changed. No longer did she see the sky of day, but the one of night. A night without moon or stars, terrifying in its emptiness. Was she dead already?

I cannot make you believe in anything. The choice is yours. I am here. I am within you. You and I are one. What do you want your last moments to be?

Flora knew. As she understood what it took to lift a plane off the ground, as she understood how to bend her voice around notes to lift them off of a page of music and into someone's heart, she knew what Love was asking of her. Not to act only if it would change the inevitable, but to act because it was the most courageous thing she could do.

The end, for everyone, was the same.

It was the choices made in the face of that, the ones made with a full heart, that could and did live on.

Flora opened herself fully to Love's presence, feeling him turn her into everything she'd feared becoming: someone no longer in control, no longer protected, no longer safe. Light and heat rose from her chest. They filled the cockpit with flame and bathed the windshield with brightness.

Death turned, a look of astonishment on her face.

And then it was not the sky around them that had changed but the airplane too. They were no longer in it, bending toward earth.

The plane, Flora asked. *What's happened to it?*

Death has stopped time. She's taken us out of it. We're elsewhere.

It took Flora a moment to take in what spread before them: a view of the world from a great distance. Galaxies unfurled like living watercolors, sending shades of blue and tan and green into the infinite black. She was unimaginably far from everything she knew.

Flora turned and saw Death as Love did. She saw the unrelenting loneliness of being the only one of her kind, the one everyone feared. She also saw the one who secretly loved every soul she devoured, keeping each one safe in the endless expanse of her memory. Flora saw her, and she could not hate her.

"Too late," Death said. "The Game is over. You lost. She's mine to take."

Love's thoughts rose through Flora's mind like air currents.

May I? He was asking if he might use her body to speak.

Yes.

"But she chose him. Moments too late, but she chose him. This victory should not make you feel proud." Love's voice felt like music in her mouth, and as strange as it was to have someone speak through her, she also loved the sound and feel of it. With so little time left, it was a final pleasure to cherish.

"I am entitled." Death's face was pale and her hands shook.

"That may be. But you can't take her," Love said. "Not as long as I'm here."

"She's mortal," Death said. "I can wait."

"You're a terrible liar. Look at your hands."

Anger twisted Death's face, and black tears welled and fell. "What do you know of suffering? I am the most hated figure in existence. I bring nothing to humanity. All I do is take. I'm a curse. Unlike you, the thing I feed on despises me. And so I'll take my solace. I will!"

She grabbed Flora by the throat.

Why aren't you saving me? Flora pushed the thought at Love urgently.

I can't. I'll only prolong your suffering. We lost. And now, we must let go. Flora felt him depart her body. Her flesh grew cold. She could not see what surrounded her, only faces, the faces of everyone she'd known and loved. She heard music and saw the blue sky. She felt hands on her body. Lips on her lips. *Henry.* These memories, especially of him, filled her mind, as vividly as photographs but in full color, enriched with the full depth of her senses. The dampness of sweat on his forehead in the heat of a performance. His hand on her back as they danced on a rooftop. The scent and touch and sound of him as she listened to his living, beating heart. Her life, every moment of it, was being pulled away as she watched.

Seeing it again, she understood what she'd failed to see earlier. Someday. Just as it wasn't only something to be afraid of, it also was not something that existed only in the future. She and Henry had their someday moments. To see them all again, to hear them, to feel them without the blunting filter of fear: It was like nothing Flora could have imagined.

To die was not the worst thing that could have happened. The worst thing was that she'd almost missed the wonder of love.

She could not speak, not with Death's hands crushing her throat, the source of her song. She sent Death a thought, one she hoped would be her final gift. *The Game means something only because we lose. That is your gift to humans. So thank you.*

Death's hands faltered. Flora took in a deep, painful breath. She swayed, and then Love was standing behind her, holding her up.

"If life didn't end," he said, "there would be no need for me. To choose love in the face of death is the ultimate act of courage. I am the joy, but you are the meaning. Together, we make humanity more than it otherwise might have been."

Death stepped away. Her shoulders heaved, and tears striped her face. She removed an envelope from her pocket. She opened it and removed a piece of paper. When she destroyed it, both players would be lost.

"No," Love said. "Please. Wait."

"It's not what you think," Death said. "Trust me. It's just that I cannot do this without you." She pressed the paper against her heart. Two names, Flora's and Henry's, had been written on it.

Death handed the paper to Love. "Keep it safe for me. Keep them safe."

"For how long?" he said.

Flora did not hear Death's answer.

And then she was gone from that space, and back inside the airplane, and it was burning. The heat and the smoke were more than she could endure. She struggled to free herself. And then she felt two pairs of hands and arms closing around her. She'd given herself to love, and then she'd given herself to death, marveling that both forms of surrender felt like deliverance. These beings who carried her, immortal both, held her to the sky for one last flight, during which her skin was soothed and made whole by a wash of blue air, air as cool as the sea under a full moon.

She felt herself being laid on the ground.

She opened her eyes as an explosion filled her ears.

Chapter 71

HENRY REACHED FLORA JUST AS THE STAGGERWING BLEW UP. HE covered her body with his, stunned at what he'd seen: the plane dropping from the sky, slamming into the runway, tearing a smoking black streak into the earth. He'd run to save her, but she'd somehow been thrown free and had materialized on the gravel about twenty yards clear of the burning wreckage. He thought he might be hallucinating, but then she shifted beneath him, and he realized it did not matter what had happened or what he'd seen. All that mattered was she was there with him.

He looked down at her, beautiful and uninjured, as though she'd been made of something unbreakable.

She blinked and focused. "Henry?"

"Flora." Her name was fire and music in his mouth. A weight flew from his shoulders, the one he'd felt on them his entire life. "The Game. Is it over?"

"I don't know."

They sat, and she brushed bits of glass from his shoulders, looking at him as if the world contained nothing else. He stood, and held out a hand. She took it, and they were side by side, watching the plane turn to ash. She shook her head at him and laughed. And then she was kissing him, the sort of kiss that they both might have thought existed only in the lyrics of songs.

The kiss: It felt like light rising through them. It was a memory and it was a promise, an enigma and a wonder. It was music. A conversation. A flight. A true story. And it was theirs.

Chapter 72
Saturday, March 28, 2015

DEATH HADN'T VISITED THE SMALL GREEN HOUSE FOR MANY years. The world had changed all around it. No longer were the cars graceful things of steel and chrome. Some were small and sleek, tucked against sidewalks. Others were great rusting hulks on blocks in overgrown lots. But the house in Death's memories remained as it ever was. Neatly painted, pleasingly compact, its windows lit with soft yellow light, filtered by gauzy curtains.

Wearing an old-fashioned red dress that had somehow managed to come back into style, Death climbed the steps. Shallow crescents had been worn into the treads by time and passing feet, but the stairs felt sturdy, well cared for, ready to help people transition from inside to out and back again.

The house was quiet but for a vintage jazz album that took Death's mind back to the days the song had been played live: "Walk Beside Me."

Once upon a time I dreamed
Of how my life would go . . .

Death turned to take in the late-afternoon sun. She waited for him to arrive, much as he'd waited for her in Venice that spring day so many years ago. The passing time felt a bit like a dream: so vivid in parts, and yet nothing she could truly hold on to.

I'd span the globe, a lonely soul
Beneath the moon's white glow . . .

Love materialized beneath a once-small oak tree that now shaded the street. He'd dressed, as ever, in his fine gray suit. And he greeted her with a wistful smile.

For years after the Game ended, he'd sat by her side, holding her hand, until the moment came and she knew she could carry on alone. That's the way of unfed hunger. It dies, even as it feels like healing.

But there was something more to it. Death couldn't bear Love's suffering. He was as hungry as she, although for something else. And so, because she loved him — she knew this feeling now, both its name and its effects — she'd let him go.

I may have dreamed before you
Of how my life should be . . .

"Did you miss me?" he asked, looking as old as she felt.

"No," she said. "Not for a moment."

It was a lie and they both knew it. But some small lies are games. Or, closer to the bone, echoes of games that no longer need to be played.

"Are you ready?" Love asked.

Death nodded and found her voice, which was rusty from disuse. "Eternally."

She despised the sound, and so, although she was weak and unsteady, she transformed herself into the Helen guise one last time. She felt better right away, as though she'd come home to a place she never thought she would miss.

"That face." Love's laugh was surprised. "I'm glad to see it again."

He shifted as well, and was once again young and glowing with irresistible light. The opponents faced each other. Death's hunger unfolded like a map of space itself, infinite. It would not be long now. She readied her hand to knock. Then she hesitated.

Love read her mind, as he now could. He stood next to her, his arm around her, keeping her steady and warm as the music played on.

> *The only thing I want now*
> *Is for you to walk beside me . . .*

Death knocked. There was a pause and the sound of slippered feet scuffing a wooden floor. The door opened halfway. Flora, her face shaped by the passage of many years, stood there as if she'd been waiting for them.

She opened the door all the way. "I thought — I hoped — it would be you. Though I wouldn't have minded if you'd come as the cat."

Death couldn't speak. As was her lot, she'd consumed lives over the years. But she had long been hungry for this soul above all others, and she hadn't known what sort of greeting to expect. She would never admit it, but being welcomed by Flora meant more than she could have imagined in all of those years of waiting. To be welcomed was rare; to be welcomed by someone she loved . . . she did not have the words for how it felt.

"May we come in?" Love asked.

Flora stepped away to let them pass as the song neared its end.

> *The only thing I'll ever want . . .*

"Henry's in here," Death's player said, gesturing toward the bedroom where her parents had once slept.

Is for you to walk beside me . . .
Walk beside me . . .
Walk beside me . . .

As the instruments played their last notes, Flora shuffled to the record player — a vintage thing, the sort most people had replaced with small digital devices that turned ones and zeroes into sound. It meant the song was the same every time it was played, something that struck Death as being simultaneously magical and dreadful. The old woman lifted the tone arm, careful not to scratch the vinyl. She'd become gentle in her old age, even when she knew it did not matter. It was a form of caring, of connection.

Love cleared his throat. "Shall I wait out here?"

He put his hand on the back of the davenport, the one that had been Flora's grandmother's. In the decades since, it had been reupholstered many times, now in a soft velvet the color of new fern leaves. But Death would have recognized it even if time had reduced it to a pile of sawdust. The wood of the curving, carved arms still sang of the tree's soul. Something about it sang of Marion's, as well.

Did she want him to see her at her most vulnerable? At her most despised? It would have been easy for her to keep him out of the room, to spare herself the shame. But there was no longer room for that in their relationship. Not when so much had been shared.

"Come with us," Death said.

Love took Flora's arm. Death followed them into the bedroom.

The setting sun was visible through the window, a dusky painting in reds and oranges and gold. These were the colors of fall, although it was an early spring evening, and this evoked a sense of a beginning and of an ending, which was as it should be.

Death didn't need the light, but she'd always liked it. The fading rays reached Henry where he lay in bed, his eyes closed, his face slack with age and exhaustion. Time had changed him, but she would have known him anywhere. Not as well as her player, perhaps. But well enough to pick his face out of the billions she held in her mind.

Henry had kept his curls, and they'd kept up their relentless march on his forehead. Flora sat next to him, placing her hand on his brow, as if feeling for fever. She moved his hair back to where she knew he wanted it to be.

"They're here," Flora said, leaning close to his ear. "Both of them."

Henry did not stir. He was too far gone to that land of waking dreams and memories. His hands twitched by his sides, his fingers moving as though he were playing his bass. His lips moved, and Death read the word they shaped.

Someday.

Someday had come. It had come in many versions. This was the final one.

"How will this work?" Flora asked. She reached for Henry's hand. "If it's all the same to you, I'd still rather you didn't kiss him."

Death turned toward Love. Could it be that Flora didn't understand she was here for both of them? That she had postponed taking them for as long as she could? Death had won the Game. She always won. This time was different. Because of love, she'd waited. But that was all.

"Flora," Love said. He walked to her side and put his hand on her cheek.

Flora leaned into him and wept. "Take me too. I don't want to live without him."

Death's heart filled with relief.

"You won't have to," Love said.

Flora lay down next to Henry, cradling his body. She put her hand on his chest. Henry opened his eyes. He found her hands with his and turned to look at her.

"Are you sure you want to be here?" Death asked Love.

Love nodded.

The planet spun; the window darkened. Death sat next to Flora and Henry. She looked at Love, and he held out the piece of paper she'd entrusted him with so long ago.

"Please," she said. "Keep holding it. Just a little while longer. I'd rather do it this way."

He held the paper as if it were the most precious thing in the world. Death reached for Flora's and Henry's hands, which were still clasped over Henry's heart. The rhythm had almost left him. His heart, the one Love had chosen, limped like a wounded soldier, but the music it made pleased Death still. She looked at Love and thanked him silently for his choice. And then Henry's and Flora's hands were in hers, and their lives began to flow away, all of those somedays that they'd hoped for, and had.

Death gasped at the beauty of it all. Sunsets that pounded Puget Sound into a gleaming copper bowl. The taste of warm gingerbread on cold fall evenings. Two lines of tiny wet footprints made by their just-bathed children. The way these two children, a son and a daughter, looked as they slept, chubby arms and legs flung wide as if they'd fallen from heaven.

And there were sounds: of airplane propellers rising into the blue. Traffic rushing down past the Hudson River in New York. The swing and blare of gigs in Seattle, San Francisco, and Shanghai. The sweet burst of their son banging chords on his piano, and their daughter blasting high notes on her trumpet.

There was silence too. Particularly that of the moon. Hanging sideways over an island in the Pacific. Gleaming like a cup of honey over an ancient temple in Rome. Rippling in a puddle in a rubbish-choked gutter.

Oh, the moon.

Everywhere the same and yet different, and so worth finding as it traveled overhead each night, scoring the passing days in the sky.

In this rush of life, Death felt the strange pain of love, something that had once been so unbearable but now felt an indelible part of her. She realized something as their lives filled her. To love: She'd had the power all along.

And this love between Henry and Flora . . . at first, it was a small, uncertain thing, like the glow of the morning sun on the horizon. And then it was its own wild animal, bucking against the world and anything that threatened it, so hot it could burn and sometimes did. And then it was quiet, as quiet as a snowfall, covering everything, certain of its place, even as it was certain it could not last forever.

And then, everywhere all around and inside her, it was still. Flora's and Henry's hearts had stopped. Which one beat last, Death could not tell. It felt as if they'd ceased their work at the same moment. Death hoped that was so, that neither had to spend a moment without the other.

She laid down their hands. Gently, even as that no longer mattered, it still felt the only way to let go.

The room was dark. And then there was the hiss of a match and the slow, steady spread of light. Love had lit a candle.

"No two flames are alike," he said.

"Some are," Death whispered. "Some are exactly the same."

He held out the paper to her. The one she'd written on in blood and tears so many years ago. The ink had faded. You could hardly read what it said anymore. But she remembered. She always would.

Flora.

Henry.

She reached for the paper. And as they touched hands, she gave him a gift: all of her memories of Flora, so that her player would continue within him. She hoped Love would not mind that she kept Henry and his perfect heart for herself. And for the first time, even as it was lost, the Game was also won by both Love and Death. For in this way, the players lived on.

Love touched the corner of the paper to the candle. He flung the burning scrap into the air. It flared, split apart, and fell to the ground, petals of a fiery rose. It smelled of smoke and lilies and blood and ash, and it made Death weep once more, tears as black as the hollows of space. But she did not mind this time, because she felt so full, not just of life, but of that other thing.

"Shall we?" Love offered Death his arm. She took it. They walked together into the living room.

"I can't bear to leave just yet," Death said, her strength returning.

"We have all the time in the world." Love found a record. He laid it on the player. The music started again, scratchy from age, but so sweet and beautiful and deep.

Someday.

And there, in the darkness, Love and Death and the ones inside of them danced until the song was done.

And then, when all around was silent and still, they disappeared.

ACKNOWLEDGMENTS

I HAVE HAD YEARS OF LOVE AND SUPPORT FROM MY EDITOR, Arthur A. Levine, as well as the rest of the crew at Scholastic: Nicholas Thomas, Emily Clement, Cassandra Pelham, Andrea Davis Pinkney, Becky Amsel, Nina Goffi, Antonio Gonzalez, Tracy van Straaten, Elizabeth Starr Baer, Bess Braswell, and Lizette Serrano.

My literary agent, Sarah Davies, is a voice of support and sanity. Likewise, the book has benefited from the professional attentions of Jill Corcoran and Elizabeth Law, as well as Jordan Brown, Anne Ursu, and Denise Hart Alfeld. I'm privileged to work with my film agent, Josie Freedman.

Katy Cenname helped me with insight into the pilot's mind. Larry Wixom provided helpful specifics about the Staggerwing. Milt Hinton's thrilling bass music kept me company as I wrote, and *Playing the Changes* by Milt Hinton, David G. Berger, and Holly Maxson filled me with admiration and respect for musicians during the Depression and beyond. *Jackson Street After Hours* by Paul de Barros and Eduardo Calderon provided insight about the African American jazz legacy in the Pacific Northwest, and the Northwest African American Museum fed my imagination with real stories. All of the inevitable errors are my own, though, along with any insensitivity, misunderstanding, or other failure of language.

Thanks go to my friends who've either read drafts, written alongside me, or talked me through the challenging parts of the story (and a whole lot else): Jesse Klausmeier, Emily Russin, Jolie Stekly, Kat Giantis, Patti Pitcher, Sofia Headley, Justina Chen, Holly Cupala, Samantha Berger, Robin Mellom, Sara Wilson Etienne, Brenda Winter Hansen, Liz Mills, Jaime Temairik, Cori Barrett, Lish McBride, Marissa Meyer, Jennifer Longo, Mary Jane Beaufrand, Sean Beaudoin, and Jet Harrington.

Thanks also to the extended Brockenbrough, McClure, Wilde, and Berliant families.

And especially to my very own family: Adam, Lucy, and Alice. If I know love at all, it is because of you.